I0690582

Sins of the Father (A Lady Marmalade Mystery)

by

Jason Blacker

PUBLISHED BY:
Lemon Tree Publishing

Visit www.JasonBlacker.com on the web to stay up to date

Editing: Dragonfly Editing

ISBN 13: 9781927623428

For my mother and father who have always been encouraging and supportive

Table of Contents

One

June of 1942 was a terrible time to be living in England. It was made all the worse if you were cooped up in London. Although The Blitz of 1940 was well behind you, the air raid sirens were a constant reminder to remain vigilant. And indeed, there were bombings haphazardly conducted whenever the Germans felt like it, to keep you on your toes.

But, by this time, of course, one had gotten used to the air raid sirens and the screeching whistles of the bombs falling, when they did. And at the moment, this was one of those times. Lady Marmalade couldn't hear any screeching whistling from any bombs and she could barely hear the air raid sirens.

She was in the bunker that Eric had commissioned in the summer of 1939, when talk of war was apparent but nobody wanted to believe it. He managed to see the construction through before he passed.

Frances was thinking about that now.

"What do you think about it, luv?" he asked.

They were both fifteen feet under the ground; the round bunker like a tube. It wasn't large, but it was as big as their living room. Enough space for sitting out a night's bombing or two. Frances looked at him and put her hand on his shoulder. His was around her waist.

"I hope we don't have to use it," she said.

It was a fragile hope, like the last leaf of summer clinging precariously to the limb of the tree. Eric looked at her and kissed her forehead.

"Better safe than sorry, though."

They looked around the bunker together. Eric very pleased with it, explaining the thickness of the concrete reinforced walls and the other specifications that Frances couldn't quite remember the details of.

It had originally only had their queen sized bed in it. But as of today, as Frances sat on the chair in the middle of the bunker, it held three beds. Alfred and Ginny wouldn't leave her, even in these tumultuous times. They had promised Eric the same. And being without family of their own there was nowhere else they'd rather be.

"This door, here," said Eric pointing to a door at the far end of the bunker, "opens up to the London tunnels. I've made a map and you'll find it in the top drawer of this table."

The table Eric had pointed at almost three years ago still sat squarely by the door.

"This tunnel is just in case we can't get back out through the house," he said. "It opens up into the tunnels, and about three hundred yards away you'll find the first underground station."

"You're so very thoughtful, my dear," said Frances to him. She leaned up and kissed him on the mouth.

"I couldn't bear to have anything happen to you, luv. I just can't imagine you not being my side."

Alfred walked off to the far end of the bunker and checked on the door. It brought Lady Marmalade out of her reverie. The pain was still sharp at moments like these. She hadn't imagined losing Eric so soon. But that was the fickle hand of fate that dealt the cards she now held.

Frances stood up from her chair and turned on the wireless. Eric had wired one down here so that they might remain abreast of the goings on while they were huddled down in the bunker. The announcer was calmly informing everyone to remain calm and to make their way to the nearest shelter. That they would keep everyone updated.

Though Frances thought that everyone should have been well hidden in a shelter by now. The poor souls who might be out on the ground might not be terribly lucky if this turned out to be a real bombing raid.

You could hear the sirens better over the wireless whenever the announcer took a moment to gather his thoughts. The ebbing and flowing of the siren was not an unpleasant sound, but it was monotonous and constant, like a moaning wolf.

Frances looked up at Alfred.

"Would you please sit down, Alfred, you're making me nervous standing there and pacing around."

"Sorry, my Lady. Didn't realize I was doing that."

Alfred came down and sat in a chair by Ginny. He looked over at Frances.

"You know, my Lady, both Lord Declan and Lady Amelia feel that you should not be in London during the war, but rather up at Ambleside."

Frances nodded.

"I know, but someone needs to take care of the London home now and then, and that's what I intend to do. It's withstood the best that the Germans have been able to throw at it and I'll be damned if I'm going to cower away because the Germans want to throw some bombs around. Besides, who else will help to clean up the mess and take care of those who suffer greatly and have nowhere to run to?'

It was a rhetorical question.

"Yes, my Lady, though I confess to believing that Lord Declan might be right. It is dangerous to be here in the midst of it."

"But, my dear Alfred, I was not here in September of '40 during those two months of consistent blitzing. And we've hardly had anything else like it since. I fear that our British stiff upper lips have taken the fight out of the Germans. Would you not agree that the bombings are becoming less and less common?"

"I would, my Lady, but I fear I could not live with losing you too, so soon after Lord Marmalade."

Alfred cast his eyes down. It had come as a sudden and quick blow to lose his master, and could he dare say, dear friend. Never in his many years of service had he worked for a peer who was as humble and as kind as The Most Honorable The Marquess of Sandown.

Eric had even encouraged Alfred to address him by his first name. But Alfred could never come to bear that. It was asking too much, though the gesture was a mark of Eric's greatness and kindness.

The raid siren stopped for several seconds and then Lady Marmalade could hear it start up again, this time as one single monotone. She smiled and looked over at Ginny. Ginny was nervous, you could tell. She always got nervous during the sirens. Her freckled face was flushed and her eyes darted around at every little sound she heard.

"How are you holding up, dear?" asked Frances.

"I'm fine, thank you, my Lady. And if I might be so bold as to agree with Alfred and Lord Declan, I fear this is no place for a Lady."

Frances smiled at her housekeeper. The two of them had been extremely loyal, perhaps even more so since Eric had passed on.

"Avalon does need upkeep, too, you know," said Frances. "I can send you up on the next train if you'd like to head on up to Ambleside and take care of Avalon for me?"

Ginny fiddled with her apron and looked at Frances.

"No, my Lady, I prefer to be right with you, if you don't mind."

"I don't mind at all."

"We have the all clear, ladies and gentleman. You may now leave the shelter in a calm and dignified manner. As always, remain vigilant, watch out for each other and listen to the proper authorities."

Lady Marmalade turned off the wireless and stood up. Alfred stood up with her, as did Ginny.

"That wasn't too bad, was it?" she asked.

"Not bad at all. I believe that makes it twenty one nights without a bombing. A new record I believe, my Lady," said Alfred.

"And let's hope it continues."

They made their way back upstairs and came out through the bookshelf in the study. Alfred closed it up after them and it was hard to tell there were stairs behind it. Looking around inside Marmalade Park, which is what Eric and Frances had come to call their London home, you couldn't tell that Frances was living during war times.

Many of the paintings and ornaments had, over the last several months been put back up after the raids had become less frequent. For some reason that only fortune knew, many of the homes butting upon Hyde Park had barely been scratched. Marmalade Park was one of them, and Frances counted herself amongst the lucky ones.

"I think some tea might be just what we need to steady the nerves, Ginny," said Frances.

"Right away my Lady."

Lady Marmalade made her way into the living room where she sat down and picked up the morning's paper which she had not yet had the chance to read. She heard a knock at the front door and looked up at her watch. It was close to nine p.m.

"Who on earth can that be at this time of night, just after a siren?"

"I'll go and find out," said Alfred.

Two

Alfred came back to the living room where Lady Marmalade was still looking at her paper. Frances looked up when he came in. He was followed in by a nervous looking woman who reminded Frances of a wounded bird. She was jittery and slight of build. She was young, perhaps no more than thirty, and she already walked with a slight hunchback. She had a mousy face with a pointed nose and thin mouth. Her eyes were brown and small, darting around like loose beads in her skull.

"I do apologize, my Lady. But Ms. Beckenswidth was adamant that she see you," said Alfred.

Frances got up from the couch she was sitting on and walked towards the two of them. She offered her hand, which Ms. Beckenswidth took. Frances shook what felt like nothing but a warm, limp and dry cushion. Eric had always told her that you could tell a lot by someone's handshake. Both men and women. He'd said it was the same for either sex.

"Welcome, Ms. Beckenswidth," said Frances. "I'm Lady Frances Marmalade. Please, call me Frances."

"Lula Beckenswidth," said the young woman finding it hard to keep her eyes on Lady Marmalade's.

"Do come in. You're just in time for tea."

The grandfather clock struck nine. Frances led the young woman back into the living room and Lula sat in an armchair across from the couch that Frances sat back down in.

"Is there something wrong?" asked Lady Marmalade.

Lula played with her hands in her lap, her eyes upon them as if they held a valuable prize. She darted a look at Frances before she spoke.

"It's my grandmother, she thinks someone is trying to kill her and she told me to come and speak with you."

Lula went back to looking at her hands.

"Who is your grandmother, my dear?"

"Ms. Margaret Hollingsberry, though she prefers Madge."

"This sounds to me, my dear, like something that you should rather be speaking to the police about."

"She doesn't want the police involved. She said they'd never believe her."

"I see," said Frances, squinting slightly.

Ginny came in with a tray carrying the teapot and two cups with saucers. There was lemon, cream and sugar on the tray, too.

"Thank you, Ginny."

"I thought I heard you had company, my Lady," said Ginny, looking over at Lula.

"This is Ms. Lula Beckenswidth. Ms. Ginny Johnson is my housekeeper."

Ginny smiled at Lula but barely received a glance from her in return. Frances took the teapot and picked it up.

"Would you like some tea, my dear?"

"Yes, please."

Lady Marmalade poured tea for Lula, leaving a little room in case she wanted to add cream and sugar. Frances poured a cup for herself and squeezed a wedge of lemon into it. She watched as Lula poured a generous amount of cream into her cup and added three sugars. It was practically overflowing and it made the stirring very difficult.

Lula was splashing tea all over the sides and into the saucer. Frances watched with incredulity and curiosity as Lula continued stirring and splashing tea down the side of her teacup as if that was the natural way of doing things.

When she was finished, Lula lifted the teacup off the saucer and poured the tea from the saucer back into the teacup, while two drops of tea dashed themselves against the edge of Lula's cardigan which she didn't seem to notice.

Lady Marmalade took a sip of her tea and placed the cup back onto its saucer and then down onto the table near to her. She watched as Lula put the teacup to her mouth to test the temperature, and finding it cool enough, she drained half of its contents into her in two big gulps.

"All right then, please tell me why your grandmother seems to think that someone is trying to kill her."

"She's not very well. She's bed ridden mostly, but she's been getting these letters from someone that she says are threatening to kill her."

Frances looked at Lula fidgeting with the hem of her dress. Her nails were bitten down to the quick and had no nail polish on them. She seemed like a woman who had been brow beaten to death, and yet she was so young and fragile.

"I see, Lula, and what do these letters say exactly?"

Lula looked up at Frances and offered a wispy smile, that vanished as soon as Frances looked back at her.

"She says they say threatening things, and she's sure they'll make good on killing her."

"So you haven't seen any of these letters, have you, my dear?"

Lula shook her head, looking down at her lap. She was wearing a rather plain cream colored dress and a gray cardigan overtop. She had on brown, flat shoes that you might find a hospital matron wearing. She wore no makeup, not that any would help. Her teeth were the same off color cream as her dress and a mess of overcrowding.

"Do you know how many letters there have been?" asked Frances, sitting on the edge of the couch to try and make Lula feel more comfortable. Lula also spoke very softly like the light whisper of wind amongst trees.

"She didn't tell me, but I've seen three letters written with the same hand writing arrive three weeks apart. I don't know if there have been others."

"So you have seen them then?" Frances was hoping the young woman would make up her mind.

"No, my Lady, I've only noticed them from the writing on the envelope when I take them up to my grandmother."

Lady Marmalade picked up her teacup and sipped from it again, before replacing it. Lula took the opportunity to drain the remaining tea in her cup in two gulps.

"Would you like some more tea dear?" asked Frances.

Frances poured her another cup, being sure to leave additional room in this one. It didn't matter, Lula made sure to fill it to the brim with an even healthier splash of cream and the same three sugars. She stirred, spilled the tea and poured it back into the cup just as she had done the first time. Lady Marmalade couldn't quite be sure if she wanted to laugh or yell at the young woman and instruct her in proper etiquette. She decided against both options.

"So, how do you know that these letters are the ones that contain the threatening content?"

Lula lifted her eyes up and looked at Frances before letting them drift down and look at the coffee table between them, as if her eyelids were made of lead. Lula gave the impression that every act was an act of great cost. To move, to speak, even to breathe seemed to her more like a penance.

"Every time I've taken these letters up to my grandmother she complains about them, saying that these are the same ones that are going to ruin her."

"Does she know who they come from?"

"She says she does, but she won't tell me."

"Have you seen a name or return address on any of the envelopes?"

Lula shook her head slowly as if to do so quickly might cause it to snap off her thin neck.

"There are no return addresses and no names on any of them."

"And how are you related to Madge Hollingsberry?"

"I'm her granddaughter."

Lula said it as if it might be the first time that she had mentioned that Madge was her grandmother. There was not a sneer or a tone that would indicate otherwise. She poured half the cup of tea down her throat in another two big sips and licked her lips. She put the teacup down on the edge of the table.

"Yes, dear, I gather that she is your grandmother. Rather, I'm wondering how you are related to her as your grandmother and how you've come to be the one to give me this message."

"Madge is my mother's mother."

"And you live with her I take it?"

A small nod of the head and the averted eyes.

"Where is your mother dear?"

Lula looked up at Frances and balled her small hands into fists which she rested upon her thighs, each fist to its own thigh.

"My mother died during the Spanish Flu in 1918. I've lived with my grandmother ever since. She raised me as her own."

"I see, I'm sorry to hear that."

Frances took her teacup and saucer into her hands and took a sip from it. She hadn't quite finished half of her first serving of tea and Lula was making quick work of her second.

"It doesn't matter, my mother is long dead and I hardly knew her when she was alive."

An odd feeling, thought Frances, looking the young waif of a woman up and down. She was hard to peg. Perhaps more than met the eye, or perhaps that was all there was to her, a broken shell of a human being, the yolk long lost and spilled.

"Has there been anyone come round the house lately who would give you reason that they were out to hurt your grandmother?"

Lula took a moment to think about it. She unballed her fists and straightened her hands, spreading them over her dress, her eyes darting over her hands as she looked at them. Then she picked up her teacup and drank the last of her tea and cradled the empty cup and saucer in her lap, and looked over at the teapot greedily.

"None but the usual guests and visitors that come to see her."

"She doesn't mind them then?"

"Not all of them. Lots of them are hangers on, now that she's dying or thinks she's going be murdered."

"You don't quite seem convinced that your grandmother is about to die. Is that true?"

Lula looked up at Frances and shrugged her small shoulders.

"She's been saying that she'll be dead for a long time now. But maybe this is different, maybe someone really is trying to kill her, but she won't let me help her. She won't let me take a look at her letters. She keeps them in the drawer by the side of her bed and when she leaves her room she locks the drawer and takes the key with her."

Lula seemed mesmerized by the teapot on the tray. Frances wasn't sure she wanted to offer the young woman another cup of tea, the spectacle was quite unnerving. One would think the young thing hadn't ever tasted tea or for that matter had anything to drink the whole day.

"More tea, dear?" asked Frances.

Lula nodded her head and thrust out her cup towards the teapot. Frances picked it up and poured just about the last of the tea into her cup. Lula poured the cream into her cup, tipping it upside down and holding the jug like that until she was certain no more cream was coming out of it. More sugar, more stirring, splashing and refilling.

"How does your grandmother think I can help?"

"She asked me if you'd come round and see her. She says she won't show anyone else the letters she's been getting, except for you."

A tip of the teacup to Lula's lips and when it was rested back on its saucer, half of its contents were gone.

"But why me in particular, Lula?"

"She says you're the greatest detective and that you'll be able to catch whoever's doing this to her before they can harm her."

Frances looked at the table for a moment and on the front page of the daily paper was an article about the ongoing Battle of Midway. An aerial photo of a Japanese aircraft carrier was shown billowing smoke. She looked at Lula and thought the young woman was having a battle of her own.

"When would your grandmother like to see me?"

Lula looked up at Frances briefly.

"She's waiting for you now," said Lula, "if you'd be willing to come."

Frances shook her head and smiled.

"My dear, we've just come off an air raid siren and it's after nine. I'll be sure to call upon her first thing in the morning, if you'll leave me her address. Give me one moment."

Lady Marmalade got up and walked into her study. When she came back out she was holding a piece of paper and a pen. She placed it down in front of Lula on the table. She noticed that

Lula's teacup and saucer were now back on the tray, empty and practically bone dry.

Lula leaned in to the corner of the table and wrote an address on the piece of paper that Frances had provided. She handed it to Frances who took it and looked at it. It was a Hyde Park address, only a couple of blocks away.

"Thank you, Lula, you can tell your grandmother that I'll be round tomorrow for nine a.m."

Lula sat stiff and upright in her chair, not moving, not taking the moment to leave.

"Is there anything else?"

"She wanted me to tell you that things are going missing too. That she's being robbed."

"I see. What sorts of things."

"Mostly jewelry from what she's told me but she says there are other things, too. A hairbrush has gone missing and her favorite lipstick. I think there are other things but she hasn't told me."

Frances nodded and stood up. This was Lula's cue that her stay was no longer welcome and there would be no more tea coming. Lula reluctantly got up. Though she stood still where she was. Frances put her arm around the young woman's shoulder and started to guide her out. She wouldn't move.

"What is it dear?"

Lula looked at her feet, her hands were knitting themselves together.

"Nothing."

"Tell me," said Frances.

"Well, it's just that Granny's been acting strange lately and I can't explain it. She seems to be getting more paranoid over the last few months."

"I see. Perhaps she has reason to be. You did say that she's been getting these strange letters."

"They don't seem strange to me except that they don't have a return address on them."

"But you aren't aware of their contents are you?"

Lula shook her head.

"I'll come by for a visit tomorrow and we'll see what I can find out."

Lula looked up at Frances and nodded. She pinched her lips together and let Frances walk her out of the living room and down the hall to the front door.

"Would you like me to have Alfred walk you home? It is getting late."

Lula nodded. Alfred was just behind them as they spoke.

"Happy to walk the young lady home, my Lady," he said.

"Thank you, Alfred."

Lady Marmalade closed the door behind them and went back into the living room. Ginny came in and put everything onto the tray and then took it away. It was less than fifteen minutes later when Alfred returned home. He came back into the living room just as Frances was finishing up with the paper.

"Quite a queer young lady," he said as Frances looked up at him and smiled.

"Quite odd, indeed."

"If I may, my Lady?" asked Alfred.

"By all means Alfred."

"She said something strange to me on the way there. It was the only thing that she said, actually."

"Interesting, and what was that?"

"She said that war does peculiar things to people, makes them remember their misdeeds and seek retribution. It also clouds the minds of those who have not lived righteously."

"Was that all? No context?"

Alfred shook his head, standing tall as he was with his hands clasped behind his back.

"Nothing else at all, my Lady. It was quite strange. I didn't know what to say, so I said nothing."

Lady Marmalade nodded her head thoughtfully and smiled at him.

"This is a puzzle, isn't it?"

"I should say so."

Three

It was a little before nine when Lady Marmalade left Marmalade Park with her butler Alfred walking alongside her. It was a bright and sunny day. The blue dabbed sky keeping everyone's moods jolly. All about, men and women were carrying on with their daily business. And even though there had not been any bombs for some time, crews were working hard at cleaning up the rubble that was still about.

It was an ongoing concern and one that would only be completed years after the war ended. But idle hands do the Devil's work, and as such there were better things to do, such as keep London as presentable as one could.

Bayswater Road held rows of expensive townhomes that looked out across Hyde Park. Hyde Park, which was such a beautiful and tranquil park, had not been spared from the German's bombs. Her face was pock marked in places, though not as badly as one might have expected. A whitewashed complex of these townhomes greeted them and Frances checked the address one more time and found the gate corresponding to Madge Hollingsberry's home.

They walked up to the front of the home and Alfred knocked on the door. A younger and more rotund man than Alfred opened the door. He was dressed in a fine black tuxedo with tails and wore white gloves that had never known dirt or grime. His face was round and cherubic with a slight sheen to it and he had a cheery disposition. A wreath of black curly hair was about his crown and the rest of it was, by contrast, straight.

"Good morning. Lady Marmalade, I presume?" said the butler bowing. "Please, do come in."

Frances and Alfred walked in, Alfred taking off his bowler hat and holding it in both hands. It was stiflingly hot inside, as if they had walked into an oven.

"This is my butler, Alfred Donahue," said Frances looking over at Alfred.

"A colleague and a friend. It is a pleasure to make your acquaintance, sir." he said, holding out his hand for Alfred to shake. "I am Jeremiah Rondleton."

They shook hands.

"May I take your coats? You might find it warm in here."

Lady Marmalade took off her coat and handed it to Jeremiah. Alfred handed him his black jacket, too. Already, Alfred could feel the prickling of sweat at the temples.

"I hope you don't find it unbearable; Madam Hollingsberry finds the cold terribly annoying. Must be her years spent in India, I imagine," said Jeremiah.

He put their coats away in the closet as Lady Marmalade took off her pale blue scarf from around her head and tied it loosely around her neck.

"Who is it, Jerry?" came a screech from upstairs.

"It's your guests, mum," said Jeremiah as he closed the closet door.

"I'll be down in a minute," came another screech.

From where Frances was standing she couldn't see the upstairs landing, only the flight of stairs.

"If you'll come with me," said Jeremiah smiling all the while, "I believe Madam Hollingsberry would like to entertain you in the living room."

They followed Jeremiah down the hall which was littered with tables and assorted trinkets and statues from India as well as elsewhere. Lady Marmalade noticed items from the Far East too. Towards the end of the hall they turned into a large living room, crammed with additional pieces of unnecessary furniture, batiks and artifacts. One had to be cautious to move carefully about.

Frances wondered if perhaps things were not so much getting stolen as broken and quietly discarded. That wouldn't surprise her in the least.

"Please make yourselves comfortable and I'll have Mollie start some tea."

Jeremiah left them and Frances sat down on a large modern couch. Alfred sat down on the same couch. From what Lady Marmalade could see, there seemed no rhyme or reason to the menagerie of trinkets and assorted pieces of art and furniture that were scattered around the home.

In the one corner sat a life sized statue of a meditating Shiva with four arms. Next to him was Vishnu, standing with a coy smile and four arms holding different items. One of his hands had broken off it seemed. Opposite them was a statue of a meditating, smiling, Buddha with his fat belly. He was half the size of the other two. There were also two tall gold ashtrays on either side of Lady Marmalade's couch that stood at least waist high and were, therefore, unusable to those seated.

A short woman, around Lady Marmalade's height, but almost as wide as she was tall, shuffled into the living room making great use of a cane in her left hand. Her face was sallow and in her right hand she held a cigarette in a long slender opera length cigarette holder made of ivory and inlaid with small jewels.

She was wearing an off white dressing gown over a similarly colored night dress. On her feet she wore gray slippers and her ankles were swollen and almost blue in color. She walked over to a Queen Anne chair and sat herself down slowly, as if she might sit on a pin cushion. Next to her was an ashtray at the height of the armrests.

Her hair was a bird's nest mess of brown that needed recoloring. A couple of inches of gray roots showed throughout as if her hair was wire that had just been stripped of its colored coating. He face was deeply wrinkled and loose with jowls and fat.

Alfred sat back down as she did, having stood up when she came into the room. The woman took a moment to catch her breath, all the while Lady Marmalade watched with a detached smile on her face. The smell of tobacco nauseated her and it was all that much stronger now.

"I'm Madge Hollingsberry," said the woman. "Thank you for coming, Lady Marmalade."

"Not at all," said Frances, "this is my butler, Alfred, and please, call me Frances."

A short round woman carrying a silver tea tray came into the living room as if she were being pulled along by it. She might have been Jeremiah's sister. Her face just as ruddy and cherubic, her hair just as black but pulled up into a bun behind her head and covered in netting. She wore a black housekeeper's uniform with a white apron in front and she wore black sensible shoes.

As she laid the tray down on a coffee table almost too small for the job, she kept glancing up at Frances and smiling broadly, as if Lady Marmalade might have a big dollop of marmalade on her nose.

"That'll be all," said Madge.

Jeremiah had walked back into the living room and stood himself in the far corner, looking like a statue as he stood next to a Mongolian warrior, which, thankfully as far as Lady Marmalade was concerned, was not real. His menacing grimace still quite frightening.

"Thank you, Jeremiah, if you'll give us a minute."

Jeremiah bowed at the back of Madge's head and walked out the living room. Madge took a long time sucking on her cigarette. Lady Marmalade thought she might finish it off in one puff. Alfred was the model of composure as he sat there next to her, his eyes fixed on their host.

Madge took the cigarette holder out of her mouth and held it in her right hand, the elbow resting on the armchair. She blew a long stream of smoke up towards the ceiling and it settled like a heavy cloud above them. Threatening rain, even if it wasn't real.

"How may I help you, Madge?" asked Frances.

Madge opened her mouth and you heard her wheezing breath.

"Someone's out to kill me, Frances, and I'd like you to stop them."

Her voice was coarse and grated on the ears, but it was more pleasant than the shriek Frances had heard coming from upstairs earlier.

"Who do you think is trying to kill you?"

"I don't know, that's why I've asked you to help."

"Don't you think this is a job better suited for the police if you think the threats are real?"

"Not at all, the police won't believe me and they're incompetent, in any event."

"Lula said you had some letters you've received that are quite threatening. May I see them?"

Madge nodded her head and then yelled "Lula!" It was the same screech they had heard earlier. It was a terrible sound, an unnatural sound and not a sound that should come from a human.

"She's a little simple and dim witted that one, takes after her mother. But I promised to take care of her and that's what I'm doing. God knows what'll happen to her when I'm dead."

Footsteps could be heard thumping down the hallway and a moment later Lula appeared in the living room. She walked up to her grandmother and stood by her side. Her head was bowed down and her hands clasped in front of her.

"Go get me my letters, and be quick about it."

Madge hooked her cane over the armrest of her chair and with her left hand she pulled off a gold chain that was around her neck and which held a brass key. She handed it to Lula but didn't release it right away.

"No snooping, missy, or you'll get it."

"Yes, mum."

Lula marched off looking quite petrified.

"She's always been a nosy one, that one," said Madge. "Got that from her mother, too. It'll be the end of her. Curiosity killed the cat I told her, and it'll be the end of her, too."

"You've raised her since she was a young girl, I understand," said Frances.

Madge nodded while inhaling smoke from her cigarette holder.

"Since she was four. Her mother was a frail thing, just like Lula. Died from the flu. Lula's been with me ever since."

"What happened to her father?" asked Frances.

"Don't know. Though likely he was some rake of sorts. Never met the man. Heard his name was Errol Crowley. A cad if there ever was one. I suppose that's my fault somewhat, sparing the rod and spoiling the child. She was very spoilt, you know."

"Who was?"

"My daughter, Celia, Celia Hollingsberry. I was too good to her, it seems."

"Lula's surname is Beckenswidth, though."

"Yes, that's right. She took my husband's name as we all did, until that scoundrel left me for the secretary. Good riddance I say, now. So I took back my maiden name."

"I see, and your daughter, Celia, she decided to take on your maiden name too?"

"Good heaven's no. Celia was born before I met Harold Beckenswidth, we never had children together."

"Do you mind telling who Celia's father is then?"

"He was Rolie Vilvalayn another ne'er-do-well. Knocked me up and then left me after a few years when he found someone else. I changed Celia's name back to Hollingsberry shortly thereafter."

The pitter patter of feet came rushing down the hall and in came Lula. She handed the letters to Madge with her hand outstretched, they were still in the envelopes. Frances noticed that there were cuts on the knuckles that had just recently started to scab. Frances hadn't noticed them the previous night when Lula had come calling.

Madge took the letters and fanned them in front of Lula. This was her cue to leave and she did. Madge handed the three letters over to Frances. Alfred had to lean far over to reach them from Madge's fat, sausage like fingers. He gave them to Frances.

Frances took a moment to look at them. She turned them over and studied the front carefully, then she looked at the back of them. Nothing was written on the back. The front was in a deep indigo ink and the handwriting was large and curly and quite beautiful with big loops. At first glance Frances thought it might be the handwriting of a woman, someone with careful penmanship that was obviously a point of pride.

The stamp was brand new and painstakingly placed so that each side was flush with the corner of the envelope. All three of the envelopes were done in the same painstaking manner. Frances looked a little more closely at the writing and faint lines could be seen that might have been ruled in pencil under each line of the address. They had been erased but not quite fully, only the slightest telltale sign of these ruled lines remained.

Even from the faintness of them, Lady Marmalade could see that they were carefully measured to be the same width apart as each other. Frances looked up at Madge who was smoking her cigarette and watching her intently. The ash was a long drooping nose at the end of her cigarette.

"You've only received three of these?"

Madge shook her head.

"No, I've received five, though the first two I burnt. I couldn't believe the impertinence and the hatred in them. But when the third one arrived about three months ago, I thought I'd best keep them, as I began to fear for my life."

Madge started coughing and it soon turned into a spasm. The ash fell onto her lap which she carelessly brushed off.

"Jeremiah!" she screeched in between her coughing fit.

Jeremiah came running into the living room carrying a glass of water.

"Here you go, mum," he said.

Madge took a sip and that helped to bring her coughing under control. She wheezed and breathed heavily for a bit.

"I should get you back upstairs, mum," said Jeremiah.

She waved him off with her cigarette holder and he went and stood in the corner of the room.

"May I pour us some tea?" asked Frances, putting the letters in her lap.

Madge nodded and Frances poured tea for each of them. She added cream and sugar as per Madge's request and did the same for herself. Alfred took a cup, just black.

A tall, lanky young man entered the living room. He was perhaps just a little older than Lula with greasy brown hair and dry skin. He had bulging eyes pushed onto his face and a small nose set between them. His mouth was thin and above his top lip he wore a feathery moustache. He would have looked better without the moustache. His brown suit was too small and his pants barely made it to his ankles. He wore large brown shoes which looked like they hadn't seen a polish since the start of the war.

He came in carrying a book in one hand and chewing the fingernails of his left hand. He took a seat in the chaise lounge that was pushed up against the wall. He used the wall to support his back and tossed his right gangly leg over the left as if his joints were only attached by thin string.

Four

Madge looked at him with transparent annoyance on her face.

"Colin," she said, "I'm having a private conversation, if you please."

He glanced up at her and smiled wickedly before opening his book back up and looking inside.

"Don't let me interrupt you."

Madge stared at him with daggers for a long while but then gave up and took a puff on her cigarette which was all but finished.

"That's Colin Abbermann, one of my boarders," said Madge, unhappily.

"I see, and how many do you have?"

"Three of them. It helps to pay the bills, you know. A place like this is not cheap."

Lady Marmalade smiled and nodded and looked over at Colin. He was doing a good job of pretending to read his book, but she had the distinct impression that he was really much more interested in their conversation.

"You were saying you had received five of these letters. How often do they come?"

Madge put out her cigarette in the ashtray and left the cigarette holder leaning into it. She reached in and took her tea from the table and placed it in her lap, held with her right hand.

"They've come almost like clock work on the eleventh of the month. Except for the first one, that arrived January the 10th, a Saturday."

"I'm impressed you remember that."

"Well, it was quite shocking at the time to receive a letter like I did. It made its impression upon me. The eleventh was also the anniversary of my parent's passing, eleven years before."

"I'm sorry to hear that, how did your parents pass?"

"They were killed. Unfortunately their murderers were never found."

"Good grief, that is terrible."

Madge looked at Frances steadily, she told it without emotion as if she was recounting a recipe.

"It was a long time ago."

Frances looked back down at the envelopes in her lap. She took another sip of tea and placed her teacup on the table. She picked up the envelopes and looked at them in turn. She opened the first one which was stamped the 11th of March. She opened it up and pulled out the letter inside. It was cream colored and thick paper of very good quality.

There was no date on the letter and it wasn't addressed to Madge. The envelope was, but the letter itself contained no salutation. The penmanship looked identical to the hand that had addressed the envelope and though the page was unlined, the faintest signs of ruled pencil lines could be seen drawn with equal width between each line of writing.

Like those that had been added and erased on the envelope, these lines were deliberate and careful. They had also been erased but the ghost of them remained. Frances thought how much trouble and painstaking care must have gone into each of these letters to make them just right.

The writing in the letter, as an example, was placed deliberately and perfectly in the middle of the page. It read:

Punish the children for the sins of the father to the third and fourth generation of those who hate me.

Vengeance is mine to be meted out. The death knell tolls. Repent.

Three dash six.

Frances handed the first letter to Alfred to look at. He raised his eyebrow.

"I say. That's Deuteronomy, if I remember carefully."

Frances nodded her head.

"Chapter five, verse nine. Also found in Exodus chapter twenty, verse five, as well as Exodus chapter thirty four, verse seven."

Alfred looked over at Frances, grinning with an arched eyebrow. He was impressed.

"I didn't know you were religious," said Madge, "I had to look that up to remember where I had seen it."

Frances looked up at her and smiled.

"I'm not particularly, but we did attend service when I was a young girl as well as Sunday school. I took all of my lessons seriously."

Frances took the second letter out of the envelope and looked at it. It was identical in all aspects to the first one except for the second and third line:

Vengeance is coming wrathfully. Your suffering will soon be over.

Four dash six.

She passed that one over to Alfred and he looked it over as Frances took a look at the third. The third letter was again identical to the first two, and like the second letter it had a different second and third sentence:

A dish best served cold. The hour for murder almost upon us.

Five dash six.

Frances handed this one over to Alfred. He read it and handed all three back to Lady Marmalade. She replaced them in their envelopes and put them on the corner of the table in front of her. She picked up her tea and took a sip.

"This is very worrying," she said.

Madge nodded.

"Exactly. Someone is out to get me. You see, I knew it."

"What do you know?"

"I'm not safe in my own home. Someone here is out to kill me."

"Who do you think it could be?" asked Frances.

"Heavens. It could be any of them."

Madge looked over at Colin and he was smiling into his book. He had heard but he chose not to respond.

"How long have your boarders been with you?"

"Colin's the newest," said Madge, looking at him and not lowering her voice. "Now that I think about it, he arrived on January the first, just before the letters started."

Madge leaned in towards Frances and she leaned in towards her.

"There's something not quite right about that boy," she said, whispering.

"I can hear you," he said, not looking up from his book.

"Colin," said Frances, looking at him. He looked up at her. "We haven't met. I'm Lady Marmalade."

"I know who you are."

"Then you have one up on me. Who are you Colin? Why are you living with Ms. Hollingsberry?"

"I am a student, my Lady, at the Royal College of Art, happy to paint your portrait if you'd like, and I live with Madge, because the rent is cheap and the drama free."

He smirked at Frances as if this was all just entertainment for his enjoyment.

"That's one of his paintings over there," said Madge, "I don't like it, but Lula does and she was adamant that we hang it up in a place of honor."

"You don't like it, mum, because you have dismal taste for the arts. I mean, just look all around this place. Full of knick knacks and assorted trinkets that show no cohesion," said Colin.

Frances looked at the painting. It was perhaps two feet by three feet. A dark moody painting of a female Christ-like figure hanging on a cross. She was naked and there seemed more blood than there ought to be. The skill was exceptional, but like Madge, Frances didn't care for the subject matter. Colin's signature was at the bottom right. Just his last name with loopy and exaggerated accents.

"What do you call it?" asked Frances.

"Murdered Madonna," he said, full of pride. "But I see you don't care for it, either."

He said it as if it made no difference to him, though Frances had the feeling if she'd shown actual distaste in it, he might have relished that.

"You show remarkable skill, but you are correct, it is not to my tastes."

"Not many people can enjoy the naked authenticity and emotive response of the painting," Colin sneered.

Frances smiled at him, not allowing herself to be baited by this young man.

"Do you sell well, Colin?" she asked, knowing full well what the response would be.

Colin looked back down at his book and mumbled, "I don't see how that's any of your concern."

Lady Marmalade's smile widened, she saw Alfred fighting with a small smirk of his own. Frances turned to Madge.

"If you were to guess, who do you imagine might have it in for you?"

Madge looked back over at Colin but his nose was deep in his book.

"Him," she said quietly, nodding her head in his direction. Colin didn't say anything. "Or perhaps Matilda, she's one of the other boarders and doesn't quite like the rules around here."

"Is she around?"

"No, I shouldn't think so. She's a nanny for a family not far from here. She should be back around six."

"And why do you suspect her?"

Madge took a moment to crane her neck around and clicked her fingers to get Jeremiah's attention. She told him, with little kindness, to get her cigarettes, which he obediently did with the same cherubic smile on his face.

"At the end of last year I told her that boarders weren't allowed guests in the home after ten p.m. I found her with a young man in her room well past that time and I ordered him out."

"It was barely after ten when you went snooping around. He was just about to leave. But you always make such a scene of things," said Colin.

"And who was this young man?" asked Frances.

"I don't know, just some hanger on who was up to no good, I'm sure."

"He was Maxwell Blacksmith and the two of them had been exclusive for some months by that time already. You have an easy way of upsetting most people around you, my dear Madge," said Colin, taking his nose out of his book.

Jeremiah came back into the living room quite hurriedly. He gave the packet of cigarettes to Madge and she took one out and placed it in the cigarette holder after taking the spent one out. She looked around for a moment, confused.

"And where is the bloody lighter, Jerry?" she screeched at him.

He bowed obsequiously.

"Sorry mum, my mistake."

He trotted out of the living room.

"The incompetence," said Madge under her breath. "Why I've kept him on all these years I sometimes wonder."

Jeremiah was back quickly and held out the lit lighter for Madge with his hand trembling ever so slightly. Frances watched the whole spectacle, thinking to herself that it was no wonder Madge was getting letters the likes of which she had just shared. She was a very difficult woman to like. Jeremiah skulked back to the far wall where he stood still as a statue, a bead of sweat trickling down his cheek.

It was stiflingly hot in here and Frances couldn't imagine how Madge could be dressed in a dressing gown and slippers. Colin, in his suit jacket too short for his long arms, was also a mystery. And he wasn't sweating at all. In fact he seemed as dry as the Sahara and oblivious to the heat in the house.

"And I take it that Matilda was quite upset with you for embarrassing her in front of Maxwell?"

"You might say that, though she's quite a sullen young woman. How on earth that man takes a shine to her, I'll never understand. She's got a camel's face, really quite awful to look at."

Frances was amused that Madge, who seemed to be no catch by any liberal standards, was quite comfortable talking about her boarder's looks. Off to the side, Lady Marmalade could see Colin shaking his head slowly from side to side and clenching his teeth.

"You mentioned that you had three boarders. Who is the third?"

"Penelope Sallow, and the name suits her to a T. Her complexion is as sallow as her temperament. Quite the wallflower and very meek and mild. She doesn't make much trouble. Keeps to herself, really, but you never know. It's the quiet ones that you have to keep your eye on. Something about her makes me nervous, though."

"Something about everyone makes you nervous, Madge. I make you nervous just being in the same room. Besides, Penelope is very kind and intelligent. If you just took a moment to speak with her you'd find she's quite well read."

Madge waved off Colin's comments with the cigarette in her hand. She reached for her cup of tea and drained it. She placed it back onto the saucer and onto the table. Frances took her last sip and also placed her teacup on the table. Alfred had finished not long ago.

"I don't care for intelligence, Colin, but rather kindness. And none of you have shown me any kindness, except for sweet Lula."

"That's because you haven't bloody well earned it."

Colin was exasperated. She was slowly getting under his skin.

"So you have the three boarders and Lula. Is there anyone else who lives here?"

"Jeremiah and Mollie, though they share a small residence in the back."

"And who might visit on a regular basis?"

"Not many visitors. My doctor, Dr. Kenyon Dankworth comes by once a week. He should be round tomorrow, actually. The postman comes around twice and the milkman comes by once a week. The boarders get assorted guests, though you'd have to ask them about that. My solicitor comes round once in awhile when I need to sign some business papers. Nobody else really."

Frances nodded.

"And do you mind if I ask how you've managed in this place. Besides the boarders, the costs must still be substantial?"

"They are. My grandmother left me a substantial sum when she passed." Madge leaned in and whispered. "Almost three hundred thousand pounds," and then her usual voice. "Still, one needs to be cautious and watch the pennies or the pounds might run away I've managed to increase it a bit since then."

She laughed at her own joke which turned into a coughing fit. She reached forward for her glass of water and took a small sip. The coughing stopped and she took her time, wheezing and catching her breath.

"Careful," said Colin, "you might cough up a lung and we can't have that."

Frances looked at the letters on the table and put her finger down on them.

"These worry me. It appears you might be due one more if whoever wrote them is serious."

Madge looked at them.

"Why do you think just one more?" she asked.

"Well, they're all signed off slightly differently. With the first one I couldn't quite make out what it meant, but then the second one gave it away. 'Three dash six', 'four dash six', and then 'five dash six'. I think the last one will be signed six dash six, indicating the end of the series."

"My God," said Madge, "then I'll likely receive it on Thursday. What do you suppose it means when I've received the last one?"

Madge seemed unnerved. There was the specter of fear draped around her like a spider web.

"I can't say. I don't believe anything will happen, if indeed whoever wrote this is committed to harming you rather than scaring you, until after you've received the last letter. Do keep your eye out for anything or anyone suspicious."

Madge nodded and then looked over at Colin. He felt her stare and looked up at her.

"If I wanted to kill you, I'd hang you up like my Murdered Madonna," he said with more relish and spite than was perhaps warranted.

"Colin, I dare say that's awfully mean of you," said Madge.

"I agree. That's not the way to speak to a lady," said Alfred.

"She's no lady."

Frances put her hand on Alfred's knee to persuade him not to do anything rash. He held steady, though what he wanted to do was box the young man's ears.

"This handwriting on the letters, do you recognize it?" asked Frances.

"No, not at all, it's not written by anyone whom I might have recognized."

"What I'd like," said Frances, "is to get handwriting samples from everyone who lives here. I'd like samples from Colin, Lula, Matilda, Penelope as well as Jeremiah and Mollie. If it's all the same to you, I'd like to come back this evening before eight and collect them. I'd also like to meet with Matilda and Penelope."

"Yes, of course," said Madge, gaining courage from Lady Marmalade's confidence and air of authority. She puffed on her cigarette and blew billowing smoke to the ceiling.

"I want to ask you about the content of the letters," said Lady Marmalade. "Do the words mean anything to you?"

"No, nothing at all really. As I said, I vaguely remembered the words were from the bible. I had to look them up."

"I know this next question might be difficult and I don't mean to be impudent, but can you think of any reason why someone might perhaps want revenge against a perceived resentment?"

Frances looked at Madge as she smoked her cigarette and looked up thoughtfully. Madge shook her head.

"I can't say, really. I suppose there have been lots of little things that might have upset some people. You can't get through life without jostling a few lost souls, you know, Frances. And I suppose some might consider my insistence upon decency and good manners as an affront to their chaotic ways."

Frances nodded and smiled at her. Colin looked up from his book and was about to say something before he thought better of it as he looked over at Alfred and bit his tongue.

"Lula also said that some things have been going missing. Is this correct?"

"Yes, that's right. Odd things, I should say. Started happening when the first letter appeared. Now that I think about it, within a week of receiving a letter an item of mine has gone missing. Been stolen by one of the riff raff, I suppose."

"So now you're taking to calling us riff raff. How charming," said Colin sarcastically.

"If it is such a pain to be here, you are more the welcome to leave," said Madge indignantly.

"I'd rather not. The price of admission is terribly cheap. And you put on such a show. You know, Lady Marmalade," said Colin looking over at Frances, "I should think that she might be making this whole thing up just for a laugh. I wouldn't put it past her to write those letters all by herself."

Frances didn't say anything.

"That's rubbish," said Madge, "and I'll give you a sample of my handwriting too."

Frances nodded.

"If you wish, though I tend to take these sorts of things seriously. In any event, I should like to have my friend, Inspector Pearce of Scotland Yard take a look at these letters, if you don't mind."

Madge smiled and puffed herself up with pride. Lady Marmalade certainly was well connected and she was terribly pleased that an Inspector of Scotland Yard would show interest in her case.

"That would be wonderful," said Madge. "I've always held the highest regard for the members of Scotland Yard."

Not bloody likely, thought Colin.

"Back to these items that have been stolen or gone missing. What are they?"

"I should say certainly stolen. I've had the house turned upside down looking for them and I can't find them anywhere. The first item to go missing was a gold chain with a cross on it. I got that from my grandmother when I was just a young girl. It's terribly valuable to me. That was in January. In February a pearl necklace was stolen that was my daughter's which I got after she passed. In March somebody stole my hairbrush, an odd sort of thing to steal..."

Frances thought that might explain her mess of hair. Though she doubted that Ms. Hollingsberry's only brush had been stolen.

"April they stole my favorite lipstick and May they took a photograph. Not a valuable photograph but one that held a lot of sentimental value to me. It was of my daughter, Celia, me, and Lula when she was just a baby."

Madge finished smoking her cigarette and squashed it down next to the first one. Then she took a moment and steadied her eyes on Lady Marmalade.

"Will you take my case then?" she asked, almost scared of the answer.

Frances looked at her, nodded her head and smiled.

"Of course, why do you think I wouldn't?"

"Well, you've come to see me and I appreciate that and you've asked a lot of questions, but you haven't jotted anything down. So I wasn't sure."

Madge wheezed as her breathing remained belabored.

"I have an eidetic memory. I find that notes just slow me down."

"I see. I've never met anyone who had such a memory, I've been skeptical of such things in the past."

"Ask me anything you wish about what I might have noticed since I've been here."

Madge looked past Frances at the wall behind where she and Alfred sat. There was an Indonesian batik in a frame.

"Behind you," said Madge, "is a prominent item on the wall, can you describe it. I know this is sneaky, you might only have glimpsed at it as you came in, but still, if you'd humor me."

Frances smiled.

"Of course. You're talking about the Indonesian batik that is indigo in color. I'd say it was two feet by four feet. I believe it depicts Vishnu, the protector. He is seated in the lotus position with his hands together in front of his chest, his index finger and thumbs creating circles and the rest of his fingers perpendicular. He sits on a small table on top of six people kneeling, three on each side of a pyramid. His head is circled by three radiating halos each with heart-like patterns around the circumference. The first halo contains five hearts, the second six and the third nine. To each side of him, in line with his body, are two squares each containing a single line. Should I go on?"

Madge's smile was getting wider as she listened to Lady Marmalade depict the batik as if it were right in front of her. Colin was looking at her with an arched eyebrow and Alfred was smiling smugly.

"I think that was very well done."

Frances smiled.

"And Colin is reading 'Psychologische Typen' in the original German by Carl Jung."

"Very good," said Colin, putting down the book and clapping his hands sarcastically.

Lady Marmalade looked at her watch. It had gone half past ten.

"If you can't think of anything else that could be of assistance, I'll be going, only to return again around eight."

"Yes, not at all. I'll make sure that I have those handwriting samples collected by then. I'll start with Colin, seeing as he's right here."

Madge started to get up, with much effort.

"No need to get up," said Frances, as she and Alfred rose.

"Nonsense," wheezed Madge, as Jeremiah came to her side to help her. She shrugged him off with much effort. "I need to be getting upstairs, lying down is so much better for my health."

"Her health is fine," said Colin, "she's a hypochondriac, I'm sure she could dance a jig around all of us if she wanted to."

Madge was up by the time he finished speaking and she grabbed her cane and shook it at him.

"Why I put up with you, I have no idea."

Frances and Alfred followed her as she shuffled herself out of the living room. Frances paused as they walked by Colin.

"I'll see you later, Colin," she said.

Colin had not stood. He was ill mannered and by all accounts appeared ill tempered as well. Frances wasn't put off and she and Alfred continued on their way. Jeremiah was exceedingly flattering in ushering them out the door, almost to the point of embarrassment.

Once outside, the two of them clutching their jackets, the spring morning felt almost frigid compared to the oven they had just stepped out of.

"Not sure I could've lasted much longer in there, Alfred. I thought I might have been cooked hours ago."

Alfred chuckled.

"It was quite stifling, my Lady."

He put on his bowler hat and folded his jacket over his forearm as they ambled leisurely towards home.

"What do you think of it all?" asked Frances.

"I think the young man, Colin, needs to learn some manners. I find him insolent and boorish, though I might add he could have useful information to offer."

"I quite agree."

Alfred looked over at Lady Marmalade.

"Having said that, mind, I think the lot of them are quite odd. Ms. Hollingsberry is gruff and ill tempered with those around her. Lula seems like a frightened bird stuck in a cage being rattled by horrible children..."

"That's a very good way of putting it."

"The only decent people in that home seem to be the house staff, and I'm not certain their good naturedness is terribly sincere."

"This is why I love to have you with me on these excursions. You have a very erudite manner about you Alfred. You'd make a remarkable sleuth."

"You're very kind my Lady, though I confess to enjoying butlering quite enough."

"I wonder what the others will turn out to be like?"

"Could be we've entered a pit of vipers my Lady, and visited the best amongst them."

Frances slapped his shoulder softly, laughing out loud.

"We shall see, though I think in all earnestness, Ms. Hollingsberry does have reason to be concerned for her safety."

Five

It was just about eight p.m. when Lady Marmalade and Alfred made it back to the Hollingsberry home. Frances was in a summer dress, she had changed into something lighter for the Hollingsberry heat. Alfred had done the same. He wore gray slacks and a white shirt with a light sport's jacket and he had left his bowler behind.

Jeremiah answered the door, beaming a big smile at them.

"So nice to see you, again," he said. "Please do come in."

And although it sounded sincere, you couldn't help but wonder if he might say the very same thing to robber or thief. Jeremiah looked as if he had changed his suit. He still had a sheen of sweat upon his face, but his suit looked dry and crisp.

Frances took off her light cardigan and gave it to Jeremiah to put away. Alfred gave him his sport's jacket.

"Everyone is in the living room," said Jeremiah, turning to lead them to it.

And as he promised, everyone was present. Everyone that is, except for Madge.

"If you need Ms. Hollingsberry, she's upstairs resting. Just let me know and I can take you up, Lady Marmalade," said Jeremiah.

He left the living room to do some chores. Lula came up to greet Lady Marmalade and invited her and Alfred to sit down. The chairs and couches had been rearranged around a couple of coffee tables so that everyone could converse more easily.

Frances and Alfred sat down in the very same couch they had sat in earlier during the day. Across from her sat Lula in Madge's smoking chair, though Lula wasn't smoking. Nobody was smoking, something that Frances was grateful for.

To Lula's right, in another low armchair, sat a young woman also in her late twenties or perhaps early thirties who had a pinched face, sallow complexion, and long, straight, black hair. She was attractive at the right angle and with the little bit of makeup she wore.

"Thank you, everyone, for being present tonight; I'm Lady Frances Marmalade and this is my butler, Alfred Donahue."

"I'd sooner speak with you than the police," chimed in Colin.

"You might get lucky enough to speak with both," said Frances.

That shut him up for a moment. The young woman with the sallow complexion and long black hair who sat next to Lula stood up and reached her hand over to Lady Marmalade who shook it.

"I'm Penelope, Penelope Sallow," she said in a soft but pleasant voice.

Frances looked over to the couch where Colin sat next to another woman. She had medium length curly brown hair. She too got up and addressed Lady Marmalade.

"Matilda Parsons," she said, offering her hand to shake, which Frances did.

"Pleasure to meet both of you."

Frances sat down and Alfred sat next to her. Matilda didn't have what Frances would consider a horse's face. She had somewhat of an overbite but it wasn't terribly pronounced, and in fact she was the prettiest of the three young women present, and probably the oldest. Her voice was warm and pleasant and her gaze steady.

Lula reached over and handed Lady Marmalade some sheets of paper.

"These are the handwriting samples you asked for."

"Thank you, my dear," said Frances, taking them from Lula.

She looked at all seven of them briefly. They had each written The quick brown fox jumps over the lazy dog. And then they were signed by each person as well as had their name printed above their signature.

All seven of them were dissimilar, the five ladies' handwriting much prettier than the men's with one exception. Mollie's, the housekeeper, was childlike and suggested a lack of formal education.

Colin's handwriting was a scrawl and quite difficult to read in general and Jeremiah's was clean and practical but hardly notable. The only hand which came close to being similar to the letters was Matilda's; being similar it was by no means identical. Frances looked at it for a while trying to determine if Matilda had been trying to mask her normal handwriting when writing this sample. It was hard to tell.

Lady Marmalade gave the papers to Alfred who took his time looking at them through his glasses before folding them and putting them in his shirt pocket.

"So," said Frances, "I'd like this to be an informal and carefree conversation. Please feel free to talk about anything you might like, though if it be related to Ms. Hollingsberry in some way, that would be much better. One question I have to start things off, is why is it so hot in here? How do you all manage?"

Frances was looking at Colin who was still wearing his small suit from earlier in the day.

"You get used to it, I guess," he said.

Then he went back to sketching in the notebook he held open on his lap.

"I haven't noticed how hot it is for quite some time," said Penelope, "I think Colin's right. You do get used to it. There's no use complaining, Madge won't hear of it."

"She's not well," said Lula, "she get's sick very easily with just the barest touch of cold air."

"Not likely," said Matilda, "I think Madge is a hypochondriac, actually. I've overheard her speak with Dr. Dankworth and he's told her the same."

"What has he actually said?" asked Frances.

"I don't remember exactly but he basically said that her ills were all in her mind. He still gives her sugar pills for them, though. Though I don't think she knows they're sugar pills."

"How do you know they're sugar pills?"

"I took one and it did nothing for me."

Lula and Penelope gasped. Matilda looked over at them and shrugged.

"Madge is always complaining about something. If she didn't have her imagined ills to worry about there'd be no end to the grief in this place."

"Why is that?"

"Because she's generally mean spirited. You've met her; you must know what I'm talking about. She's an uncouth, mean spirited woman who thinks only of herself and what's in it for her."

"Then why do you live here, Matilda?" asked Frances.

"There aren't a whole lot of boarding homes available in London due to the bombings and I need to be close to work. I'm doing my bit for the war effort, working in the factory making munitions, and I like living with others. It feels safer."

"And you, Colin, you're at school. I would have thought they might have cancelled the non-essential programs."

"And you'd be wrong. So long as you're fit for war you can't study art. But seeing as how I'm not fit for war, I can."

"You look like an able bodied chap to me," said Alfred.

"Looks can be deceiving."

"He's got terrible asthma and he suffered rheumatic fever as a child, exercise of any vigorous sort would be the death of him," said Lula.

Colin looked over at her sternly.

"And I'm a conscientious objector," he said.

"Painting violent works. That seems out of character," said Alfred.

Lady Marmalade put her hand on Alfred's knee.

"Yes, well, we've already determined that the two of you don't have an appreciation for modern art."

"And you, Penelope, are you not concerned for your safety, working in London?" asked Frances.

"Sometimes, during The Blitz of '40 I was quite nervous, but I made it through then, and it's funny how you get used to it. Everything seems so calm now. I mean, we haven't had any bombs drop in over a couple of weeks isn't it?"

"It'll be twenty two nights if nothing happens tonight," said Alfred.

Penelope nodded and smiled widely.

"Yes, right, that's quite long. In a perverse way one misses them, I suppose. Not really misses them, but I guess the rhythm of things. Anyway, I need work and my employer won't leave, can't leave really, and so I'm stuck here. But as Matilda says, I like the company, it makes me feel safer, even if Ms. Hollingsberry is a bit overbearing at times."

"And you, my dear Lula?"

"My grandmother needs me," said Lula, fidgeting with her hands in her lap, "she's the only family I've got around here."

Frances looked at Lula's hands, the knuckles of both were still crusted in blood.

"What happened to your hands, Lula?" asked Frances.

Lula looked down at them and bunched them into balls and when that didn't hide the injuries completely she folded her arms and tucked her hands under her armpits.

"I scrapped them outside when taking out the rubbish," she said. "Silly me."

Her eyes wouldn't meet Frances', she kept them on the table.

"That's not what you told me," said Penelope.

"Shhh!" said Lula, looking very angrily at her friend.

"It's no secret that Madge beats you, Lula, everybody knows it," said Matilda.

"No, she doesn't!"

Matilda rolled her eyes and shrugged.

"You can't help those who won't help themselves," she said.

Lula looked up at Frances with pleading eyes and a quivering lip.

"She doesn't mean to. She just gets angry sometimes and she can't help herself. She's very sorry after."

"It's still not right, my dear," said Frances.

"Have any of you tried to help?"

"We called the police once, last year sometime I think it was," said Matilda. "Fat lot of good that did. Lula here denied the whole thing and made us look like idiots. That's what you get for trying to help."

Lula wasn't looking at anyone, she still held her hands under armpits.

"Has Madge tried to hit anyone else?"

"She threatened me once with her cane, the stupid old woman," said Matilda, "but I just pushed her down onto the floor. It was quite hilarious really. I don't know why Lula allows her to keep doing it. Beyond me really."

Frances looked at Lula.

"I don't imagine this is the first time she's done something like this to you, is it?"

Lula shook her head sadly.

"No," she whispered, "but she's not well and she doesn't mean it."

Matilda rolled her eyes again and sighed. She couldn't understand how Lula could allow herself to be treated so badly.

"How old were you when she started hitting you?" asked Frances.

Lula looked up furtively and then dropped her eyes from Lady Marmalade.

"Five or six I guess, if I remember correctly."

"You know you don't have to put up with it anymore."

"Where would I go? I don't have a job or money, nobody likes me and nobody wants me except for my grandmother."

Lula was mumbling, her eyes wet with pain.

"There are services out there that would help you, and as I understand it, the factories are in desperate need of young women who can work hard."

"They are," said Matilda, "I'm sure I could get you in, we have so many spots available, and you could find another boarding house to live in."

"But I don't think I'm very good at anything. I don't even know how to use a hammer."

"You'll get shown," said Matilda.

And this was the problem with poor, frail Lula. Not only had the beatings left physical scars, but they'd also beaten all confidence out of her. It was a terrible and criminal shame.

"Why have none of you stepped in when Lula's been hit by Madge?" asked Frances, looking around the room at the young faces.

"We tried, like I said, to call the police once. But we only find out about it afterwards. Madge always waits until none of us are around."

"Well, I'm going to talk to Inspector Pearce about this and see what we can do to help. You shouldn't be letting anyone hit you, Lula, not at your age and not for any reasons whatsoever."

Frances looked at her sternly as a mother might to her child. Lula was licking her lips and biting them.

"Why did she hit you this time?"

Lula wouldn't look up at Frances, she couldn't find her voice.

"Because Lula wasn't able to bring you back with her last night when she called upon you," said Penelope.

Frances shook her head. This whole situation was madness, she'd have to get Lula out from under Madge's hand. And she was going to speak to Madge about it too.

"When I'm finished down here I'm going to go upstairs and talk some sense into Madge."

"No, don't!" exclaimed Lula, finding her voice quite suddenly.

"And why not, my dear?"

"Because it'll just make things worse."

"You can come and live with me until you get on your feet," offered Frances.

"That's very kind," said Lula, glancing at Frances, "but I couldn't dare leave my grandmother, she needs me."

And this was the plight of the abused, somehow Lula had got it into her mind that this was her journey and her just deserts. It was wrong, but it could only be Lula who could change her own mind about that in time.

"I'd like to ask you all about Madge at this time. Anything you can share about her that you might think important would be helpful. I'll start with you Penelope."

"Well, if I can speak frankly..."

Frances nodded.

"Of course, anything you say will be held in confidence unless I should need to break that confidence due to you committing a criminal act."

"Madge is not a pleasant woman. She's not kind and she's spiteful. As I said, the only reason I'm here is because of the company. Not hers, but Colin's and Lula's and Matilda's. That and it's cheap, too."

"What do you think of these letters that she's received?"

"I don't know what to think of them. I haven't seen them, but from what Lula says, they've upset her quite a bit. Though ever since I've known her, she's been in bad sorts. Always a black mood, thinking she's about to die at any moment. That's why she brings her doctor round almost every week it seems."

"What if I told you the letters seemed quite threatening. They quote Deuteronomy, 'punish the children for the sins of the father'. They also threaten vengeance."

Penelope stuck her tongue in her cheek and tilted her head in thought for a moment. She pushed her hair behind her ear before she spoke.

"I suppose they do sound serious. But part of me wonders if she hasn't set this up herself. Everything's always about Madge around here and how bad she's got it. A plain example is with Lula. She hits Lula and then makes it sound like its Lula's fault for making her angry enough to lash out at her. She's crazy enough to pull a stunt like this herself. I wouldn't be surprised."

"So you can't think of anyone who might want to threaten her like this?"

Penelope shook her head and her black hair waved slowly from side to side.

"No. Though I suppose I wouldn't blame Lula for wanting her dead..."

"I would never," said Lula, looking quite shocked at the thought.

Penelope put her hand on Lula's arm and nodded.

"I know Lula, I'm just saying, you'd have good reason to."

Penelope looked back at Frances.

"I don't care for her, but honestly, my Lady, I couldn't be bothered to threaten her let alone find the energy to murder her."

"So nobody comes around who you might suspect of something like this?"

Penelope chuckled.

"Maybe the postman, he's the one that brings the letters. Or perhaps the milkman. Madge is forever crying over spilled milk, however little he might spill as he leaves the milk out."

"What about a gardener, I haven't heard mention of one."

"Oh, she has one, only he just comes around once a week or once every couple of weeks. Jeremiah deals with him mostly and I've never seen him in the house. Jeremiah pays him too, not much, from what I can tell. He's always whining about how much he doesn't get paid, yet he keeps coming back."

"And her doctor, Dr. Dankworth, what's he like?"

"He's quite pleasant. And quite good looking too..."

Colin looked at her and raised an eyebrow. She winked at him.

"He spends most of his time upstairs with Madge when he's visiting, but he keeps us informed about her treatment before he leaves."

"And Jeremiah and Mollie, how do they seem?"

"They're nice enough. Always so happy, especially Jeremiah, though I have no idea why. It's quite strange really. She treats them both abysmally. I can't for the life of me understand why they've stuck around as long as they have."

"Has she ever hit them that you know of?"

"No, I don't think so. But she's very rude and dismissive of them. Treats them worse than animals sometimes."

"I see, can you give me example?"

Penelope nodded.

"One time we were all having dinner and Madge didn't like it. It was spaghetti with meatballs. She said it was too cold and she threw her plate of food at Jeremiah. She didn't throw it hard, I mean he was standing right there, she more or less pushed it into his stomach and made him clean up the whole mess. She went on and on about how incompetent he was and how he'd be lucky to find work anywhere and that she was always paying him too much, though truth be told, from what I understand he's underpaid as a butler, especially in London."

"What do you think Lula?" asked Frances.

Lula shrugged her shoulders and fiddled with her fingers.

"I don't know. About what?"

"About Madge, about how she treats others, and about the possibility she might have written these letters herself to drum up sympathy for herself."

Lula shrugged her shoulders more.

"Well, then, she'd be silly to do that, wouldn't she, because she'd be found out soon enough?"

"Perhaps not. If nothing ever came of it she might get away with something like this for some months."

Lula looked at Frances and then at Penelope.

"I don't think she'd do that. I mean, she seemed very upset when she told me about them and when I brought the letters to her. I can't imagine why she'd do something so ugly."

"Because she's an ugly woman," said Matilda.

They all looked at her for a moment before looking back at Frances.

"For what it's worth, I tend to believe that these letters are not her own doing. But what about the way she treats you and others? What do you think about that?"

Fiddling fingers in her lap, it looked as though Lula might be trying to knit herself a cloak of invisibility. It was apparent, looking at her, the awkward gestures, the furtive glances, that

Lula was uncomfortable in social situations and perhaps more so speaking about her grandmother publicly like she was being asked to do.

"I think she's just misunderstood. I understand that she had a difficult upbringing. It was only her grandmother whom she was close to. She has a temper, but she doesn't mean it. I know that, even if nobody else does."

"You've never seen her hit anyone else?"

Lula shook her head.

"Tell me what you think about Jeremiah and Mollie and the gardener."

"They're nice. Jeremiah has the patience of Job and Mollie too. You'd almost think they were related..."

"Are they?" asked Frances.

"No, and the gardener I've only met briefly whenever I'm out in the yard or talking to the milkman. He seems nice enough even if he is a bit gruff."

"What do you mean by that?"

"He's not as friendly as Jeremiah and Mollie and he talks to himself, sometimes he's even arguing with himself, too. I've heard him out back."

"And what does he argue about?"

"I've only ever heard him argue about Madge and how stingy she is with her money. A real Scrooge he says. He says he should take something of hers to make up for it. But I don't think he's quite right in the head."

"I see, and what's his name?"

"Silas Pound."

"Tell me, Lula dear, can you think of anyone who might want to hurt your grandmother?"

Lula looked around at the faces all staring at her, except for Colin. He was sketching something and looking at Lady Marmalade intermittently.

"Anyone here, really. Like Penelope says, Madge isn't the kindest and she doesn't know how to treat people well, but she's trying. It's just that sometimes people don't know that deep down she's got a decent heart..."

Lula looked at Matilda and Colin quickly before looking at her hands knotted together in her lap.

"Colin and Matilda spoke of bumping her off not long ago..."

"I ought to wrap your knuckles myself, for everything I've done for you!" said Matilda.

"I'm sorry, dear, I didn't quite hear you," said Frances.

"Colin and Matilda were talking about bumping my grandmother off. I heard them, they were laughing about it."

Colin glanced up, hearing his name and shrugged his shoulders.

"It's not what it sounds like," said Matilda.

Frances looked at her.

"Then what was it like, exactly?"

"Look," said Colin, "Madge gets into these moods. She curses up and down the house, screeching like a banshee and putting everyone in a foul mood. I was just trying to let off some steam so I turned to Matilda one time and said we should bump her off and be done with all the drama, the wailing and gnashing of teeth."

"Still, that's quite a serious thing to admit to, especially under these circumstances," said Frances.

"I don't care," said Colin shrugging and looking back down at his notebook. "I'd welcome her death if I can speak plainly."

Both Penelope and Lula gasped.

"Colin!" said Matilda.

He looked up at her and tilted his head to the side.

"Listen, all I'm saying is that she's a horrid woman, I wouldn't miss her if she were bumped off, now I didn't say I'd do it."

"But that's just the problem," said Frances, "you admitted to saying the very thing just now."

"That's not what I mean, that was only in jest to try and alleviate the mood. Ask Matilda here."

Frances looked at Matilda.

"It's true, I didn't take it seriously and it did help ease the tensions. I don't think he'd do something like that. He's an artist, he's very sensitive beneath his angry exterior."

"I see," said Frances, looking over at Lula again. "What about the milkman or the postman?"

"They're very nice. I spend some time speaking with them when I have the chance. Grandmother gets me to pay Tom, he's the milkman, Tom McMeritt. He's an older man, very sweet. He takes good care of his horses too. You can always tell a man by the way he treats his beasts. That's what grandmother always says."

"And the postman?"

"He's a busy man, busier than the milkman for he won't stay as long and talk with me. But he's nice when he does have the time. He's old too, maybe even grandmother's age, and fat. I don't know how he can be so fat when he's walking around all day, but I've never asked him that. His name is Raymond Thompson, with the 'p' as he says."

"Can you see either one of them harboring any ill will towards your grandmother?"

"No, they've hardly ever met her. Certainly not more than a handful of times that I know about."

"What about Jeremiah or Mollie?"

Lula looked up at Frances with wide eyes.

"Good heavens, no, I can't imagine them hurting her. They've been with us over ten years each and they certainly could've left if they wanted to. No, I don't think they'd hurt her at all."

"But we just heard that Madge doesn't pay them very well, that might be incentive enough?"

"I don't get paid anything to look after my grandmother and I do it happily, I'd never think of hurting her."

"Does your grandmother have any other family you know of?"

Lula shook her head wearily.

"Not that I know of... wait, I did hear her talking about someone once in her sleep. Michael, Michael she kept calling out. I went to comfort her and asked her about it, but she wouldn't say anything. One day I found a picture of her in one of her drawers, holding a small baby. The back of it was written 'Michael 1 month, Christmas 1893'. Other than that, I never could find anything else out about Michael. I asked her once more but she got very angry and told me to never speak of it again."

"And there's nobody else who might know anything about that?" asked Frances.

"No. Her parents both died when she was seventeen I believe and her grandmother has been dead for quite some time. She's never spoken about any siblings that I know of."

"It's all very strange," said Frances, looking around at everyone and then at Alfred. "The most likely suspects are all in this room, and that would make them very foolish to harm Madge now that they know I've taken an interest in it."

"Indeed, my Lady," said Alfred.

"Or they'll do it so carefully that you'll never be able to pin it on them," offered Colin.

"There has never been a case that I have not been able to solve, given enough time."

"There's always a first time for everything then, isn't there?"

"You're an insolent and annoying young man," said Alfred getting a little hot under the collar.

"No need to get upset, Alfred, underneath all that gruff exterior is a sensitive artist, don't you know."

Frances smiled sweetly at both Colin and Matilda. Matilda attempted what might have been a smile but ended up being a face she might make while sucking on lemons. Colin was unperturbed and went back to his sketching.

Six

It was getting late. The clock had struck ten and the boarders were getting restless, but Lady Marmalade needed to finish her questioning while she had them all under one roof. She turned to Matilda.

"How long have you been a boarder here?"

"Penelope and I arrived about the same time. I started in June of last year and Penelope came the following month. I was the first I believe..."

Lula was shaking her head. Matilda and Frances looked at her.

"Is that incorrect?" asked Frances.

"Yes, my grandmother has had boarders as long as she's had me, practically."

"Well, in any event, there was nobody here when I answered the advertisement in the paper."

Frances looked back at Lula who nodded her head.

"Just a minute please Matilda, if you don't mind," said Frances putting up her hand to stop Matilda and looking at Lula. "How long do the boarders stay, on average, would you guess?"

Lula shrugged her shoulders and clenched at her dress. She looked furtively up at Frances.

"I can't say for certain, but I can't remember anyone lasting longer than a year."

She turned to look at Matilda.

"I'll be here longer than a year, I can promise you that. She's not going to scare me off."

That made Lula smile and she went back to looking at her hands in her lap. Frances put her hand back up to stop Matilda.

"Why hasn't anyone lasted longer than a year, do you suppose?"

Lula shrugged again and bit her lip. It was hard to tease out the information that Frances needed from her. Perhaps she felt self-conscious speaking about her grandmother in front of others, perhaps if Frances got her alone it might be easier.

"If you were to really think hard, Lula, why do you think nobody want's to stay after their lease is up?"

Lula looked up with flittering eyes that darted around the room like scared birds.

"I guess because most people don't understand Granny like I do..."

For some reason, Lula was reluctant to use this informal name for her grandmother, though it rolled off her tongue easily, perhaps the more formal 'grandmother' was mostly for everyone else's benefit, thought Lady Marmalade.

"I mean, my grandmother," Lula continued. "Nobody knows her like I do. I've been with her the longest. She's told me as much. Nobody else in her life has been with her longer than I have, not even her parents or her grandmother. Like everybody else says, she has a bit of a temper and she can be unkind, even though she doesn't mean it. I guess she has a way of pushing people away even though she doesn't mean it..."

"Oh, I think she means it very sincerely," said Matilda.

"Thank you, Lula, for your honesty."

Frances would have to speak with Madge about her treatment of Lula. It had been a long time since she'd heard anybody make such resolute excuses for such bad behavior on another's part. Though the hour was getting late, it would have to wait until Lady Marmalade's next visit. Frances looked back at Matilda.

"Sorry to interrupt you. You were saying that you arrived almost a year ago in June and Penelope in July."

"Yes, that's right," said Matilda, eager to return to her point of view. "Then Colin arrived in January of this year, didn't you Colin?"

She looked over at him and glanced down at his sketch which was almost complete. Colin nodded.

"And as I said, I'm not leaving anytime soon. So long as the three of us remain friends."

She looked at Penelope who smiled and nodded her head and then at Colin who was lost in his sketchbook and didn't say or do anything, and then she looked over at Lula.

"So you don't have to worry about that," she said, still looking at Lula.

"You feel quite protective of her don't you?"

Matilda leaned back into the couch and looked at Lady Marmalade.

"I do, she's almost like a younger sister to me. I try to watch out for her and if Madge's not careful she's going to have to deal with me if she continues hurting Lula like she does."

"And yet, not long ago you threatened to wrap her knuckles yourself."

Matilda looked down and folded her arms across her chest. Then she looked over at Lula.

"Yes, well, I just get frustrated sometimes. Lula knows that I would never lay a finger on her though, don't you?"

Lula nodded, smiling broadly.

"Really, Lady Marmalade, Matilda's got a big bark but she's toothless, really. She's been so terribly good to me this past year. You must believe me."

"I do." Turning to Matilda. "And now back to the matter at hand. Penelope mentioned that she wouldn't be surprised if Madge wrote these letters herself. What do you think about that as a possibility?"

"I wouldn't be surprised at all. Madge is like a child in some ways. If she's not the center of attention she creates 'incidents' to put herself in the center of attention. Like the time she threw her food at Jeremiah as Penelope recounted, she did that, not because the food was bad, it was quite good really, but because she wanted attention. And so she'll get herself worked up into these tantrums. It's quite hilarious if it wasn't so awful."

"So you think that her feelings of persecution are exaggerated?"

"Well, I can't think of who'd want to hurt her other than the three of us. And we'd be extremely foolish to do anything of the sort. The easy solution is for any of us just to leave if we're really fed up with her, but I don't get that sense that any of us are there yet. So to answer your question, I suppose that, yes, I probably do feel that these threats are grossly exaggerated."

"Let's play a game of what if. What if, these threats are serious and sincere? Who might you think capable of pulling them off?"

Matilda unfolded her arms and smiled cheekily at Frances before turning to look at Colin for a moment.

"I suppose that would be Colin and I."

Colin looked up at her and grinned like the cat that just caught the mouse.

"Please, Matilda, let's be serious. I happen to think these threats are sincere and I hope you'll take them seriously too, for all our sakes. Because if someone means to do harm to Madge in her house, I fear that none of you might be safe."

That lowered the temperature in the room quite quickly. Matilda's grin fell off her face silently and she looked down in thought at something on the floor.

"It's just unnerving, that's all. I'd hate for something to happen to her after what Colin and I joked about a few weeks ago. The last thing I need is for the police to be interested in me and having work find out. I need my job."

She looked up at Frances with pleading eyes, sorrowful as a Basset Hound's.

"I understand under the circumstances you and Colin were making light of the matter. But now, we need to look at things more soberly, so if you could help me with the answer to my question, that would be a good start."

"Well, other than Lula, I'd say that Jeremiah gets the worst treatment from Madge and he's always so damn cheerful. It seems quite insincere and forced. I don't know what it is about him, but there's something under his facade of docile servitude that just sends shivers down my spine."

"Have you ever seen him angry at anyone?"

"Not to anyone, but I have seen him lose control."

"Tell me about that."

"A few months back, I was coming downstairs to start my day and I heard all this yelling and screaming coming from the kitchen. So I went in to investigate and what I saw horrified me..."

Matilda steadied herself, she swallowed and blinked her eyes and knotted her fingers.

"He had taken a broom and he was thrashing it about on the floor. When I got closer to look, he was bashing a rat and her babies to smithereens. Now, don't get me wrong, I'm terribly afraid of rats and their big buck teeth, but there was a maliciousness and perverse enjoyment that was shown all over Jeremiah's face that horrified me the most."

"And did he see you?"

"He did, and just like that, as if you would flick a switch, he regained his composure and became his sickly sweet cordial self as if nothing out of the ordinary had happened. But the way he took after the rat and her little babies was excessive, but it was more than that. He showed a macabre pleasure and delight in finishing them off. It was horrifying really. I've never forgotten it; it haunts me to this day, too."

"But it was only a rat," said Colin.

"Yes, you might say it was only a rat, but to get such perverse pleasure from violence like that, it made me tremble, and I dare not think about what else a man like that is capable of."

Matilda had her arms folded and she was visibly upset by the ordeal. She stared at a spot on the tables in front of all of them.

"I agree, Matilda," said Frances, "that is indeed quite upsetting, and worrying."

Matilda looked up at Frances and then glanced away. Perhaps she was trying to determine the sincerity of Lady Marmalade's statement. But what she didn't know, was that Lady Marmalade was nothing if she wasn't sincere.

"What about Mollie? The two of them, Jeremiah and Mollie both seemed quite similar. I find them both a little... odd."

"Yes, I find that too. I've often wondered if they're siblings, but Lula assures me otherwise. Mollie has that same unctuous tone as he does, though I have never seen her angry or upset. Unlike Jeremiah, I sometimes wonder if Mollie just isn't a little slow."

"Grandmother thinks she is, too, but says she works well, even if she is less than competent," offered Lula.

"I suppose you get what you pay for," said Penelope.

“What about the milkman or the postman. Have you had a chance to meet either?” asked Frances.

Matilda shook her head.

“No, though as Lula says, she’s pretty friendly with both of them. They seem all right, but I’ve never really paid attention to either of them.”

“And what about Silas, the gardener?”

“I wouldn’t trust him with very much at all. I’ve never seen him in the house, but I wouldn’t be surprised if he’d swipe things if he had the chance. Maybe he’s snuck in and stolen some of the items that Madge claims have gone missing.”

“But nobody’s seen him in the house, have they?”

Frances looked around to grim nodding faces. Nobody had seen Silas in the house.

“He sure is odd, in a sinister way. He talks to himself like Lula says, but he’s scary with it.”

“How so?”

“On one occasion, I was in the garden minding my own business. Trying to enjoy the weather and reading a book in peace and quiet. He was out there pruning the bushes and pulling weeds. He had worked his way up close by to where I was sitting and I heard him talking to himself. I asked him what he was saying, as I thought he was talking to me. He said ‘you’re a pretty little thing, you are. You’d make a fine payment for my troubles.’ Very upsetting; I asked him what he meant, and he said ‘for all the trouble there’s been you’d make the proper sacrifice.’ I got up and left then and he called out after me, ‘she’ll pay she will, mark my words.’”

“That is quite upsetting, my dear,” said Frances, “what do you think he meant by that?”

“I don’t know and frankly I don’t care to know. I thought he was just soft in the head, but he’s scary too. I don’t go near him, now, whenever he’s around.”

"That's what you get when you pay people so poorly," said Colin, looking up from his sketchbook.

"What have you been sketching, Colin?" asked Frances.

Colin picked up his sketchbook and showed the drawing to Lady Marmalade. It was exceptionally well done and Lady Marmalade immediately knew what it was of. It showed her standing up looking at Madge who appeared dead in a bathtub. Frances was holding a magnifying glass as she peered at Madge's drowned body.

"That's quite macabre," said Frances.

Colin smiled as if Lady Marmalade had just given him the finest compliment he had ever heard.

"Not as macabre as my Murdered Madonna," he said placing the sketchbook back down on his lap and smiling admiringly at his own work.

"Why is she in a bathtub?" asked Frances.

Colin looked up at her, still smiling.

"Because I imagine that would be an easy and satisfying way to murder her, if you were going to do it."

"Colin!" said Matilda, slapping him across the shoulder. "We're in enough trouble as it is."

"You are indeed, and if anything should happen to Madge, the police will be very interested in you," said Frances.

"Look, it's just a joke and a sketch. No harm meant by it. And anyway, I happen to agree with Penelope and Matilda, I think that silly old cow is setting you up, Lady Marmalade, and nothing is going to come of this. I think she likes the attention. No, I know she likes the attention and I imagine this is her coup de grâce."

"I hope you're right, because, God forbid, anything happens to her and you'll be the first on my list to speak with," said Frances.

"I'm an artist not a killer," said Colin, appearing genuinely wounded that anyone should think otherwise.

"You're also impudent and callous, young man, and that will get you into a whole lot of trouble if you don't mind your manners," said Alfred.

If he weren't here with Lady Marmalade, Alfred felt certain he would have already boxed the lad's ears. Colin closed the sketchbook and laid it on his lap with his hands on top of it.

"If you were to look back over the year you've been here at Madge's home as a boarder, do any other names come to mind as someone who might have an axe to grind with Madge?"

Matilda looked off to the ceiling for a moment trying to sift through a year of life under the constant threat of bombs and the haranguing of Madge.

"There was an older gentleman who came calling at the end of last year. I think it must have been around the middle of December."

Frances nodded.

"He was a little older than Madge. He was a tall and large man. Not fat mind you, but big and he had thick gray hair with bushy eyebrows. That's the impression he left on me. I overheard Jeremiah speaking with him at the front door. He was very well dressed and said his name was Hiram Gaspar."

"And what did he want?"

"He wanted money."

"Are you sure, you said he was well dressed?" asked Lady Marmalade.

"I'm quite sure. I had the distinct impression that he was a man who went through money quite liberally. He convinced Jeremiah to let him go upstairs and visit Madge, even though she didn't want to see anyone. My bedroom is upstairs, all of ours are actually, but my bedroom is right next to Madge's and I could hear them arguing through the wall. It got quite heated."

"What did you hear?"

"He demanded the money that he said was rightfully his. He said if she didn't give it to him that he knew about her secrets and that she would regret it. He'd tell everyone he knew about it."

"What was this secret?"

"He didn't say, but it made Madge very upset and she started yelling at him to get out and eventually she called for Jeremiah. It was at that point that he left. He was quite odd. I watched him leave as I stood just inside my doorway. He saw me and stopped and smiled. It was a kind smile but a sad one. He held his hat in his hand and he reminded me of a very well dressed undertaker as he stood there and spoke to me."

"What did he say?"

"He said, 'I'd be careful if I was you, dear, there're bad things bound to happen in this house.'"

"Was that all?"

"Yes. I didn't know what to say so I said nothing. He just turned and walked out and I haven't seen him since."

"Do you know who he was?"

Matilda nodded, looking at Lula.

"He said he was Jasper's son, earlier in the conversation he was having with Madge. That set her off, too. She said something about him being no relation to her."

"Do you have any idea of who that might be?" asked Frances.

Nobody spoke up. Matilda shrugged and said that maybe it was somebody related to Madge somehow. Frances noticed that Lula was fidgeting with her dress again.

"Do you know, Lula?"

Lula looked up and nodded.

"I think Jasper might have been her uncle. When I found that photograph in grandmother's things I found a couple of others, too. One of them was of her mother, Phoebe, when Phoebe was a young woman. It must have been before she was married. The date on the back said 1867. I think her mother must have been about ten or eleven. It showed a picture of a man and woman, must be Phoebe's parents, along with Phoebe and a boy called Jasper. It looked like he was older by just a bit and he must have been her brother."

"So Jasper would have been Madge's uncle?" asked Frances.

Lula nodded her head.

"I think so, though, when I asked about him at the same time I asked about Michael, she slapped me across the face and made me wash my mouth out with soap."

"That would make Hiram and Madge first cousins, I suppose," said Frances.

"If you say so, I find this whole thing quite complicated," said Matilda.

"Who was the mother of Phoebe and Jasper then?" asked Frances.

Lula chewed her lip and furrowed her brow.

"I think the parents in that picture were Charles and Lilly Gaspar. Yes, that's right," said Lula nodding, "because my grandmother always spoke so well about her grandmother whose name she said was Lilly." Lula was nodding her head vigorously now. "That's right because she said she always remembered her grandmother being as pretty as a flower. She really admired her."

"The picture is becoming clearer, thank you Lula. So how did she get the name Hollingsberry? Who were Madge's parents?"

"Phoebe married Rufus Hollingsberry."

Frances nodded.

"All these family relationships are quite puzzling. And her parents died when she was quite young, right?"

"Yes, I think she was seventeen when her parents died. At least that's what I recall," said Lula.

Frances paused for a moment to collect her thoughts and put all the pieces of the puzzle in place. There was now an incredible cast of characters that she needed to either find out more about or discard completely. Only time would help with that.

"Now, I've heard," said Frances, looking back at Matilda, "that Madge threw out a gentleman friend of yours, Maxwell Blacksmith, and that you got quite upset about it. Is that true?"

"Yes, that's quite true. Max was just about to propose when she came barging in. It was barely past ten and she was just looking to make a fuss. He was on bended knee and reaching for his ring when she just walked straight into my room, without knocking I might add, and told him that curfew was up and that he'd best be going."

"And, what time was that?"

"It was barely past ten, I don't imagine it was past five after ten. I was spitting mad. These are the sorts of things that she does that just drive you batty."

"And did Max not propose after that?"

"No, he did," said Matilda, putting out her left hand for all to see the small solitaire diamond that was on her finger, "but still, the impertinence of it."

Lula looked at her with squinted eyes.

"You are going to leave, aren't you," she said, sounding visibly upset.

"Not for at least a year, and by then, we'll get you out of here, too. Max doesn't want to marry until after the war and he's been discharged, and I agree. It was still sweet of him to propose as a promise to me for when he returns."

"When did he propose?" asked Frances.

"St. David's Day, the 1st of March, he's Welsh you see."

Frances nodded.

"And I take it he's not here at the moment; he's on the front, is he?"

"Yes, though he says he's safe. I got a letter from him recently and he says we're making good progress keeping the Japanese back. Last I heard he was in Madagascar writing to say that they were making good progress in wrestling it away from the Japanese and French."

"Well, as we've heard, we've gone a few weeks without any air raids, so perhaps things are indeed boding well for the future and the end of this war," said Frances. "Is Max getting leave anytime soon?"

Matilda looked down at her ring on her wedding finger and shook her head sadly.

"No, I don't think so, at least not for some months. He didn't give any indication."

"Well," said Frances trying to offer reassurance, "the two of you will have the rest of your lives together once this war is over and done with. And hopefully it will be the war to end all wars."

Matilda looked up at Frances and nodded eagerly, as if agreeing to the hope might make it so. Even though in the back of her head she had the niggling doubt, she didn't wish to give any notice to.

"So, to try and keep everything straight, Matilda, you can't imagine who might want to harm Madge, other than Jeremiah, whom you think is quite odd, and dare I say frightful. Or perhaps the gardener, Silas, or maybe even this strange, big man you met once, Hiram Gaspar."

"Yes, I suppose if I were forced to guess, those might be my three best suspects, but I've never met the milkman or the postman so I can speak about them."

"Right, though we've all heard from Lula that they're quite pleasant and it has been my experience that those who murder, most often, though certainly not always, have more than a casual acquaintance with their victim."

"But like I said, I really think that perhaps Madge is doing this herself to create more drama, as if there isn't enough already, with the war and all the stress that goes along with it."

Frances turned to Colin.

Seven

"Do you have anything to add, Colin?" asked Frances.

Colin looked up at Frances and stopped tapping on his sketchbook with his long, slender hands. He shrugged.

"I don't think so. Like Matilda and Penelope, I think that Madge is having you on. I find this whole idea of someone wanting to harm her quite preposterous."

"Why is that?"

"Well, let's look at things objectively, and no disrespect, Lady Marmalade, I know that your reputation precedes you, but let's look at the facts."

"That's often a good way to start," agreed Frances.

"Okay, then. The facts are that you have received, what, three letters?"

Lady Marmalade nodded.

"Three letters that apparently contain damming and threatening content. I doubt very much that you'll find anybody's handwriting to match that in the letters..."

"How can you be so sure?"

"Because you've already looked at the samples we've given you and I can tell that nothing jumped out right away or you wouldn't have stayed so long asking us these questions."

Frances hadn't realized that Colin was more observant than she had originally given him credit for.

"But perhaps somebody has masked their handwriting in the samples," said Frances.

Colin squinted his eyes and looked down at the floor briefly.

"Perhaps, but that will be hard to uncover. As I said, we have to stick with the facts."

"Carry on."

"So you have three letters, given to you by Madge, that contain threatening content. But yet, who would have good reason to harm her. You might say any of us, so let's take a moment to look at each of our motives."

"Please."

Colin nodded his head.

"Good," he said, and looked over at Penelope. "I'll start over on my right with Penelope. What is her motive? Frankly, I can't think of one for Penelope. She's quiet, to be certain and doesn't like Madge, that's no surprise, but I wouldn't say Madge treats her any worse than the rest of us."

He looked at her for a while and she smiled at him sweetly and nodded her head.

"Yes, I agree, on the exterior, Penelope doesn't look like she has much of a motive. But I have often found, Colin, that there are ulterior motives, secrets sometimes, that need to be uncovered before one can find the motive."

"But let's stick with the facts as we know them to be right now. Penelope doesn't have much of a motive."

"Fair enough, though I think you do protest too much. It is plain to me as the twinkling stars outside in the night sky, that you and Penelope care very much for each other."

Penelope blushed and Colin stalled for a brief moment.

"Well, we're not trying to keep that a secret, still, it doesn't change the facts."

"Very well, go on."

"Now we get to Lula. Here we can actually start to dream up motive. As you know, Lula's treatment at Madge's hand is abysmal and atrocious. I have no idea why she puts up with it, and it's been ongoing since I arrived. At least four months, though I dare say it's actually been going on for years."

Lula looked uncomfortably at the coffee table and fiddled with her fingers, gently rubbing the scabs that had crusted her knuckles.

"It's been at least a year," said Matilda, "and I'm sure it's been going on for much longer."

Everybody looked at Lula but she just wanted to curl up into a little ball and be blown out of the living room by any token of breeze.

"You were reading Carl Jung's book earlier today, Colin, the psychology of abuse is not well understood and we should rather offer Lula compassion than judgment if we are to help her at all," said Frances.

Colin nodded his head.

"Yes, I suppose, but let's stick to the facts again and not the psychology. All I'm saying is that Lula has motive. Perhaps she wants to harm her grandmother for all the harm that Madge has caused her."

"I would never hurt my grandmother," mumbled Lula.

"Not to worry dear, this is just an exercise in sleuthing," said Frances.

"So Lula has motive, but then one has to ask, why go to all the trouble of writing these letters, or more likely have someone write them for you? I mean it doesn't make sense to me. You're putting the limelight on yourself and making it easier for the police, or you," said Colin looking at Lady Marmalade, "to catch her. Why not just be done with it, poison the old woman and not leave a trail?"

"Well, that's where the facts aren't very helpful Colin. In my experience, the facts can help you identify the killer but aren't always helpful in uncovering motive or why they plan or plot or carry it out as they do."

Colin ignored what Frances had to say.

"Lula has motive, and God knows I'd not blame her for wanting to hurt the old lady, but she hasn't, and she doesn't strike me as someone who would, either. She's as meek and mild as a summer breeze."

He smiled at her and she offered him a weak smile in return that could easily have been blown off her face by the lightest of the summer breezes he had just spoken of.

"Dear Colin, you're going from facts to speculation. If you're going to stick to the facts," said Frances, "then you can't discount Lula based just on your feeling."

"Right, I agree. The facts are, Lula has motive, but she hasn't carried it out yet and I can't see her going to all that trouble."

Colin then looked at Matilda and smiled. He put his hand on her shoulder.

"Forgive me," he said, and she scowled at him. "Matilda has motive, too. She was embarrassed by Madge when Madge kicked her boyfriend out, and she's plainly not happy with the old woman. So Matilda has motive."

"Yes, but why would I go to the trouble of writing letters that started before Madge kicked Max out?" asked Matilda.

"How do you know they started before March?" asked Frances.

"Lula told us that she had started delivering these letters to Madge back in January."

Frances looked at Lula and she nodded her head in embarrassment.

"And that's just the thing," said Colin, "why would you write these letters starting before March when Madge embarrassed you, unless there was some other reason."

"Such as?"

"I'm not going to speculate, I'm just going to stick to the facts. And there are no facts that would offer a reason as to why you might write threatening letters to Madge beginning in January. Other than ever since I arrived in that month, you've plainly complained to me about how awful she was. Perhaps you wanted to give her a little scare and then with what happened with Max, it gave you more fuel for the fire?"

Matilda shrugged and folded her arms across her chest.

"You see how easy it is to start speculating?" said Frances.

Colin looked at her and nodded.

"And that's why I think we should stick with the facts. The facts are that Matilda has a motive, perhaps just as strong or stronger than Lula's. A woman scorned, after all, has a fury greater than hell, as Bill, the other old bard, said."

"Are you talking about Shakespeare?" asked Matilda.

Colin looked up at Penelope who grinned back at him.

"No," she said, "he's talking about the other Bill. William Congreve."

Colin beamed.

"You see, I told you she was well read and intelligent."

Frances smiled. One could warm to even the prickliest of people when they were in love as Colin was expressing just then.

"Then wouldn't we need facts as to why Matilda wrote these threatening letters?" asked Frances.

"Yes, we would, and that's to come, I suppose, if all evidence points to Matilda."

"How nice of you to say," Matilda said, "to hang a friend out like that."

"I'm not done," said Colin, "as we turn to me. I have motive and perhaps I have even been caught somewhat red handed having said that we should bump her off."

"Yes, you admitted to that, and you were overheard speaking it. And though you now proclaim it was just in jest, perhaps it wasn't. And the letters did conveniently start just after your arrival here," said Matilda, relishing the chance to put Colin's feet to the fire.

"Agreed. But what's my motive?"

"You just plainly don't like her, you paint violent and disturbing paintings and you generally enjoy, and dare I say, relish, the drama in this house."

"Guilty as charged," said Colin, holding both his hands up towards the ceiling. "And yet, I doubt very much my hand resembles the writing in those letters."

"Perhaps, though you could have changed it, you are, after all, an artist," said Matilda.

"I doubt you'd need to be an artist to change your penmanship in situations like this," said Colin.

He turned to look at Lady Marmalade.

"So we have the four of us here with only three having motives based on fact. And yet, I fear, that all three motives are weak and held up by feeble sticks of fact."

Frances looked at Colin with bemusement on her face for a moment and then looked at the others.

"I think Colin is an absolute genius," said Penelope.

"But that's only because you don't have a motive," replied Matilda.

"I can't believe that any of us would really want to hurt my grandmother," said Lula meekly.

"Well done, Colin. I think your exposition of the facts are quite well done. But it isn't just the facts that matter but sometimes emotion and motive are more important. But based upon your facts, let me ask you one question. If you had to choose, who would you choose to be the one?"

Colin looked around, taking a moment to pause on everyone's face. Then he looked at Lady Marmalade.

"Honestly, I'd have to say I'm probably the best candidate. Looking at the facts and also the circumstantial evidence, I think I'm the only reasonable choice."

"Explain that a little more, if you will?" asked Frances.

Everyone was looking at Colin intently now.

"Well, let's start at the beginning. I arrived just before the first letter was written and sent to Madge. And I imagine it's easy for any of us, really, to change our handwriting especially if we're going to be sending threatening letters to anyone, but perhaps Matilda makes a good point and being an artist, maybe it's easier for me than anyone else."

Colin paused for a moment and looked around.

"So right from the start it looks terribly suspicious. And as everyone here will tell you, I've made no secret of my distaste for the old lady since I arrived. Yet, I stay. Why is that? Because I enjoy the macabre and the drama? Perhaps, or, could it be I'm really plotting her demise. I think that's a better reason."

Frances nodded in encouragement.

"Then there's the art I'm painting. It's expressive and full of passion and depth, but most don't see that, most see violence and anger, so there's another mark against me. We all don't care for her, but none of us except for me, seems to have a taste for the macabre. And lastly, I'm a man. I'm the only man amongst us, excepting Alfred, who doesn't count anyway because he's here on your behalf, Lady Marmalade."

"Why do you think being a man is so important?" asked Frances.

"Wouldn't you agree that men are most often more likely to commit murder than women?" asked Colin.

"As a rule, yes," said Frances, "but it also depends on how murder is committed. I try not to be dissuaded one way or the other by trying to predetermine the sex of the murder but rather allow the murder itself to point me towards a likely candidate. But if I were to go by your sketch, then I'd have to say, that yes, drowning, being a violent method of murder would most likely be committed by a man."

"And there you are," said Colin, offering his hands out, wrists together, "handcuff me and take me to gaol for I'm obviously guilty."

He looked around with a wicked grin on his face.

"Ah, yes, I quite forgot, there hasn't been a murder yet, has there?"

He put his hands back on top of his sketchbook and looked around. Matilda was grinning but shaking her head in disappointment. Penelope was smiling broadly, quite delighted with Colin's act, and Lula was looking furtively about.

"This might seem very funny to you at the moment, Colin, but if anything should happen to Madge, you might find yourself in deeper trouble than you'd like to think, even if you haven't anything to do with it," said Frances.

"Look," said Colin, glancing at Frances, "all I'm trying to say is that I have no idea why we're spending so much time on this. Nothing has happened except for a few, apparently threatening letters. And if I were a betting man, I'd put money on Madge as being the one who wrote them to herself."

"By a show of hands then, who believes that to be the case?" asked Lady Marmalade.

She looked around as Colin, Matilda and Penelope all raised their hands.

"And who thinks that someone else wrote these letters?"

Frances, Alfred and Lula put up their hands.

"Looks like we are at an impasse," said Frances.

"You can hardly count Alfred, no disrespect, but I'm certain he'll just do as you expect of him," said Colin.

"Not true, Colin. In matters like these, Alfred's input is often different to mine and very valuable. In any event, the only opinion around here that really matters is mine."

"Then who did it?" asked Colin.

"I haven't determined that yet, but I will in time. But more importantly, I'd like to hear what you have to say about some of the other potential people we've heard about. For instance, what about Jeremiah? As we've heard from Matilda he seems to have quite a temper."

Colin shrugged and tapped his fingers on his sketchbook, in a rhythm.

"I can't say. Certainly he seems odd to me, but then doesn't everyone? We're living in odd times. Most of you would think I'm quite odd, too. Yet, I'm hardly a murderer."

"But you haven't shown anger or violence like Jeremiah did."

"Right, but you've seen my art..."

"That's not the same."

"Well, maybe it isn't, but only Matilda saw Jeremiah acting out that way, and no offence Matilda, but perhaps she read more into it than was really there."

"I most certainly didn't," said Matilda crossing her arms over her chest again.

"Then you'd say that you don't think Jeremiah would harm Madge?"

"I'm not saying that at all. Look, I suppose anyone could harm anyone else if it came down to it and they had good reason for it. I just don't pay much attention to him, that's all. Yes, he's sickly sweet with his exaggerated servile facade, but that doesn't make him a monster."

"All right then, what about Mollie?"

"As someone else mentioned, I think it was Matilda, she could be Jeremiah's sister, but really, I pay less attention to her than I do to him. She's almost a non-entity around here. I barely notice her."

"The milkman, the postman and the gardener?" asked Frances.

"Aha, there's your triumvirate of harm."

Penelope giggled and Matilda smirked, looking down at her feet. Colin looked up at Frances and could see that she was not amused.

"Sorry," he said, "I can't help myself. I find this all very taxing and tiring when nothing of note has really happened, except more drama which Madge seems to thrive on. I swear the woman would be dead if it weren't for the drama around here that keeps her going. It's almost like her air. I haven't had enough to do with those three to really say anything about them one way or another. Though, as Matilda says, Silas sure seems a little odd."

"Have you met the doctor or this fellow, Hiram?"

"Yes and no in that order. The doctor is a very gracious and, dare I say patient, man. To put up with Madge's whinging and hypochondria for all these months. He's almost a saint, except I imagine he gets paid well for his troubles and sugar pills."

"How long has Dr. Dankworth been visiting your grandmother?" asked Frances.

"A few years at least, I'd say," said Lula.

Frances turned back to Colin.

"And Hiram Gaspar?"

"Never met him, don't know him other that what Matilda shared. Again, quite odd what he said to her, and menacing too, I suppose. But everything about this bloody place is odd and menacing when you're talking about Madge."

Now Colin was crossing his arms over his chest. He was plainly getting exasperated and had his legs thrust out under the table in front of him. Frances looked at her watch, it was after ten thirty, the clock had just chimed not long before.

"You've all been terribly patient and I'm very grateful for that. I'm also grateful that you've shared your handwriting with me and your thoughts on who might be responsible for these threats, if in fact they are real."

"That's the clincher, if they are, indeed, real," said Colin, still looking miffed at the wasted time that he was sure Madge had created for her own perverse enjoyment.

"And that's how I'd like to end our visit, and let you get back to your evening. Penelope, if I can start with you. I know we've spoken extensively about who might be a candidate for having written these letters and you've mentioned Lula..."

"Yes, but I wasn't quite serious."

"But you said her name first so one must take that into account."

Penelope looked at Frances without saying anything.

"For argument's sake, you've suggested Lula..."

Lula was fidgeting and her eyes were flitting from person to person in the room.

"...and you've also said that you wouldn't be at the least bit surprised if you found out that Madge had orchestrated this whole thing herself. So my question to you is this. If you have to choose just one of these options, which one would it be?" asked Frances.

"I'd have to say it was Madge doing this whole thing herself just to create more drama."

Frances nodded.

"And you Lula, you seemed to think that if it could be anyone it might be Colin or Matilda."

Lula looked at them both. Colin looked up at her with a blank expression on his face. Matilda looked at Lula and gave her a small smile.

"She also thought that Silas was quite odd and had spoken of robbing Madge," offered Matilda.

"Right, thank you Matilda. So, Lula, you've offered up Colin, Matilda and Silas. But what about the idea that your grandmother is doing this herself? I'll ask you the same question I asked Penelope. You can only choose one option or person, who would you think most likely?"

"She's leading the witness my Lord," said Colin. "You can't tell her to choose one option and then tell her which person she thinks that is, that's only giving her one option which is to say that it was someone else who did this to Madge, not herself."

Frances looked at Colin coldly.

"She knows what I meant."

Lula looked around the room.

"I'm sorry Colin," she said, and then she looked at Frances. "I'd have to say if it was anyone it'd be Colin."

Colin smirked and nodded his head.

"You would say that, wouldn't you?" His voice dripped with sarcasm.

"But I don't think he'd really do such a horrid thing to Granny, um, I meant grandmother."

"It's okay, dear, you can call her whatever you're most comfortable using," said Frances.

Lula looked down, her face was flushed, most likely out of embarrassment. Perhaps she felt too old calling her grandmother 'granny', and she wouldn't be wrong thinking that. But such were the ways of dysfunctional relationships.

"Matilda, you mentioned how upset you were by seeing Jeremiah kill that rat and her babies as well as the upsetting things that Silas said to you. You also thought that Madge might do something like this herself. So again, one choice out of these options. Who or what do you think it is?"

Matilda held out her left hand in her right and examined her engagement ring. It sparkled in the light of the living room and she was pleased. For she'd be getting out of this place soon enough when Max got back. Little did everyone else know, but they were going to move in together. Times were changing and they were on the forefront of it, they weren't going to wait until they go married to live together.

"Definitely Madge. I'd have to say she set this whole thing up for her own amusement. Though you being the sleuth and all, and getting paid for it, I guess it's only your opinion that matters."

Matilda smiled at Frances sweet as the first peas of summer.

"Yes, only my opinion matters, but what matters above everything are the facts. And I'm not convinced of any facts yet, nor am I getting paid."

"Well, you should. She surely has the means to pay you," said Matilda.

"And I have the means to choose what I do for free. Lastly you, Colin. The same question as before."

"Well, it must be me. I mean Lula said so, so it has to be true."

He looked at her, his mouth dripping with sarcasm as if he'd just tipped a jar of honey all over his face.

"Now, now, Colin, that's not nice nor necessary," said Matilda.

"I don't recall being nice or necessary the whole evening," he said.

"I'd like nothing more than to see you locked up by the police should anything happen to Ms. Hollingsberry," said Alfred.

"Yes, well, nothing's happened to her, has it? In any event, I was only joking and Lula knows that. I'm with Matilda and

Penelope. I'd put money on the fact that Madge has set this all up for her own amusement and to inconvenience all of us. Including you, I dare say, Lady Marmalade."

Colin stood up and tucked his sketchbook under his arm.

"Now, if you'll excuse me, I need to catch up on my beauty sleep before those bloody Germans start bombing again."

He didn't wait for any response. He marched smartly out of the living room and they all listened to his footfalls echo down the hallway and become softer and softer as he climbed the stairs to his bedroom on the second floor.

Frances stood up, as did Alfred. The other ladies stood, too, as soon as Frances did. They all wished her a good night and Frances and Alfred left into the black night. As dark as the lack of light that had shone onto this case so far. Frances felt certain that Madge had not written these letters herself, but who might have done it and for what purpose was not very clear as she walked silently with Alfred at her side. Not very clear at all.

Eight

The house was lit when Alfred and Lady Marmalade made it home. There should only have been Ginny keeping watch and if so, she had a lot of lights on that weren't needed. Especially during the war. Frances appreciated the gesture but thought she needed to speak with her housekeeper about it. Even though they could afford it, there was no need for the extravagance. Particularly during wartime.

Alfred opened the door for Frances and she walked in. She heard men's voices coming softly from the living room. The voices stopped and she heard the shuffle of feet as she and Alfred entered the house and Alfred closed the door behind them.

"Mother, dear," said a young man walking up to Lady Marmalade and embracing her in a warm hug. "I'm very cross to find you here. Father wouldn't approve, and you know it."

He stood back from her, holding her at arms distance. He was handsome, tall and slim, just like his father. He was six foot one, the same height as his father. He had the same thick, black, curly hair and the same bright-blue eyes. He grinned from ear to ear.

"Oh, Declan, my dear boy, how nice of you to visit, though it's frightfully late," said Frances.

"Only because you're home so late. Everard and I have been waiting over two hours, haven't we?"

Declan looked over at his friend who stood next to him. Everard was almost as tall and almost as handsome with brown hair and masculine, Germanic features with a square jaw and dimple. Though there was no German in him. Everard also had the most piercing green eyes, the color of pure garnet gemstones. He reached in and hugged Lady Marmalade, kissing her on both cheeks.

"So good to see you again, Frances, you look absolutely ravishing," said Everard.

"Lord Marmalade, Master Silsbury," said Alfred beaming at the two young men as he shook both their hands in turn.

"Where have you been, mother?" asked Declan.

"I've been down the street with Alfred, seems there's some frightful business going on with a poor woman and her boarders. Perhaps you can help me with it. Let's go into the dining room and see if you can't help me sort it all out."

"I let Ginny go already, seeing as I was here. Shall I get us a fresh pot of tea?" asked Declan.

"Please, my Lord, I can get the tea ready if you'll go and speak with your mother," said Alfred.

Declan looked at Alfred and smiled.

"Thank you, Alfred, that would be lovely."

Declan put his hand around his mother's shoulders and she put her hand around his waist and they walked liked that towards the dining room with Everard close behind them. They took a seat around the one end of the dining room table and Lady Marmalade put her handwriting samples face down on the table.

"This is very exciting," said Everard, rubbing his hands together eagerly. "What do we have here?"

"These are handwriting samples from the people who live in Ms. Hollingsberry's home," said Frances.

"Never heard of her," said Declan rolling up his sleeves under his sleeveless jumper.

"No, neither had I, and I don't imagine she'd be someone I'd care to remain on friendly terms with."

"Why is that?" asked Declan.

"She's prickly, rather, and uncouth and rude, to be frank with you, my dear."

"I see. Tell me then how you've come to know her?"

"A young woman by the name of Lula Beckenswidth called on me last night, quite late actually. She told me the story of her grandmother who has been receiving these letters that are quite upsetting."

Frances looked into her handbag and pulled out the three letters in question and placed them on top the handwriting samples.

"To make a long story short, Lula wanted me to head over to Ms. Hollingsberry's home late last night. It was after ten when I finally had Alfred walk her home. So I've just come back from visiting them tonight. Actually for the second time. I was there this morning visiting with Madge Hollingsberry who received these letters and then this evening I was visiting with her three boarders as well as Lula, who is her granddaughter."

"Fascinating, do tell," said Everard.

Alfred came in carrying a silver tray with silver teapot and milk jug and sugar bowl as well as three bone china teacups. He placed the tray down just off to the side but within reach of Lady Marmalade.

"Would you like any lemon, my Lady?" asked Alfred.

"No, thank you, Alfred. You may retire for the night, if you wish."

"That's not necessary, my Lady, I'd be happy to sit and visit and discuss the day's events with you, if that would be okay?"

"Yes, do stay, Alfred," said Declan, "I'd love to hear what you thought of the matter, too."

Frances looked at him and smiled.

"If you don't mind Alfred, that would be lovely."

"I'd love to," he said, and sat down next to Everard.

"So," said Declan, "Madge Hollingsberry is the woman who had received these threatening letters and Lula Beckenswidth, her granddaughter came to you last night to speak about them. Today you went over and discussed them with Madge and this evening you spoke with her boarders and got those handwriting samples," he said pointing to the pile of papers in front of his mother.

"That's correct."

"Give us the juicy bits, Frances. I want to hear all about the boarders. I bet that's where the stain lies," said Everard looking over at his partner, Declan, and grinning. Frances took the letters out of the envelopes and handed one to each of them.

"I find these letters to be quite upsetting. There is something about them that seems to suggest a secret and if I can uncover that secret then I might be able to determine who wrote these, or perhaps if not who wrote them, then who is behind the threats. But I fear time is running out. Thursday is the eleventh of June and that's when the next, and I fear, last letter should arrive."

Frances waited for everyone to share the letters around and she poured them all tea. There were only three teacups.

"Are you not joining us for tea, Alfred?" asked Frances.

"I wasn't sure, my Lady. Let me go and fetch a cup now."

Alfred got up and disappeared for a few moments until he returned with a teacup for himself. Frances poured him a cup and they sat in silence as they added the condiments to their tea just as they liked. Except for Alfred, who drank his black.

"These letters are quite menacing in tone," said Declan. "I can see why you're taking them seriously."

"What is this cryptic bit about the sins of the father?" asked Everard.

Frances nodded.

"Yes, I think that is the secret that, if revealed, will be the key to understanding this whole matter and perhaps determining if the threat is real, which I think it is, or not."

"I think one has to take this sort of thing very seriously. Don't you agree?" asked Declan looking around the table.

"I agree whole heartedly, my Lord," said Alfred.

"That's just the thing, Declan," said Frances, "None of the boarders think this is really all that serious. In fact, they all believe that Madge might have written these letters herself as some sort of silly game to create more drama in their lives."

"Why on earth would they think that?" asked Declan.

"Because Madge is not the nicest woman I've ever met. It appears that she beats her granddaughter and makes life generally miserable for everyone around her. And frankly, I didn't like her very much either."

Frances looked over at Alfred, who nodded.

"Quite a disagreeable woman," he said.

"Hmm, I see," said Declan.

"That's horrible. How can she get away with beating a grown woman, I assume Lula is grown?" asked Everard.

Frances nodded her head.

"Such is the psychology of abuse and power I suppose," said Frances. "I'll be talking to Madge about it the next time I see her and give her a stern warning. Though I imagine that if Lula is not willing to move, there is not much we can do to help her."

"Tell us about these boarders, mother, dear," said Declan.

"Matilda is the oldest one, recently engaged and has been there since June of '41. Then there's Penelope, who arrived in July and lastly is this very difficult young man, Colin, who arrived in January of this year. Coincidentally at the same time as when the letters started."

"And they all think that Madge wrote these letters herself?" asked Declan.

Frances nodded.

"That's quite a ghastly thought, really," said Everard, "I mean... you'd have to be an awful person to put others through such a horrid fiction."

"I agree, and although some might say that Madge is indeed a horrid woman, I didn't get the impression that she'd do something like this," said Frances. "What are your thoughts on the matter, Alfred?"

"I quite agree, my Lady. She is definitely a difficult woman, but I got the sense that she's quite upset by these five letters."

"So there were five?" asked Everard.

"Yes, she burnt the first two," said Frances.

"The writing on the letters is quite feminine," said Everard, "I'd think it was written by a woman. That would be my first guess."

Declan nodded picking up and looking at one of the letters.

"Quite feminine and very pleasing to look at. Artistic even, despite the message that is written," said Declan.

"Do any of the samples match the writing on the letters?" asked Everard.

"Not quite, though I thought one of them looked similar," said Frances.

She turned up the handwriting samples and shared them around. They each took turns looking at the samples.

"This one I think," said Declan, pointing at the handwriting sample of Matilda.

"I agree," said Everard.

Everybody looked over at Alfred.

"That's who I think comes closest, but by no means is it identical."

"Agreed," said Frances. "Matilda's hand is the sample most closely resembling the sample on the letters. But as you say, Alfred, it isn't identical, and I wouldn't expect it to be. I suspect whoever wrote these letters would have done one of two things. Used their real hand to write the letter or their real hand to write the sample. I think it's the latter. I think the writing used on the letters has been embellished."

"Does Matilda have a motive?" asked Declan.

"Well, that's where things get a little awkward. They all have motives, however frail they might be. Matilda, for example, was embarrassed by Madge when Madge kicked out her boyfriend, now fiancé. She and Colin were also overheard laughing about bumping off Madge by Lula."

"That sounds quite serious," said Everard.

Frances nodded.

"Colin is an odd one. He's combative, likes to stir the pot, and seems to delight in making a scene. He's an artist who paints quite ghastly images. One of his works, which he had called Murdered Madonna, was up in the living room. It was a painting of a female crucifixion. While we were there he sketched me looking with magnifying glass at a drowned Madge in her bathtub."

Declan shook his head.

"He seems dangerous, mother, I think you should be quite careful."

"I always am, dear, that's why Alfred comes with me."

Frances put her hand on her son's forearm and smiled at him.

"I wouldn't, on my life, let anything happen to your mother, my Lord," said Alfred.

"I know, thank you, Alfred. I rest much easier knowing that you're around to look after mother."

"I keep coming back to this idea of the sins of the father," said Everard. "I wonder what it might mean."

"I think it is the key," said Frances.

"But whose father and what sins?" asked Declan, looking over at Everard.

"Is Madge's father still alive?" asked Everard.

"No," said Frances. "Both her parents were murdered when she was a young woman."

"Was the murderer found?"

"I don't know, I plan on visiting Inspector Pearce tomorrow at Scotland Yard and asking him all these sorts of questions."

"What about Lula's father?" asked Declan.

"Not sure if he's still around, either. Madge certainly felt he was a ne'er do well," said Frances.

"What about Lula's mother then?"

"Her mother died of the Spanish Flu and that's how Lula came to live with her grandmother when she was a young girl."

"Poor thing," said Everard.

"Yes, she's quite the meek and timid young woman. Probably due to her grandmother's abusive and overbearing manner."

"I've got to imagine that a father of some sort is playing a role in this," said Everard. "Obviously not Madge's own father because he's been dead some time. What about Lula's father? We don't know what happened to him. Perhaps he's learned of his daughter's mistreatment at Madge's hand and is now trying to exact revenge or to send a warning?"

"That's not a bad theory," said Frances, "but we haven't heard from him in some time and from Madge's account, he was a bit of a cad. She seemed to think that he left as soon as her daughter was pregnant with Lula."

"Or did he," said Everard grinning. "Perhaps he's been in the wings all this time."

"Just to play devil's advocate. What if Madge just reminds someone close to her of his or her mother and that's triggering something. Could be, let's imagine, that someone's mother was unkind, or worse, to them and their father stood by and did nothing. Sins of omission instead of commission," said Frances. "And so what we have is something being triggered by a traumatic childhood event and now this person is out for revenge on the very person, Madge, who reminds them of their own mother."

"Good heavens, mother, you do have an active imagination. Perhaps it is nothing more than a cryptic message to lead everyone off the trail that will lead to the killer."

"You could be quite right, Declan. It is late and I'm tired, perhaps I'm getting too fanciful with my imagination. Perhaps I'll see things more clearly in the morning."

"It seems, my Lady, that the problem is that his puzzle has so many pieces and we can barely get a corner of it together just at the moment to make any sense of what the picture might even begin to look like," said Alfred.

"Sigh, I think you could be right, Alfred. And yet time is running out, I fear, before the final letter arrives later this week. So many pieces on the chessboard and the queen remains unprotected."

"You've never failed yet, mother dear, on a case you've put your mind to, and I'm certain you won't fail now."

Frances smiled at her son and patted him on the hand.

"Yes, but will it be before anything more serious happens?"

"Not to diminish the threat that these letters contain, but perhaps that's all they are. Just threats. Perhaps that's all that was intended, and not something more sinister."

"I hope you're right," said Frances, and then changing the subject. "Are you two staying tonight?"

Declan looked over at Everard and then at his mother.

"If you don't mind," he said.

"Of course, I could use the company. Your room is ready and always willing to have you," said Frances.

"I wish father had been as understanding as you are, about who I am," said Declan looking vacantly at the table.

"I know. But believe me, Dec, he tried. In his way, he tried to understand."

Frances had taken Declan's hand in hers and squeezed it gently.

"It's just that I miss him, and I wish that I'd gotten to know him better."

Frances nodded. There wasn't much to say to that. It was one of her greatest regrets that Eric could never fully come to terms with his son's sexuality. Not that he was ever unkind about it. He just didn't understand it. And not understanding, he felt awkward and unsure of how to conduct himself around his own son. Yet, they had worked professionally together in the family business and that was something. It was better than nothing. But it surely could have been more.

Nine

It was nine thirty and Lady Marmalade had announced herself at the main desk of Scotland Yard. She had come down to see Inspector Devlin Pearce, an old and dear friend, though not old in age. He was forty two years old, a fact that Lady Marmalade knew about because he had told her, a long time ago when they had just met, that he was the first baby born in London in 1900.

Lady Marmalade sat stiffly in the chair, waiting for the young constable to call upon Devlin which seemed to be taking some time. She was wearing a yellow summer dress with yellow shawl over her shoulders and a soft red scarf over her hair. She heard the sound of footsteps coming down the hall and as a door opened she saw the young inspector appear, a big smile upon his wide face.

He walked up to her and held out his hand.

“So sorry to keep you,” he said, “the young lad doesn’t know who you are. I’ll have a word with him.”

Pearce was dressed in his favorite ensemble which was a brown suit with brown shoes. A white shirt and University tie. It was the Churchill College’s colors of brown and pink. Understated, but elegant.

“Please, Frances, right this way,” said Pearce as he showed her towards the door he had moments before exited. He opened the door and she stepped into the hallway. To her left was the main reception area where the desks of the intake constables were.

"Harris," said Pearce pointing to the young constable who had telephoned him about Lady Marmalade, and curling his finger. The freckle faced young man came over, knowing full well, from the tone in Pearce's voice, that he was about to be reprimanded.

"Yes, sir," he said, standing as stiff as cardboard.

"This is Lady Marmalade. If she comes calling again, don't keep her waiting. Call me and show her in right away. Is that understood?"

Inspector Pearce was standing toe to toe with the young man and his tone was curt. The constable looked down for a moment.

"Yes, sir, quite clear, sir."

Then he looked up at Lady Marmalade.

"Sorry, my Lady."

"It's quite all right," said Frances smiling at the young man who looked more like a boy than a man.

Inspector Pearce took Lady Marmalade's elbow and guided her down the hall to his office. He pulled the chair out from in front of his desk and tucked it in as Lady Marmalade sat down. He went to his side of the desk and sat down.

"How can I help you, Frances?" he asked.

Lady Marmalade looked down at her handbag and pulled out the handwriting samples and the three letters, still in their envelopes.

"I had a strange visit by a young woman named Lula Beckenswidth on Sunday evening around nine p.m. She lives with her grandmother, Madge Hollingsberry..."

"I know that name," said Pearce.

"You do. How?"

"There's been some trouble in that house before. One of the boarders...Colm perhaps..."

"Colin?"

Pearce nodded.

"Yes, Colin, an artist, had complained about Ms. Hollingsberry having destroyed one of his paintings and thrown his paints and brushes out some months ago. He wanted us to charge her with theft."

"Did you?"

"No, we couldn't prove it was theft as she wouldn't admit to it. As for the destruction of his painting, she said it was a painting he had given her. He admitted to that and so we couldn't do anything about it. The two made quite a pair. A miserable couple if I ever met one."

Pearce twirled the left side of his moustache.

"Yes, she is. And she hasn't changed one bit. Still quite, miserable as you put it."

"So what did this Lula want?"

"She wanted me to visit her grandmother as her grandmother has been receiving some very strange correspondence lately. These letters, here," said Frances pointing to them on the table in front of her.

"They're quite frightening really and threatening. I'm trying to determine who might have sent them. The boarders seem to think that Madge might have done it herself to spite them or to create additional drama in their lives. Personally, I think they were written by someone else. And I'm taking them seriously; I believe that Madge's life is in real danger."

"May I see them?"

Lady Marmalade handed them over to Pearce and he took each one out of the envelope carefully and held it as delicately as a flower in both of his hands. Frances watched as he read them each, thoughtfully, his lips moving silently as his eyes slipped over the words. He folded each one up after he had read it and put it back into its envelope. He took out his monocle from his breast pocket it and secured it in his right eye. Then he studied the envelopes, turning each over before handing them back to Frances and replacing the monocle.

"Interesting," he said. "I think you are right to be concerned. These sorts of letters are often followed through with the threats they contain. I see we are due for one more. So that buys us a little bit of time."

"Yes, I noticed that. Madge said that they have all arrived on the eleventh of the month except for the first which arrived on the 10th of January, which was a Saturday."

"I see, so what happened to one of six and two of six?"

"The first two she burnt, not thinking much of it and being, rightly so, quite upset by them. It was only on the third did she become really concerned and thought she might need to keep them as evidence."

Pearce nodded his head thoughtfully.

"What did the other two say?"

"She didn't recall exactly but she said they carried the same threat and tone."

"What's on the other papers you have there?" he asked.

"These are handwriting samples that I've collected from Madge herself as well as the boarders, along with the butler and the housekeeper."

"And did you find any match?"

"Not exactly but I found one similar that might be worth looking into further."

"May I see," said Pearce holding out his hand.

Frances handed him the seven pieces of paper.

"Can I take a look at one of the envelopes, too, as comparison?"

Frances slid one of the envelopes over. Pearce put his monocle back over his right eye and studied each sample in turn, looking at the envelope and then back at the sample. He didn't say anything. He just took his time and studied each one carefully as though he were looking at counterfeit money.

"I'd say that it looks like Matilda's sample is the closest one that matches."

Frances nodded her head.

"I agree."

"What I'd like to do is hang on to these and have them studied by our expert graphologist if you don't mind."

"Not at all, I'd like to get some sense of who might have written these."

"And you think it might have been Matilda from the looks of things. But why?"

"That's what I'd like to know. She has a weak motive, that much I've managed to ascertain, but as to something stronger, I just have no idea."

"What is the motive?"

"She was embarrassed by Madge one evening, barely after curfew, just when her boyfriend was about to propose to her. Madge kicked him out. She's also the longest staying boarder in the home, coming up on a year or thereabouts."

"Well, if it was Matilda or one of the other boarders, then I'd be more inclined to believe that the threats in these letters won't be followed through. That would be out of character for someone so close to go to all that trouble and then follow through with it. That might sound counterintuitive, but they're simply too close. The risk of getting caught is too high."

"Agreed, although the threats are very serious in nature and quite threatening. I think the one piece of the puzzle I want to solve is to try and find out what the sins of the father means and whether it has any bearing on Madge or the letter writer at all.

And that's one of the reasons why I wanted to speak with you about this puzzling case. I wanted to see if you can't give me some clarification on one particular thing."

"And what would that be?"

"I've heard that Madge's parents were murdered when she was a young woman. I'd like to know what you might have on that case?"

"When do you think this might have occurred?"

"That's hard to say. I think she's in her sixties, so perhaps the mid nineties."

Inspector Pearce started writing on a pad of paper that was on his desk. He looked up at Frances in between his scribbles.

"Do you know their names?"

"Yes, I was told that Phoebe Gaspar married a Rufus Hollingsberry."

"And you don't know their date of marriage or death or even when Phoebe might have been born?"

"I'm afraid not Devlin. But I'm sure you'll be able to find out all you can with the information at hand. You are the best, you know."

Frances smiled at him and he couldn't help but grin like a proud school boy who'd done very well on his Higher School Certificate Examinations. Even though he realized that she was complimenting him to oil the sticky wheel of bureaucracy, she was certainly sincere with it.

"Let me see what I can do," he said still grinning at her. "You know that flattery will get you everywhere around here."

Frances smiled.

"I do," she said.

Inspector Pearce picked up the phone.

"Get me Homicide Command."

He waited for a moment to be patched through and he looked at Lady Marmalade. Frances had her handbag on her lap and waited patiently, quietly, looking at Pearce as he tapped his pen against the pad of paper on his desk as he waited.

"This is Inspector Pearce... yes, hello. I'd like to have you look up a case, a murder involving Phoebe and Rufus Hollingsberry. Phoebe née Gaspar... I don't know exactly, sometime in the nineties... yes, here in London... Good, thank you."

He put down the phone and looked back at Frances.

"That might take a day or two, depending on who gets the task. I'll ring you up when I have anything."

"Thank you so much, Inspector, you're always so terribly kind."

"Not at all. This is certainly a serious matter and I'll help you get to the bottom of it. If it turns into something more serious, like these letters suggest, then of course we'll have to take over."

"Of course."

"With your exceptional help."

Frances bowed her head ever so slightly.

"Tell me more about the characters involved with Ms. Hollingsberry. I'd like to do some background work on some of them to see what sorts of spiders we might find under overturned stones."

"That's a terrific idea, Devlin. I think Lula Beckenswidth might be someone to start with. As I mentioned, she's the granddaughter of Madge and has been with her grandmother since she was quite young. I'd like to verify if her mother did in fact die from the Spanish Flu or if there was something more sinister involved."

Pearce was taking notes as Frances spoke.

"Do you think she might have anything to do with this business of the letters?"

"I don't believe so, Devlin, but one never knows for certain until you rule them out."

Pearce nodded his head.

"I do know that her grandmother is unkind to her and beats her. Just yesterday I saw that she had cuts on her knuckles from her grandmother because she couldn't get me to come over right away and visit with Madge on Sunday evening when Lula first came over to see me."

"That's quite unfortunate," said Pearce. "And who is Lula's mother?"

"Celia Hollingsberry, and while we're at it, I wouldn't mind finding out whatever we can about Lula's father, a man by the name of Errol Crowley. Madge didn't have much to say about him. She said she'd never met him."

"Errol Crowley," repeated Pearce, scribbling on his pad of paper. "Never heard of any of these men and women."

"Perhaps that's good news."

"Or they're more devious and we've never come into contact with them. Who else? I'm going to put down Colin Abbermann the artist, we'll definitely have something on him."

Pearce wasn't looking up, he continued writing.

"Right, well I think all the boarders should be vetted. Colin's one of them. Then there's Matilda Parsons, the oldest of the three and the one who's been a boarder the longest. Also Penelope Sallow. She's very intelligent but soft spoken and seems to take a fancy to our man Colin."

Pearce nodded his head as he wrote down the names that Frances was giving him.

"Matilda told me an interesting story about a chap that came by once a little while ago. His name was Hiram Gaspar."

Pearce looked up, stopping his writing.

"Interesting. I wonder if he's any relation to Jasper Gaspar."

"Apparently so, Hiram claimed to be Jaspar's son and he wanted money from Madge, something about being paid what was his due. What do you know about Jasper Gaspar?"

"He was known as the London Lurker during the seventies and eighties. You might not remember that."

Frances shook her head.

"No, I think I was too young, and I certainly know that you were."

"Yes, I read about it as I'm wont to do with older files now and then when I get bored. He used to lurk around homes, spying on ladies as they were bathing or getting ready for bed. He was never caught in the act but a couple of constables spoke to him and wrote a couple of reports about it."

"Interesting."

"Yes, quite. However, it seems that he never ventured beyond that into more serious crime. At least not that we were able to pin on him. I'll see what else we might be able to find out about him, though I imagine he's long dead by now."

Frances nodded.

"Yes, I imagine so."

"What was it about this Hiram chap that was so interesting?"

"Matilda had heard him getting into an argument with Madge. Matilda's room is upstairs next to Madge's and she heard the two of them arguing about money and that he wanted some money from Madge which he thought he was owed. He also told her that Jasper was his father."

"Why is that so important?"

"I believe that Jasper was Phoebe's brother. In other words, Jasper would have been Madge's uncle."

"Right," said Pearce, scribbling more notes.

"But perhaps the most interesting part of his visit was when Hiram left Madge's room and saw Matilda standing in her doorway. He said, according to Matilda, 'I'd be careful if I was you, dear, there're bad things bound to happen in this house.'"

Pearce paused and looked up at Frances, resting the tip of his fountain pen on the pad of paper. It started to bleed out, creating a black circle of wet ink.

"That sounds threatening to me. Did Matilda feel threatened by it?"

"She didn't say so, and I got the impression that she wasn't."

"I see," said Pearce, nodding and lifting his pen off the paper to staunch the flow of ink.

"I almost forgot, but one of the more interesting things Matilda overheard Hiram saying was that he would tell her secret to everyone he knew

. Her being Madge. That's what really infuriated her and she yelled for Jeremiah, her butler, and kicked Hiram out of her home."

"Fascinating. So we have secrets and sins. I have no sense of clarity about this whatsoever."

"It is quite the puzzle I agree. We have Colin, Hiram, Penelope and Lula to look into. Also, Madge's parents and her uncle, Jasper. There are a couple of others who might be worth looking at too."

"I couldn't agree more, there aren't enough sordid sorts involved as it is."

Pearce was grinning.

"I know, but we'll get to the bottom of it soon enough. Just one plodding step at a time."

"So, who else?"

"I have handwriting samples from both Madge's butler, Jeremiah Rondleton, as well as the housekeeper, Mollie Smouthwary. I'm not sure about Mollie, but Matilda has seen a vicious and violent side to Jeremiah that needs further inquiry."

"I see. He's been violent to her?"

"No, but he seemed to take great pleasure in beating to death a rat and her babies."

Pearce looked at her with an arched eyebrow.

"I know what you're thinking, but this was a perverse, cruel and unnatural pleasure."

"Very well, so Jeremiah and Mollie it is. Not to mention Errol, who is Lula's father. But what about Celia's father, did Madge mention him?"

"Yes, I suppose we should speak about that, too. Rolie Vilvalayn was Celia's father. She wasn't with him long, from what I understand. Madge was also married to a Harold Beckenswidth. That's how Lula got her surname. Madge doesn't have much good to say about him, but I wouldn't mind talking to him about Madge and Lula. Apparently he left Madge for a secretary, I was told."

"Charming."

Pearce was writing all over the top sheet of paper by now, drawing arrows and circles to make sense of the mess of names on the sheet of paper.

"What about children?" asked Pearce.

"Harold and Madge never had children together."

"That's a small mercy," said Pearce focusing on his writing. Frances smiled.

"Yes, Madge is a very difficult woman to like, Devlin."

He looked up at her then.

"Then why are you taking on her case?"

"Well, she's not evil even if she is mean spirited and cruel. And as you know, Devlin, there are other ways of settling differences that don't include threatening letters and, God forbid, violence. It also helps take my mind off this awful war that's been dragging on for far too long."

"Couldn't agree with you more. Though it's bad for business."

Pearce smiled softly.

"What do you mean?"

"I'm being facetious really. But what we have noticed over these past few years is that there's less crime generally and especially less violent crime. It appears that having a national enemy to focus on has brought Londoners closer together."

"Really? That's quite interesting and fascinating. Though I dare say a terrible price to pay for having less crime at home."

Pearce nodded his head.

"Yes, I agree, it is rather sad, really."

Pearce paused his writing for a moment and looked up at Frances again.

"Is there anyone else we need to include or are these..." Pearce started counting all the names on his list, his lips moving silently, "fourteen names sufficient?" He smiled cheekily at her. She smiled back.

"No, I'm afraid there are a few more who are worth noting. Silas Pound, the gardener. He comes by every couple of weeks as I understand, had some upsetting words for Matilda when she was out in the garden reading one day."

"Go on," said Pearce, writing and not looking up.

"Silas said to Matilda, at least according to her, 'you're a pretty little thing, you are. You'd make a fine payment for my troubles.' Though what troubles those were I can't say, though Matilda asked him what he meant and he said, 'for all the trouble there's been you'd make the proper sacrifice.' At that point Matilda got up and left when she heard him say, 'she'll pay she will, mark my words,' after her. Lula also heard him say he should rob Madge because she doesn't pay him well enough."

"And has he?"

"Don't know. It appears that Madge is quite stingy from all accounts. She did mention a few of her items have gone missing. A hair brush, lipstick, pearl necklace, a gold necklace with cross and a photograph of Celia, Madge and Lula. One item seems to go missing each month around the time the letters arrive."

"I see."

"Whether Silas took them, though, is another matter. I can't say one way or the other."

"And lastly?"

"Lastly, if it's not too much trouble, could you check into the milkman and postman, just to be thorough?"

"Really, the postman and the milkman?"

"Well, yes, why not. Just to be thorough."

"Okay. What are their names?"

"The milkman is Tom McMeritt and the postman is Raymond Thompson. The postman I'm particularly interested in. He is, after all, delivering these letters and perhaps he knows more about them than we realize."

"And the milkman?"

"Well, you never know. Perhaps he's crying over long ago spilled milk."

Frances looked at Pearce grinning. He raised his eyebrows.

"That's the best you can do?"

"No, Lula has heard Madge complaining to the milkman about deliveries and spilling the milk when he leaves it."

"There seems nobody that this Madge Hollingsberry hasn't managed to upset in one way or another is there?"

"I suppose not."

Frances paused for a moment and looked down at her bag.

"Madge seems to be inclined to all sorts of hypochondria from what the boarders seem to think. So I'm going to see if I can't call upon her doctor this afternoon and see if he has anything of value to offer. Perhaps she's confided in him more than she has with me or Lula."

"And I suppose you want me to take a look into his background too."

Frances laughed as Pearce grinned at her.

"Oh no, thank you, Devlin, I'm not sure there's much to be concerned about there, though if I find anything fishy I'll certainly let you know. Matilda has overheard Dr. Dankworth tell Madge that her ills are all made up. He gives her sugar pills for them, though, perhaps to placate her."

"How do you know they're sugar pills?"

"Matilda said she tried one."

"That's not very wise."

"No, it's not, but a few of these young people don't seem to be interested in wise choices as much as selfish ones, it seems to me."

"You might not get much out of this Dr. Dankworth even if Madge has confided in him. I've found doctors to be particularly tight lipped about those sorts of things."

"I have my ways, Devlin, you know that."

"All too well," he said smiling kindly at her. "But I've always had a soft spot for noble Ladies and grandmotherly types."

Frances smiled warmly at him.

"Any doctor worth his salt takes the Hippocratic oath very seriously and it speaks to doctor patient confidentiality."

"I know. But then we're dealing with serious and perhaps significant threats to Madge's safety. I'm sure he might find his way to seeing that."

"That's fair," said Pearce scrawling and scribbling on his notes, looking at them.

"I think I've given you a lot to work on," said Frances.

Pearce stopped his scribbling and looked at the results on the page. He studied them a moment before he looked up at Frances.

"Yes, quite a bit. Seventeen names to investigate before the end of the week. Not sure I can manage that, but we'll see. If nothing else comes up then perhaps I'll manage."

"That would be so kind," said Frances.

Off in the distance the whining of mosquitoes could be heard. It wasn't long before both Frances and Pearce knew what that was. It was the start of the air raid sirens. It was a strange time for attempting an air raid, right in the middle of the morning. It was coming on towards ten thirty.

"Come with me Frances," said Pearce with an air of authority.

He got up from around his desk and ushered Lady Marmalade out of his office. He locked the door behind him. The air raid sirens usually gave at least five or more minutes to get to shelter. Frances followed Pearce as he jogged down the hall, meeting up with other members of Scotland Yard.

When everyone was out, a constable locked the door behind them. Scotland Yard was now locked down. Some had stayed behind, and would, until the last minute to take in any stragglers before disappearing into the underground shelters. Four constables were stationed outside and would wait to ensure that the streets were clear and everyone had found shelter.

Most of them, including Frances and Pearce made it to the nearest underground and shelter and waited. As they dashed inside, Frances looked up and noticed a flight of four spitfires zipping by at incredible speed, not terrible high above them.

"Go get them, boys," she said, waving, not they saw her.

Another flight of spitfires followed shortly after as Frances and Pearce made their way into the underground shelter. They were packed into the station like sardines, but it was very orderly and the mood was calm but optimistic.

They found a small bench to sit on while the ebbing of the sirens continued and more people poured into the shelter from above.

"How are Ethel and the boys?" asked Frances, trying to make small talk.

Pearce looked around at the citizens of London all huddled together in this station as others were huddled in other underground stations around the city. His men were helping to keep order and find quieter areas for women and men with children.

"She's fine, though she worries about me, as you can imagine. She's with her sister up in Blairgowrie, not far from Dundee. The Germans don't seem to get that far north, thanks to our flyboys. It's also a smaller community and it's safer for everyone concerned."

Pearce put his hands together and rested his elbows on his knees. He looked around at the faces all huddled together. Some of the children were scared, you could see it. A few of the girls were crying and being consoled by mothers. Some of the men had long faces. It had been a long war, made longer by the poor start Britain had made at first. Though things were starting to edge in her favor.

"Nigel will be eleven on the twenty second. He's very excited about his birthday, he hopes to be a pilot one day. We'll see if that lasts. I'm hoping to make it out for his birthday if I can get the time."

"I'll make sure you get the time, Devlin," said Frances. And she meant it too. Though Eric was no longer with her, she had kept up their friendship with the Commissioner. She would make sure he got the time to spend with his sons and wife.

Pearce looked at her and grinned.

"Do you always get what you want?"

"When it comes to helping my friends, usually."

A young girl being dragged along by her mother walked by and then stopped just in front of Lady Marmalade. She was scruffy and her dress had a tear in it. Her face had a couple of dabs of dirt on her cheeks. She smiled at Frances. She clutched a bear to her face and chewed on its ear.

Frances smiled at her and dug into her handbag. She usually kept a few sweets in it just in case she might be able to hand out one or two to any children looking like they could use a sweetie. She found a packet of Rowntrees' Juicy-Fruits and offered it to the little girl. She let go of her mother's hand and pulled out a candy. The girl's mother looked down and smiled, seeing Frances give the young one a candy.

Lady Marmalade lifted the packet up to the mother. She smiled for a moment and then shook her head sadly.

"No, thank you," she said.

"Go on, you'll like them," said Frances, offering the packet up higher. The young women gave in and took one out of the bag.

"Thank you," she said and looked down at her daughter. "What do you say, Beck?"

The young girl looked up shyly at Lady Marmalade, hiding her face behind her weather beaten bear. She closed her eyes and stuck the candy in the corner of her mouth.

"Thank you, ma'am," she said.

"It's my pleasure," said Frances, smiling at the young girl.

"Why don't you take them all, my dear," said Frances offering the bag up to the young mother, who protested by putting her hand out.

"I couldn't."

"Please, share a little sweetness in this time of madness. There are lots more where these came from."

"Are you sure?"

Frances nodded and the young woman took the packet of sweets from Frances, smiled a sad smile and then moved on farther down towards the end of the shelter. Frances watched them go, hoping that this war would end soon so that the young girl and those her age would have nothing much to remember it by except for distant memories and the kindness of strangers. Frances turned to Pearce.

"And how is Miles?"

Pearce looked up at her and his eyes sparkled and his face brightened just thinking of his family.

"He's wonderful. He'll be seven in August. Different to his brother, you know. He much prefers to play with his toy soldiers. Every time I have a chance to speak with him he tells me that we're winning."

Pearce looked off and the expression on his face changed to one of resignation. Frances put her hand on his forearm.

"I think we are, you know, Devlin, I think we are. Things are turning for the better this year. I'm sure we're halfway through, if not better."

Pearce looked at Frances through eyes covered with the mist of misgivings.

"I hope you're right."

"I most certainly am," she said, patting his arm and looking off at all the faces gathered there in that shelter to take comfort from each other from the brewing storm. The storm of war, a storm that would never end quickly enough.

Ten

The air raid sirens had come and gone like unruly schoolchildren hauled back inside after the lunchtime bell. Frances had left Pearce at the underground shelter to help some of those who had momentarily lost children and loved ones.

Frances had gone back home to an empty house, except for Ginny and Alfred. Declan and Everard had long left. Declan to the family business and Everard, as Frances remembered, worked at Cambridge as a reader in antiquities. But that was earlier in the day.

It was now past lunchtime and Frances and Alfred were standing outside Dr. Kenyon Dankworth's surgery offices. It was four p.m.; Alfred opened the door for Frances and they walked in.

"Good afternoon," said the receptionist behind the front desk.

She was a bright and happy woman with red hair done up in a bun. She wore a modest amount of makeup that subdued her freckled face. She had the kindly look about her of a sister or young aunt.

"Hello, dear," said Frances, "I'm here to see Dr. Dankworth. I telephoned earlier, and he should be expecting us. Lady Frances Marmalade and Mr. Alfred Donahue."

"Yes, of course. Please have a seat my Lady and I'll fetch him right away."

The receptionist left her desk and entered through a door to the side of it, where she disappeared. Lady Marmalade and Alfred took a seat and waited. It wasn't a long wait. The receptionist came back out followed by Dr. Kenyon Dankworth.

"Thank you, Peggy," he said to her as she went back to her desk.

Dr. Dankworth looked to be in his late forties. His hair was jet black and one couldn't tell if it was dyed or natural. Dr. Dankworth was tall at around six and a half feet, but he carried it proudly, no slumping shoulders or bowed back. His nose was sharp and pinched and his jaw square. He was ruggedly handsome with a high widow's peak and thin hair that was combed back slickly. He had deep creases from his nose to the corners of his mouth.

He held out his hand as Frances and Alfred stood.

"How do you do, I'm Dr. Kenyon Dankworth."

"Good day, doctor," said Lady Marmalade smiling sweetly, and shaking his hand. "I'm Lady Frances Marmalade. Please call me Frances."

"Alfred Donahue," as they too shook each others hands.

Frances couldn't help but notice that Dr. Dankworth's hands were soft and slender for such a big man. More like a pianist's hands than a surgeon's. Though how the two might differ she wasn't quite sure. Dr. Dankworth didn't smile. His tone was cordial but lacked warmth.

"Let's talk in my office," he said, as he led them through the door he had just recently exited. On their first right was a large spacious office with a buttoned leather couch against the far wall and two similarly buttoned leather chairs across from his desk. He walked around and sat himself down in his leather chair and reached for a silver cigarette tin.

He opened it up and offered cigarettes to both Frances and Alfred, and they both declined. Dr. Dankworth took one out and tapped it against the side of the case. He put it in his mouth and picked up a Ronson Grecian lighter which he lit it with. He inhaled deeply, pulled at what appeared to be imaginary tobacco on his lips and then pulled a glass ashtray towards him where he wiped whatever might have been on his fingers, off onto the lip.

He was bladed towards them and had his right forearm on his desk which held his cigarette, and was within reach of the ashtray. Frances couldn't help but notice that the ashtray was empty. She wondered if he was just a casual smoker or whether he didn't get much time in the day to take a cigarette break. The tin of cigarettes he offered was only two thirds full.

To Dr. Dankworth's left was a large window that opened onto a small garden that held a variety of roses. The window was open and even against the tobacco smoke, Frances could smell the sweet rose perfume being nudged into the office by the gentle breeze.

"You mentioned you wanted to speak with me about Ms. Hollingsberry," said Dr. Dankworth.

"Yes, I did. Firstly though, I would like to thank you for your time doctor, I know you must be a very busy man."

He waved it off with his hand. The one that held the cigarette, and the smoke streaming from it jiggled like a belly dancer.

"Not at all. It's not often I get to entertain a real Lady. But please, call me Kenyon."

"Thank you, Kenyon."

"What is it that I can help you with regarding Ms. Hollingsberry."

He took a puff of his cigarette and blew the smoke towards the ceiling. He tapped the barely grown ash onto the ashtray where only a few flakes fell off.

"I don't know if you've been told, but Madge has been receiving some threatening letters over the past several months."

Frances stopped and looked at Dr. Dankworth. He took another puff on his cigarette and inhaled. He nodded and the smoke trailed out his nose like vapor.

"She has mentioned that, yes. She hasn't shown them to me, perhaps because I felt indifferent to them."

"I take them quite seriously."

"Then the police should likely be involved," he said matter of factly.

"I have met with Inspector Pearce just this morning and he'll be looking into it. I'd rather uncover the culprit who has written these letters sooner rather than later."

"Why is that?"

"Because they seem to threaten her very life, and I can't overlook that. I won't overlook it."

"Understandably so."

"Why are you indifferent to these threatening letters?"

"Because, Frances; Madge, if I might speak candidly, is a hypochondriac and she's always complaining about something or someone. At least that has been my experience. So when she mentioned these horrible letters she had received, I suppose I patronized her about them and she didn't bother to pursue it any further."

"Well, as I said, I'm taking them quite seriously."

"May I ask you, Frances, how you've come to be involved with this matter."

Dr. Dankworth smoked his cigarette and tapped a more quantitative amount of ash into the ashtray. He blew the smoke at the tip of his cigarette, watching it glow angrily.

"Oh, I'm sorry, Kenyon, I didn't introduce myself properly. I'm what you might call a part time sleuth. Sort of what Sherlock Holmes or Miss. Marple are, only I'm real."

Dr. Dankworth looked up at Frances and raised his eyebrow. "Fascinating. So, a sort-of-sleuth, then?"

Frances nodded. She watched him smoking, wondering how a man dedicated to medicine and healing would want to smoke cigarettes, which seemed to her like a bad idea if your goal was the best of health.

"I'm curious, Frances, if you don't mind me inquiring. Why would a Lady want to interest herself in the miseries of others? I deal with death on a weekly basis, and it's not my favorite part of my profession."

"You're quite right, it is difficult sometimes, dealing with human misery and cruelty. But my goal has always been to find justice for the victims, even if they are no longer with us to enjoy the justice. I feel it is my way to give back to society. And if I'm effective, which I usually am, then perhaps there is less incentive for the criminals to commit their crimes. So long as I'm on the case I believe that there is a greater chance of success in capturing and bringing to justice the rogues involved."

Dr. Dankworth nodded inhaling a puff from his cigarette.

"I suppose you and I are in a similar profession of bringing healing, though perhaps yours is of the more spiritual variety."

"That's a good way of putting it."

"How did you get involved in this sort of work originally?"

Frances looked down at her handbag in her lap. Her hands were folded over it neatly and she still wore her scarf from earlier in the day.

"A dear family friend was murdered many years ago and for the longest time I felt she hadn't received justice, and I went on to prove that an innocent man had been sent to jail for the crime he didn't commit. I managed to set him free and bring the real murderer to justice. I found that I was quite good at it."

Frances smiled at him. Dr. Dankworth nodded slowly, not smiling, still wearing his poker face. He took a last puff from his cigarette and squashed it out. There was a quarter of it left which he bent over itself.

"Peggy!" he said, rather loudly.

It took Frances by surprise. His voice carried with great volume and authority that she hadn't expected. To this point he was cordial and his voice was friendly enough, even if it was quiet. Peggy came into the room moments later. He held up the ashtray to her and she came over to Frances' side of the desk and took it from him.

"Can you clear it out for me, please?"

"Yes, doctor."

And just like that she left.

"I enjoy smoking, but I can't stand the smell of dead tobacco once I've finished."

Frances didn't know what to say to that.

"I see."

Dr. Dankworth swiveled his chair round so he was facing Frances and Alfred. He clasped his hands in front of him making a V of his arms, pointing towards Frances.

"What did these letters say?"

"All of them quoted Deuteronomy chapter 5 verse 9..."

"Thou shalt not bow down thyself unto them, nor serve them: for I the Lord thy God am a jealous God, visiting the iniquity of the fathers upon the children unto the third and fourth generation of them that hate me..."

Frances smiled and nodded her head.

"They don't quote the scripture literally, but they do mentioned punishing the children for the sins of the father to the third and fourth generation. Are you a religious man, Kenyon?"

"Not particularly, but I was raised by a clergyman and his wife, and each year I was expected to read the bible from cover to cover. I managed to do that over twelve times. Some verses stick with you."

"So you weren't raised by your parents."

Dr. Dankworth closed his eyes and lowered his head. He shook it quickly, much like a dog might shake his head to wring the water from his coat.

"No, sorry, that came across incorrectly. My father was the clergyman and my mother his wife... of course," Dr. Dankworth smiled quickly for the first time. "My father was a religious man. You could say I knew him more as a clergyman than as a father."

Frances nodded.

"I understand. Not the warmest childhood then, I imagine?"

"That is a kind way to put it."

"My father was no teddy bear, either," said Alfred.

Dr. Dankworth looked over at the old man and nodded.

"Right, and you play the hand that life deals you. I've turned out all right, I've got a productive surgery and I'm content. You can't ask for much more."

"I think children should be able to ask for more and be given it. Kind and loving parents should be the minimum," said Frances.

Dankworth looked up at Lady Marmalade then leaned back into his chair and put his hands on the top of his head.

"It's a nice dream," he said. "But not all of us get to live easy lives born with silver spoons in our mouths. My father, the clergyman, could only find work in Swansea, a rough town full of coal miners, whores and drunkards."

Alfred raised an eyebrow at the strong words Dr. Dankworth was using. Frances didn't bat an eyelid, she'd heard worse. She just shrugged.

"That's just how it was. No soft pillows to catch my falls."

"I thought I detected a slight Welsh accent," said Frances.

"It comes out more when I'm angry," said Dankworth.

"I'm sorry for the difficult childhood you had. Still doesn't make it right."

"I'm not. Made me who I am."

Frances didn't believe him. There was a bitter pill that still sat in the pit of his stomach like a hard stone. Some children can pass it, others, the more sensitive, and she felt that Dr. Dankworth was of those, never got over the trauma of childhood.

"I can quote you two other passages where the sins of our fathers are mentioned."

"Tell me," said Frances.

"Exodus chapter 20 verse 5 and chapter 34 verses 6 and 7."

"Very good. I remembered those verses too. Perhaps from all the Sunday school I took as a young girl. What do you think it might mean?"

"Clearly, I'd say whoever wrote them has issues with their father."

"Similar to the problems you had with your father?" asked Frances.

Dr. Dankworth looked at Frances sternly and furrowed his brow.

"Hardly. I've come to terms with the tyrant in my life who wore a white collar. And I made a careful decision that I could either hold on to the anger or move beyond it. I've moved beyond it and I have chosen allopathy. The care and healing of people."

Dr. Dankworth had relaxed his hands and was resting them on the leather armrests.

"What do you think it might mean?" he asked.

"The same as you. Though who might have written these letters is the question that most troubles my mind at this present time."

"How many letters of this sort has she received?"

"She has received five, though she destroyed the first two."

"Why?"

"They were upsetting to her and it was only upon receiving the third that she became worried and concerned for her safety and therefore decided to keep them."

"Will there be others?"

"I am expecting a sixth one on this Thursday. They have all arrived on the eleventh of the month except for the first which couldn't as the eleventh of January was a Sunday."

Dr. Dankworth nodded.

"I see. This is all quite fascinating, though I am not as concerned as you obviously seem. As I've already mentioned, Madge is quite the hypochondriac."

"Yes, I've heard, and not just from you."

"I see."

"One of the boarders heard you tell Madge that she was a hypochondriac."

"Not exactly, I told her that she was quite exaggerating her ills, and that she was in fine fettle. That was probably Matilda."

Frances nodded.

"Why do you say that?"

"She's incredibly nosey and quite upset with Madge every since Madge kicked out her gentleman friend, Maxwell, I think his name was."

"Yes, I had heard about that."

"I don't trust her, frankly. She seems to me to be a woman constantly scheming. Hardly ever has more than a few syllables for me each time we speak. I get the sense she's always plotting and planning something foul."

"Anything you've seen specifically?"

"No, but I've heard her and Colin whispering about putting spiders in her bed and snakes in her dressing gown. Ugly stuff. I've reprimanded them about it."

"And what did they say?"

"That they were joking. That Madge is just terribly difficult and needs to be straightened out."

"Do you find her to be difficult?"

"Matilda?"

"No, Madge."

"Quite, though of course, being her physician she's very good to me. But yet, I've heard the way she treats her employees and her granddaughter. Not a lot of kindness there. Though nicer than my father treated me, I'll tell you that much."

"Did you know she hits Lula?"

Dr. Dankworth looked at Frances as if they were discussing general cleanliness and hygiene. Not a shade of emotion crossed his face.

"Not surprising, but no, I didn't know that."

"Just yesterday, Lula had scabs on her fingers from Madge hitting her."

Dr. Dankworth clenched his teeth.

"I see," he said.

"And that doesn't bother you?"

"I didn't know about it until now. In any event, Lula is not my patient and she's a grown woman. I imagine she could leave if she wanted to. But I'll speak to Madge about it."

"That would be helpful, Kenyon, she's a shy and insecure young thing."

"Yes, she is."

"How long have you been Ms. Hollingsberry's physician?"

"About a year, I believe."

"And have you treated her for any serious illnesses or diseases?"

Dr. Dankworth smiled quickly for the second time.

"You know I'm not comfortable sharing any information of that sort. It isn't relevant to these threatening letters. Though I will say that she is currently in good health."

"I understand, but if she is getting poisoned, slowly, then that is something you'd notice and be concerned with, wouldn't you?"

"Of course."

"Good. I just want to be put at ease."

"You should not worry yourself, Frances, as Madge's physician, my primary and only responsibility is to her health and to do no harm as my oath clearly states."

Frances smiled.

"I'm much relieved. But I've heard that you have prescribed sugar pills for her."

Dr. Dankworth nodded his head.

"Why is that?"

"Because there is nothing wrong with her."

"Then why prescribed anything at all?"

"Frances, I don't like the tone of your questioning. Would you rather I give her real pills for things that do not bother her?"

"I'm sorry, Kenyon, I don't mean to be impertinent, I'm just trying to understand."

He looked at Lady Marmalade sternly.

"I give her sugar pills because she's adamant that there's something wrong with her. One week it's stomach ulcers, the next she's having trouble breathing, another time it's her heart. Just today it was her circulation. What she really needs to do is walk more, but she won't hear of it, and I get tired of fighting with her so I've given her sugar pills for what she thinks ails her. That's better than harming her with real medicine that she doesn't need."

"I understand, Kenyon, thank you for you honesty."

"If I might take up just a little bit more of your time and ask about your opinions on the boarders who live with her, I'll be out of your hair right after."

"Very well."

"But first, if I might ask a quick question about your visit with her today. How was it?"

"It was fine."

Dr. Dankworth's face had taken a turn for the worse. His mask of ambivalence was turning into the soured look of frustration.

"Can you share any details about it that might be helpful?"

"She spoke of you, of course, and how much better it made her feel, knowing that someone with your reputation was taking this seriously. I thought she inferring that I hadn't taken it seriously. Which was true."

"So you did know who I was?"

Dr. Dankworth smiled.

"Yes, but I prefer to hear things first hand. As I've said, Madge is prone to great leaps of logic and conspiracies."

"Who else was home today?"

"Can't say really. I only saw Madge, Jeremiah who let me in and Matilda who always seems to be hanging around her bedroom whenever I'm upstairs visiting Madge. She's incredibly snoopy."

"How is Madge doing, health wise?"

"As I've said, her health is good. She suffers no obvious ailments though she is on hypertension medication if you must know, in addition to her sugar pills."

Frances could tell that she was using up Dr. Dankworth's good will, but she wasn't quite finished with him, yet.

"If I might, Kenyon, why do you continue to see her as your patient if she's prone to hypochondria and continued to be an all round unpleasant woman to be around?"

"The one area where she isn't stingy is with her physician. She pays me very handsomely for my troubles and if not me, there'll be someone else. And quite frankly, Frances, she's one of the easiest patients I've had."

Dankworth opened up a drawer on the right side of his desk and pulled out another glass ashtray. He took another cigarette out of his tin and lit it. He half heartedly offered the tin to Frances and Alfred and they turned it down for the second time. He blew smoke rings to the ceiling, like empty thought bubbles. Perhaps praying that, from his lips to God's ears, Frances would hurry up and finish. He was clearly bored by this point.

"What about the boarders?" asked Frances. "Have you had much contact with them?"

"No, not much. Though of the three, Penelope seems like the most reasonable, but it's hard to tell, she's fairly quiet. Though I have the distinct impression that she's quite fond of Colin, the painter. Why, I have no idea."

"You don't care for him?"

"No, I don't. Not him or Matilda. Matilda is too meddling and always seems to be up to no good. Colin, it appears, is happy to egg her on and he has his own sense of the macabre. I imagined you've been introduced to his Murdered Madonna, which he takes great delight in showing to others and watching them become squeamish."

"Yes, we have seen it. But you must admit that he is an exceptional talent."

Dankworth puffed on his cigarette, blew the smoke at the tip and watched it glow angrily. He had bladed himself sideways to Frances and Alfred, so the smoke he was inhaling was trailing far off the right side of Lady Marmalade.

"Yes, a good talent. But a raw and undisciplined talent and those are the ones that I should watch if I was you."

"Do you think he has nefarious intent?"

"I do."

"But he'd be mad to do anything right under our noses and in the very same house as Madge."

"Exactly, I wonder if he doesn't have a sort of madness. Look at the Dutch chap, Vincent Van Gogh, cut off his ear and sent it to his lover. Then when she spurned him, he shot himself in the stomach. He could as easily have shot her."

"Van Gogh never showed a propensity towards violence against others. No doubt he was a tortured soul, but I don't understand how he is relevant to Colin. Colin seems in no way tortured, and if anything, he appears to delight, as you say, in drama and making others uncomfortable."

"Exactly. I fear he is much more dangerous than someone like Van Gogh. And the two of them, Matilda and Colin have both plotted against Madge."

"Yes, but that was a mean and unkind prank. It wasn't plotting her murder."

Dankworth inhaled on his cigarette, tapped ash into the ashtray, and steadied his gaze on Frances for a moment.

"I get the impression you hold back a lot. You're either unaware, or perhaps not willing to admit that you know that Colin and Matilda had been overheard thinking of murdering her."

He watched Frances' reaction. She smiled simply.

"Yes, Lula mentioned she had overheard the two of them. And as you became aware, why didn't you contact the police."

"Because they denied it when I asked. And I wasn't about to trouble the police with something that couldn't be verified. Why haven't you done anything about it?"

Dankworth blew smoke rings at Frances that didn't make it across the table, but he looked at her through them as though he were sighting along a barrel.

"I've spoken with them and I've mentioned it to the police. They denied it being a serious threat, just a way of letting off steam."

"And you believed them?"

"I am not convinced either way."

"And yet here you are, speaking with me, when they might, right now, be plotting to kill her or committing the very same act."

Frances shook her head slowly.

"No, I do not believe that for a moment."

"Why not?"

"Because I believe that whoever is planning on harming Madge, and if they are sincere in their commitment to the act, they will wait until after the sixth letter has been delivered. Nothing will happen before Thursday. Of that I am sure."

"Very well, it is on your hands then."

"No, I don't think so Dr. Dankworth. It is on the hands of the one who seeks to harm her."

Dankworth smoked his cigarette and crossed his left leg over his right and blew the smoke towards the far wall. Neither of them speaking with the other for some time.

"Do you know if Madge has a will? Has she spoken to you about that?"

Dankworth nodded his head and tapped more ash into the ashtray, swiveling around to face Frances.

"I witnessed her most recent will. At least the most recent that I am aware of. That was back at the beginning of the year."

"Who are the beneficiaries?"

"There is only one. St. Bartholomew's Hospital."

"Barts? Any idea why?"

Dankworth shook his head.

"No idea. I've never admitted her there and as far as I know, she's never been treated there."

"How much is she leaving?"

"Well, the home of course, that must be worth three hundred thousand pounds, conservatively. And then there are her investments which totaled about three hundred and fifty thousand pounds if I recall."

"So she'll leave nothing to her granddaughter Lula?"

"No."

Frances glanced down and looked at the Ronson lighter on the table. She wondered if Lula knew that. Poor thing.

"And I suppose the boarders will be allowed to remain while the estate is cleared?"

"No," said Dankworth, "they'll be evicted right away upon Madge's death. The will is clear on that."

"Then what is their incentive to harm her?"

Frances was asking the question mostly to herself.

"I have sometimes found that incentive is a mercurial quality when it comes to emotions and violence."

Frances nodded, not looking at Dankworth.

"That's quite a substantial sum, and not to leave any to your heirs seems..."

"Unkind?"

Frances looked up at Dankworth.

"Yes, I suppose. Thoughtless at the very least. I wonder how Lula will get along."

"She is a grown woman after all, perhaps it'll be exactly what she needs," said Dankworth taking the last puff on his cigarette and meticulously extinguishing it as he had done the first one.

"Have you heard of a Hiram Gaspar?" Frances asked.

Dankworth looked up and shook his head.

"No, who is he?"

"He's a cousin of Madge's, as I understand. Came by some time ago and demanded money from her. Money that he said was rightly his. He's the son of Madge's uncle."

Dankworth raised his eyebrow and curled his mouth downward.

"She did mention something like that to me, but she wouldn't go into specifics."

"Did you get the sense that she'd be giving him money?"

"No, she was adamant nobody was getting her money, especially considering everything she'd been through."

"What did she mean by that?"

Dankworth shrugged and pushed his ashtray to the far side of the table, towards Frances and off to her right.

"I don't know, but you know she inherited her wealth from her grandmother? Most of the money and the house she lives in was her grandmothers."

"I knew about the money."

"Well, if this chap, Hiram, is a cousin as you say, then perhaps he feels entitled to some of that wealth. Madge's grandmother would have been his grandmother too, right?"

Frances nodded.

"Yes, that's quite correct. But there was more to it. Hiram suggested he knew a secret of hers that he would tell everyone he knew if he didn't get his money. She became quite upset and agitated by that."

Dankworth looked up at Frances, his eyes wider than they had been.

"That's interesting," he said. "What was this secret?"

"I have no idea, but I'm going to try and find out. She's never given you any indication that she has a deep dark secret?"

"No, but then she's not a very transparent woman. What she is though, is belligerent, unpleasant and brash, to put it mildly. I'm certain that she has had an unhappy life mostly brought upon by herself, I would guess."

"Has she ever spoken to you about her husband or any other men in her life?"

"No, I didn't know she had been married."

"Yes, a Harry Beckenswidth which is how Lula got her surname. They never had any of their own children though. There was also a Rolie Vilvalayn with whom she had Celia."

"Who's Celia?"

"Celia was her only daughter, the mother of Lula."

"I see, that all sounds quite complicated. Did she have any other children?"

Dankworth looked at Frances steadily.

"I believe so. Lula mentioned a baby boy, Michael that she saw a picture of Madge and the baby when he was very young. But Madge won't speak of it."

"I see, so we don't know what happened to this poor chap?"

"Not yet, though I'm hoping to find out what happened to him."

"This is perhaps why I don't become too familiar with my patients. This sounds like quite a mess."

"Yes, it is a puzzle."

Dankworth sat back in his chair with a soured look on his face. He might have been trying to move himself as far away as possible from the stale tobacco smell. He put his hands on the armrests and leaned back as far as he could go.

"Would you have any opinion on her staff?" asked Frances.

"Not particularly. Jeremiah is the only one I've had a lot of contact with and he seems exceptionally nice. Too nice actually, considering how she treats him. I think there might be something else going on behind that plastic smile he wears all the time."

Frances nodded.

"She pays them poorly. Now don't misunderstand me. I'm not the most generous man about, but I pay my staff fair and current rates. Madge doesn't, and I have no idea how she finds people who will work for half to three quarters the going rates."

"Yes, that is odd, and yet from what I understand Jeremiah in particular has been with her for many years."

"Yes, that is my understanding as well. Mollie on the other hand just seems a little daft and simple minded. I think she just doesn't know any better. But Jeremiah, he's the odd one. I always keep my eyes peeled when he's around."

Dankworth had almost relaxed, sitting as he was, at the far end of his desk, practically up against the wall.

"What about the gardener, Silas? Have you heard of him?"

"Heard of him but never met him. He seems to be a complainer though. Madge is always telling me how she's going to get rid of him, but I don't think she will. So long as he keeps showing up and doing the work, I don't think she'll find anyone who can take her abuse or the paucity of pay she's offering."

"Well, Kenyon, you've been terribly kind with your time and I shan't keep you any longer. Do you have any questions of me?"

Dankworth stood up as Frances stood up and shook his head.

"No, but I do urge you to keep your mind open to the possibility that Madge might have something to do with all this nonsense herself."

He shook Lady Marmalade's hand and then Alfred's and ushered them out the door, and as he did so he picked up the ashtray and held it under his hand, his palm covering it.

"Please take care of this, Peggy," he said, handing her the ashtray as they entered the reception area. Frances and Alfred looked over to where Peggy was sitting at her desk, typing up a letter written by Dr. Dankworth that lay on the table. They couldn't read it, but they could make out his signature. The words were small and tight.

Frances and Alfred showed themselves out and when they had exited onto the street, Frances turned to Alfred.

"I wonder why he smokes if he can't stand the smell."

"I suppose some habits are harder to break than others."

He held open the door to Eric's 1939 Aston Martin 15/98 that Frances sometimes used when she was feeling sentimental. It was a fast and sporty car, but not the most comfortable. But she always remembered the first time Eric had driven her in it. Driving much too fast, the two of them laughing like youngsters. Eric gripping the steering wheel with his brown leather driving gloves and glancing over at her occasionally through his racing goggles.

Alfred climbed in next to her and started up the engine.

"Where to, my Lady?"

"Home, Alfred, and through the park," she smiled at him. "I want to telephone Inspector Pearce, there is a piece of the puzzle I forgot to mention to him."

"And what would that be my Lady?"

"Michael. I want to see if he can't find out whatever happened to the little boy Michael. I think that somehow he might be at the center of all of this."

"I don't follow, I'm afraid."

"The sins of the father. Perhaps the sins of his father, or he is now the father sinning. Somehow, I think Michael plays a role in all of this mess."

"Anything else?"

Frances looked at him and smiled.

"A visit to Harry Beckenswidth might be in order, too."

Eleven

Not far from Regent's Park in St. John's Wood is a lane of stately townhomes. Built with bright rust colored brick and white stone trim, this area of London has long been sought after. It was just after seven p.m. and Lady Marmalade hadn't felt like taking the Aston Martin this evening, as much as she was reminiscing about Eric. Tonight, she sat in the back of her white Rolls Royce Phantom III, as Alfred drove up and found a parking spot in front of Mr. Beckenswidth's home.

It was an expensive area in London to live. Not as much as Kensington/Hyde Park area where Marmalade Park was, but you had to be extremely well off to live here. And Lady Marmalade hadn't a clue as to how Harry Beckenswidth made his fortune, if indeed he had a fortune worth knowing about.

He had been agreeable and very friendly on the telephone and insisted that Lady Marmalade join him and his wife for dinner. Ginny was in the midst of preparing dinner when Frances had called so she politely declined. She was coming over for tea and dessert.

Alfred opened the back door for Lady Marmalade and held her white gloved hand as she got out. She was dressed in a white and black dress suit with white shoes and she wore a white hat with a black veil. She wasn't sure why she had dressed up so much, it wasn't usually like her, but she had a feeling that dressing the part when visiting Harry was going to pay off.

"You look simply marvelous, my Lady, if you don't mind me saying," said Alfred.

Frances smiled at him through red painted lips. Along with the dress and gloves, she had spent a bit of time doing up her face. Although she was a small woman, she had always kept herself trim and at sixty years of age, she could still turn the heads of men decades younger.

They walked up to the main door and Alfred knocked on it thrice. From inside the house they heard footsteps coming towards the door. It was opened from within without having been unlocked.

A man of average height opened the door. He was well fed. Exceptionally well fed, with a ruddy complexion and spidered nose. He was likely in his late sixties. He smelled as if he had rolled out of an oak wine barrel where he had been living for the past twenty years. He wore brown pants and brown shoes with a brown checked sweater. His hair was short but curly, still the brown of his youth, thanks to the miracle of modern science.

His cheeks were thick, like putty stuck onto his face and his eyes twinkled like wet gray stones. His eyebrows were well groomed and trimmed, painted with the same brush that most likely painted his hair the brown of his youth. Cracked, broken red veins, like small insect legs floated on his cheeks, commiserating with those on his nose.

He smiled broadly and his thick baritone voice was as strong and as well polished as a brass bell. He extended his hand.

"What a treat," he said. "It isn't often I've had the pleasure of a Lady in my home. I hope you enjoy port, we're just opening the best one in the house. A 1912 Niepoort Colheita."

"Sounds marvelous," said Frances.

"Forgive me, I am Harry Beckenswidth. I gave my butler the day off for a family emergency.'

"Lady Frances Marmalade. Frances, if you prefer."

"Why of course. I've heard so much about you and of course your husband, Lord Marmalade, was very well known."

"Kind of you to say."

Harry shook Alfred's hand.

"Alfred Donahue," he said. "I am Lady Marmalade's butler..."

"And my dear Watson as well," said Frances smiling at Harry.

"Please, do come in. Gladys is dying to meet you. She's never met a Lady before."

Frances and Alfred walked in after Harry and he closed the door behind them. He led them into the living room where a woman in her mid forties sat. She got up when Frances and Alfred entered. She wore a red dress and white cardigan over white blouse. She was about Harry's height and her face was made up carefully. She looked good for someone in her forties, when the light was subdued and the faculties numbed by wine. Her hair was platinum blonde and her nails long and painted the same color as her dress.

She held out her hand and Frances shook it.

"Gladys Beckenswidth, Harry's wife. So nice of you to visit. I'm just tickled pink," she said.

She was a very self conscious woman who spoke through thin lips hardly showing any teeth. The teeth that could be seen were as yellow and crooked as a farmer's fence. She shook hands with Alfred, too, and showed Frances and Alfred to a couch that ran perpendicular to the one she had just got up from.

Harry went over to the bar and brought back the bottle of port which was empty, and the decanter which now held the tawny liquid. Harry went back and returned with four port glasses. As he settled down onto the couch the housekeeper came into the living room with a tray of four individual servings of strawberry Savarins, drizzled with strawberry puree.

"Thank you, Madeleine," said Harry as she lay the tray down and returned to the kitchen. "She's the finest housekeeper I've found. French, too. Makes the absolute best desserts. I think you'll love these."

"My figure couldn't afford a French housekeeper and all that marvelous French cuisine," said Frances smiling at the two of them.

"I know, I have to exercise extreme judgment," said Gladys. "But Harry loves it and it keeps him happy."

Gladys tucked her hand around his elbow and leaned in to give him a squeeze. He beamed back at her.

"She's one of a kind. My life was empty before I met her," he said.

Frances smiled at them.

"That's so nice to see. All the world could use a little more love nowadays it seems."

"I know, this war is dragging on terribly. I wish it would just end," said Gladys.

"Well, we are fortunate not to have any more bombings for over three weeks now, right Alfred?" said Frances looking at him.

"If we get through tonight it'll be 23 days my Lady."

"Really, I fear it feels like only a few days. Mind you, I've only been back in London for what, two months?" said Gladys, with her arm still around Harry's.

"Just about three months, my dear," said Harry.

"There you go, I can't keep track of time."

"I urged her not to come," said Harry, "I thought it much safer for her to be up in Aberfoyle where we have a small cottage in the park."

"But I've been listening to the wireless, and I knew the bombings have been quite intermittent since The Blitz," said Gladys, "I've missed him so, and he's had a bunker built under here to keep us safe, so I don't fear for my life."

Gladys was looking at Harry adoringly. Frances smiled in the glow of their love. It seemed genuine and unforced. They made a happy couple and that was all the Frances would wish for them. Harry poured himself a splash of port. Swirled it around in the glass and then stuck his nose into to smell.

"Hmm," he said, quite pleased. He took the cup to his mouth and sipped. Letting the port coat his mouth for several seconds before swallowing.

"If I don't mind saying so myself, this is the best port I've tasted in some time."

Harry poured a glass and handed it to Lady Marmalade. Then he poured one for his wife, a third for Alfred and lastly he topped up his own. They all sat silently together for a moment sipping on the port.

"That is very good, Harry. So kind of you to open this bottle to share with us, tonight," said Frances.

"Only the best will do for nobility, my Lady," he said.

Feeling more comfortable with Harry and Gladys, and having had the chance to size them up Frances requested that he call her by her first name. Gladys reached for the plates of Savarin and handed one each to Frances and then to Alfred. She handed them forks, too, and Frances took a bite before putting the plate back down on the table next to her port.

"I had such a wonderful dinner tonight," said Frances, "that I feared I might be too full for dessert when you offered me over, but I must stay, this Savarin is divine, and I'll be determined to enjoy it all."

Harry chuckled and raised his glass. Frances and Alfred picked theirs back up.

"To new friends and those missing."

"Hear, hear," said Alfred.

"Agreed," said Frances and they all leaned in to clink together and sipped more port. The nutty, sweet, and warm flavor with a body much like honey was pared remarkably well with the Savarin's buttery lightness.

"This Savarin," said Alfred, "and I can't remember the last time, if ever, I've had a Savarin, goes remarkably well with the port. I wouldn't have expected such."

"There are snobs, Alfred, and then there are those of us, and you seem to be in the latter like I am, who just enjoy the bounty that life has to offer. I like to experiment with pairings. Though I don't often enjoy port with my dinner, who says it has to be savored only as a dessert wine?"

Alfred nodded his head.

"I quite agree. If something is pleasant, then why let formality stop you."

Frances took another bite of her Savarin and set the plate back down.

"You had mentioned that you had wanted to come speak with me about Madge," said Harry.

Frances looked at him and smiled, just having finished her mouthful.

"Yes, quite right, and to be honest, I wasn't sure how well you'd take it."

Harry nodded and chuckled before speaking with his warm baritone and looking at Frances through his twinkling eyes.

"Probably, because I assume that Margaret didn't have very nice things to say about me."

He smiled at Frances and she smiled back, nodding ever so slightly.

"That woman, I still get upset at how poorly she treated my dear Harry," said Gladys.

Harry put his hand on her knee and tapped it gently.

"She was difficult, agreed."

Gladys looked at him.

"Difficult, Harry, she practically ruined you and your business."

Harry looked down at his plate of Savarin, picked it up and severed a large chunk with his fork and put it in his mouth. He chewed slowly and finally swallowed.

"What did she say about me, exactly?" he asked.

"Not a great deal, but she made it plain that she thought you were a cad for running off with your secretary."

Harry nodded and smiled. Gladys looked a little upset.

"That's not exactly how it happened, is it dear?" she asked him.

He looked over at her and smiled.

"No, it isn't." Then Harry looked over at Frances. "You've met her, I assume."

Frances nodded.

"She's not the nicest woman. We were married from 1919 to 1922. Just after the Great War. Everyone was happy and joyful and full of hope in those days. So perhaps we made a poor decision."

"And Lula was with Madge by that time?" asked Frances.

"Yes, her mother, Celia, died in the Spanish Flu, the year before. Lula was, is, such a sweet young woman. Painfully shy though, and I can't blame her, living with her grandmother who is quite overbearing."

"And how old was Lula at that time?"

"She must have been five. She was born in 1914."

"So you didn't have a chance to meet Lula's mother, Celia?"

"No, I didn't. And the odd thing is that Margaret never spoke of Celia much, didn't keep pictures around. I couldn't quite understand, still don't. And in some ways I think she begrudged her dying and leaving Lula in her care."

"Why do you feel that way?"

"It's nothing concrete, just the way she's short tempered with Lula. But not just her though, with everyone, really. Margaret, I now realize in hindsight, is just a deeply unhappy woman. At first I thought it was me."

"It's not you darling," said Gladys, "you make me as happy as can be."

Harry looked down at her and smiled.

"Yes, I realize that now. But at the time, I thought perhaps it was me, that somehow, I was the cause of her unhappiness."

"That's a short time to be married," said Frances.

Harry laughed.

"Yes, looking back it is. But at the time, I felt like I was eternally stuck in Dante's inferno. Without trying to exaggerate, those three years were perhaps three of the worst years of my life. And I don't mean to speak ill of Margaret."

"If I might probe," said Frances, "how and why did you and Madge divorce?"

"She withdrew from me and the last year we were nothing short of boarders. In fact it was worse than that. She was mean spirited and couldn't be bothered to find a kind word to say about me at all. Naturally, I slowly gave up on the marriage myself and as it happened I found myself drawing closer to Gladys who was the kind of woman whom I had been seeking all my life."

Gladys squeezed his arm and smiled like a proud schoolgirl.

"Madge said you ran off with your secretary," said Frances.

"Grr, that's not how it happened, at all," said Gladys. "That woman just loves drama and putting the blame on everyone else."

Harry patted her knee.

"What Gladys says is true. I didn't run off with my secretary, though the last part is true. Gladys was, at the time, my secretary.

And it must be known, that Gladys and I never committed any sin. I was faithful to Margaret until the last day of our marriage."

"So, how exactly did it end?"

"I sought divorce in the summer of 1922 and by the end of the year it was finalized. That's when I proposed to Gladys. Yes, it might seem sudden, but for the year previously, Margaret and I had been estranged. And Gladys and I were never 'together' until after we got married. That's important to know. I like to think I'm an honorable man."

Frances nodded.

"It does paint a very different picture than the one that Madge painted."

"Yes, well, as I said, I think she's a deeply unhappy woman."

"Do you have any idea why?"

"Not really, in all the time we were together she never opened up to me. But she was young when she had Celia. Seventeen I believe and the father left soon after, so I imagine that she struggled a bit until her grandmother passed and she got a bit of money."

"A bit," said Frances, looking up at him with an arched eyebrow. "She received almost three hundred thousand pounds."

"Good grief no. Nowhere near that. I don't think it was even one hundred thousand pounds."

"Are you sure?"

"Yes, I'm very sure. Her grandmother passed in 1905, quite some time before we met, but in the beginning when things were good she told me she had received almost one hundred thousand pounds."

"I wonder why she would have said three hundred thousand pounds?"

Harry took a sip of his port and placed his glass down again.

"Well, I do know that I gave her two hundred thousand pounds. There wasn't any other way, not if I wanted a fairly quick divorce."

Frances nodded.

"But the home she lives in was her grandmother's was it not?"

Harry nodded.

"Yes, that's true. Her grandparents were quite successful in the last part of the nineteenth century. But through some bad bets in the early nineteen hundreds, they had practically ruined themselves."

"I see, but even so, a hundred thousand pounds is not a small amount of money."

"No, of course not, but from what I gathered they had over one million pounds just before the turn of the millennium."

"And was the money they left Madge the only money they had left?"

"Yes, from what Margaret told me, nobody else got anything."

"That would make for some unhappy relatives."

"I imagine that it would."

Frances leaned in and took a sip of port and then a bite of Savarin.

"But we never had any trouble when we were together. At least not that Margaret ever shared with me. Though on one occasion she did receive an alarming letter."

"How so?"

"She wouldn't tell me about it, but I could see that it upset her greatly. She said someone was demanding money from her. Hiram, I believe his name was, if I recall correctly. Jasper... maybe, something like that."

"Hiram Gaspar?"

Harry nodded his head to the side and stuck a piece of Savarin on his fork and held it steady.

"Could be, I can't recall."

Then he popped the cake into his mouth.

"She practically ruined Harry though, in those three years. Didn't she darling?" said Gladys.

Harry looked over at her and smiled.

"She certainly knew how to spend money very liberally."

"Back to Hiram. Did she ever mention him to you again? Tell you who he was?"

Harry shook his head.

"No, she didn't. To this day I have no idea who he is or was. I only remembered now that you asked. It was one of the few times when I felt I was able to comfort her. It was one of the few times that we had any emotional connection in a kind and caring manner."

"Hiram Gaspar came to see her again quite recently. At the end of last year."

Harry nodded politely. It didn't really make any difference to him.

"I see."

"Hiram is Madge's cousin. Slightly older than she, from what I understand."

"Interesting. I suppose it makes sense now. He might feel entitled to some of their grandmother's money."

"Exactly. He was the son of Jasper Gaspar. Jasper was the brother of Phoebe, and Phoebe as you might know, was Madge's mother."

Harry was nodding his head while stuffing his mouth full of the last morsel of Savarin. He scraped the strawberry puree onto his fork and put that into his mouth, too.

"Like I said, though, I'm pretty certain that Margaret got everything, including the house. The funny thing is," Harry put his fork down on the plate, picked up his glass of port and leaned back into the couch, "that Margaret didn't even get along very well with her grandmother, from what I recall."

"That's interesting. I wonder why she was left the estate, then?"

"Good question. I'm not sure. Margaret's parents were both dead, but I don't know about her uncle. This Jasper chap. Margaret never made any mention of him and certainly no mention of his son Hiram, other than on that one occasion when she mentioned him in passing relating to that letter."

"You'd think that the son would be first in line rather than the granddaughter," said Frances thoughtfully, sipping on port.

"Could be bad blood, I suppose. Margaret's not a nice woman. Perhaps it runs in the family, maybe it's in their blood. Maybe between her son and granddaughter, the granddaughter was the lesser of the two evils? I'm just speculating of course."

"You could be right."

"Here's another idea, seeing as how I seem to have a few of them available this evening. Maybe the grandmother had always favored her daughter. She got her son first, as you said, he's older than Phoebe, so perhaps when she got her daughter, the son had to play second fiddle or no fiddle at all really."

"But the daughter died."

"Exactly so, but she left a granddaughter who perhaps was enough of a replacement for her dead daughter. Either way, the son still gets spurned and the daughter's lineage, ending up at the granddaughter, gets the spoils."

"I do like how you think. You'd make a pretty good detective, I do believe," said Frances, smiling whimsically and looking off in thought.

"That's a very great compliment, coming from you. Thank you."

"I had the sense, speaking to you earlier, that you had a soft spot for Lula, Madge's granddaughter."

"I still do," said Harry.

"And yet, I wonder. Did you know that Madge hits her?"

Frances steadied her gaze at Harry. He centered his on his port which he swirled slowly around in the glass. He then looked up at her.

"Yes," he said nodding slowly, "and that's been one of my deepest regrets that I've had to live with. I tried to protect her when Margaret and I were together, and believe I had some success. Very seldom did she hit Lula when I was around. But when I left... I feared for that you know."

He took a sip of port and stared solemnly into his glass.

"Did you do anything about it?"

"Yes, I did. I called upon the police and they investigated on two occasions, but Margaret has always been quite clever and it was never the physical abuse so much as the mental cruelty that upset me the most. It leaves marks, though they can't be seen. As such, on each occasion that the police interviewed both Margaret and Lula there were no physical marks to back up my story. And Lula, bless her heart, always denied it. Still, to this day, she thinks well of her grandmother."

"I know."

Harry leaned in and rested his elbows on his knees. He looked up at Frances, and for the first time that evening his eyes were damp with sadness.

"I've always done what I could under the circumstances. I've spoken to Margaret. I've warned her that I'll take the child away, but I have no legal standing and they're hollow threats. She knows it, but still, it seems to help minimize the abuse she heaps upon Lula. But you must understand. It wasn't like Margaret was terribly abusive. She just got carried away on occasions with the wooden spoon or ruler. Her abuse was always mostly mental. And I'm not diminishing that; perhaps in some ways it is worse."

Harry hung his head, and slowly shook it from side to side. He looked up again and drank the rest of his port. He decided he needed more fortification so he poured himself another. He offered it around but Lady Marmalade and Alfred were still busy on their first. Gladys, who had been rubbing his back, held hers out which he topped up.

"Did you know, that Madge is not feeling as generous with Lula as her grandmother was to her."

"What do you mean?" asked Harry.

"I've spoken with Dr. Dankworth. Do you know him?"

Harry nodded.

"He told me that he witnessed Madge's will and she's bequeathing her whole estate to Barts. Worse than that, she's made sure that everyone is evicted on her death, including Lula."

Harry turned his mouth upside down and nodded his head.

"That's not surprising. Perfectly in character for her. But I've been taking care of Lula for some time."

"You have?"

"Yes, ever since I left I made a commitment to her that I would always watch out for her. I've sent her letters at least once a month, often biweekly to stay in touch. And since she became the age of majority, we've met once a month for tea."

"That's very decent of you."

"Yes. When she was younger I set aside one hundred pounds each month in an account for her. When she turned eighteen I transferred that over to her and I've been giving her three hundred pounds since then. When Margaret found out, she got absolutely furious and demanded that Lula start paying for room and board. An outrageous one hundred pounds from her own granddaughter, and she requested it to be backdated to when Lula turned eighteen."

"As you said before, that fits into her character."

Harry chortled as Frances smiled.

"Yes, but still. That's over twelve thousand pounds that Lula paid Margaret. In any event, I implored her to leave and set herself up in a nice flat. Three hundred pounds would get her something nice. I offered five hundred if she needed, but she wouldn't hear of it. I think she's a saint, that poor Lula. She said she needed to be there for her grandmother as thinks Margaret needs her help. Poppycock, I say, but she won't hear of it. What can you do?"

"I don't think there is much else that you can do. You've done the decent and kind thing."

Harry shook his head.

"Yes, well, I just wish sometimes she'd pop off. I'm sorry, but I do."

"He doesn't mean it," said Gladys squeezing his shoulder, "but you can't blame him. Margaret has been such a thorn in his side, ever since he met her."

"Yes, I sometimes think I'm sorry for that. For having met her. But Lula is sweet and makes up for it."

"Actually, that's where I wanted to get to with this conversation. You speak of wishing that Madge would step off this mortal coil and that is my concern."

"Well, yes, but I wouldn't do anything of the sort to usher her untimely end."

"I know, but I believe there is someone else who does wish for that."

"Really," said Harry raising his eyebrows. Gladys' interest pricked up too.

"Yes. Madge has been receiving letters every month since the beginning of the year that are quite threatening. She'll receive one more, I believe, likely on Thursday, and then after that I fear her very life could be in trouble."

"You don't say."

Frances nodded her head.

"I'm afraid so."

"I can't say I'm astonished. A little surprised to be certain, but Margaret has a way of turning people against her. What do these letters say?"

"They quote Deuteronomy chapter five verse nine," said Frances, waiting to see if Harry knew of it. Harry shrugged.

"I'm afraid I barely have a nodding acquaintance with the bible."

"Deuteronomy five verse nine speaks of the sins of the father being punished through the third and fourth generations of the children."

Harry nodded.

"Yes, I think I might have heard that before."

"What do you suppose it might mean?"

"I can't say. I have no idea, really. Though I do recall Margaret not getting along well with both her mother and father."

"But they were both dead by the time you met her, weren't they?"

"Yes, long dead. I never met them."

"But you knew she never got along well with them?"

Harry looked at Frances and took a sip of port. He nodded at her.

"Yes, more than that really. It was odd, but Margaret told me one of the happiest days of her life was when she found her parents murdered."

Frances knitted her eyebrow and took a drink from her port. Alfred looked at her with a raised eyebrow.

"That's quite dreadful, really."

"I agree," said Alfred.

"Yes. I was quite shocked. I didn't know what to say, but then, that was a long time ago. What do you say to someone who's happy their parents were murdered?"

Frances kinked her head to the side.

"I can't imagine there's anything to say really."

"I guess what I'm saying, is that perhaps there's a story there about someone's father. Maybe Margaret's."

"But why Margaret's father. If Margaret had been abused by her father, why would someone else want to punish her for it?"

"Perhaps because the treatment she received at the hand of her father she meted out on others?"

"That's an interesting thought. I think I'll need to focus on that aspect a little more."

"Makes me think that we should seek out Hiram," said Alfred.

"Exactly."

"Why Hiram?" asked Harry.

"Hiram said he knew of a secret that Margaret had," said Alfred.

"That could be your answer then, I suppose."

Frances nodded.

"I wanted to ask you about Madge's children. You mentioned Celia. Did she have any other children?"

"No, she never had any other children, and we never had any either."

"Are you sure?"

"I'd know if I had fathered any children," said Harry, chuckling and then taking a drink of port.

"So it would surprise you then that Lula found a picture of Madge with a son named Michael. At least we suspect he was her son."

Harry raised his eyebrows and leaned in a little, away from the back of the couch.

"Wonders never cease. I suppose she wasn't all that honest with me, completely, as you would expect a wife to be with her husband. Like Gladys is with me."

Harry looked over at Gladys and gave her a peck on the lips.

"We don't have any secrets from each other," said Gladys.

"Then you wouldn't be of any help in identifying the father of this young Michael."

"To this day, I still don't know who Celia's father was. And frankly, it's not that important anyway."

"Now, you mentioned earlier that you knew Dr. Dankworth."

Harry nodded and sat back into the couch.

"Dr. Kenyon Dankworth used to be my physician. I found him in 1919, shortly before I met Margaret. He was setting up a practice, having just received his degree to practice."

"And so what happened?"

"Well, Margaret was adamant that she would continue seeing him as her doctor after we broke up. I wasn't crazy about that idea, and so I decided to start seeing Dr. Williamson who was Gladys' doctor."

"I see, and there's nothing else that you might like to add about that?"

Harry shrugged.

"I don't know what else there is really. Dr. Dankworth always seemed like a terrific surgeon to me. His bedside manner could use some polishing, but that seems to be an endemic problem with doctors across the board, not just with him."

Frances nodded.

"I did find him a little aloof," she said.

"That's a good way of putting it. Perhaps withdrawn and aloof. Certainly he doesn't exude warmth."

"No, I didn't get that impression. Did he treat Lula, too, while you were with Madge?"

"He did. For all I know he still does."

"If I might ask, Harry, what sort of business are you in?"

"I'm in the business of providing smiles to children and patients to dentists," said Harry laughing heartily. "I own a sweet business. Beckenswidth's Bonbons."

"Yes, I've seen them around."

"I have a whole bunch of new flavors if you'd like to take some home."

"That would be lovely."

Harry got up and left the living room to collect them.

"He's a good man, Harry," said Gladys. "Margaret, on the other hand, is just short of evil if you ask me."

"I think people are often molded from a young age into the monsters they become, if I can call it that."

"Perhaps. But she just seems to rub everyone the wrong way."

Harry returned carrying a small packet in his hand. It was a white packet with Beckenswidth's Bonbons written in a stylish cursive. It had not been opened.

"I hope you enjoy them. These are a new collection of toffees that we're trying out. Mint, chocolate, both white and milk, as well as double cream."

Harry handed the packet of sweets to Frances.

"Thank you so much, I'll be sure to try each one."

"I was just telling Frances how evil Margaret is," said Gladys looking at Harry. "When they divorced, she took him for all his life savings."

"Well, almost. The two hundred thousand pounds was practically my life savings then. But we've done very well since then, haven't we sweetpea?" said Harry looking at Gladys.

"So your business survived?" asked Frances.

"More like it thrived after Margaret left. She was like an anchor in many ways, I suppose, looking back now. Beckenswidth's Bonbons did even better during the depression.

Strange as it might seem. But I suppose during difficult times people are comforted by sweets and sweets are very inexpensive."

"And where were the two of you living when you got married?"

"Where Margaret is currently. She wouldn't hear of moving. And as I had just bought this place, I decided to rent it out. It was an easy transition to come back here."

"Were there boarders when the two of you were married?"

"Good grief, no. I would have put my foot down about that. But as soon as my bags were packed she practically started inviting them in."

"Boarders?"

"Yes. Good heavens knows why. It's not like she needed the money."

"I think it's because she no longer had anyone to boss around and so she started taking in boarders to replace you in a way, darling. So she could continue to be mean spirited," said Gladys.

Harry smiled at her. Frances thought for a moment. The one thing she'd gotten out of this meeting with him was his innocence. At least she was fairly certain he wouldn't have been the one to send the letters. Though the stylish cursive on the packet of sweets he had given her looked very similar to the handwriting of the letters that Madge had received.

"Harry and Gladys," said Frances. "The two of you have been most kind, and I thank you for your time. I fear that we have overstayed our welcome."

"Nonsense," said Harry, "you're welcome to stay as long as you wish."

Frances took the last sip of her port and put it down. Alfred who had sat silently by her the whole evening had been, for some time, holding an empty port glass in his hands like a begging bowl. Frances got up.

"I hope that our conversation has been helpful, at least," said Harry standing up and walking around to Frances' side of the table.

"It has been. At the very least, I think I've eliminated you from the list of suspects."

"Ah ha, so this was more about me than Margaret," said Harry with the twinkle back in his eye.

"I suppose it served dual purposes. Though to be honest, my path to the letter writer still seems rather murky. Perhaps tomorrow will bring better news."

"Yes, I do hope so. If I can help in anyway, please let me know."

Harry and Gladys walked Frances and Alfred to the front door and showed them out.

"It was so good to meet you," said Gladys. "I hope we can do this again."

"I hope so, too," said Frances, and she genuinely meant it. She had enjoyed the company of Harry and Gladys more than she had imagined she might. "Good night."

The men shook hands and the ladies pecked at the air on either side of each other's cheeks. Alfred took Frances' elbow as he guided her down the stairs to the path. He opened the car door for her and closed it behind her. He got into the driver's seat.

"What did you think?" asked Frances.

"I thought the port was exceptional," said Alfred.

"No, not about that," she said, taking off her glove and playfully slapping his shoulder with it.

"Frankly, my Lady, the more people we speak to, the more confused I seem to get. I hardly think Harry is the type to carry a vendetta like that which the letters would suggest. And yet, on the other hand, that writing on the bag of sweets he gave you looks eerily like the handwriting of the letters."

"I know."

Twelve

Lady Marmalade hung up the phone and walked out of her living room and onto the patio outside. Her roses had started to bloom and the aroma was fragrant and sweet in the cool breeze. Alfred came out carrying a silver tray with silver teapot, cream jug and sugar bowl. There were two teacups and saucers as well as a plate with two wedges of lemon. He laid the tray down on the table that was next to Frances. He sat down across from her. At this time in the morning they were sitting in the shade, thanks mostly to the umbrella sticking out of the middle of the table.

"Are you sure you don't want any pastries my Lady?" asked Alfred.

"Yes, thank you Alfred."

It was Wednesday morning, just after ten and Lady Marmalade wore a light summer dress with a wide summer hat the color of bleached straw. She had not slept well the night before, for obvious reasons. Thursday was knocking at the door and bringing with it unpleasant news. And still she had no clearer idea of who the culprit might be who was sending those letters.

"Did you get a hold of Mr. Gaspar?" asked Alfred.

Frances nodded. She had been on the phone with Inspector Pearce earlier in the morning. He was making slower progress than she would have liked on the subject at hand. But in fairness, she had asked him the evening before to look into Hiram as well as to see if he could find any information on the baby boy Michael.

There was no news about Michael yet, he was still trying to look into the murders of Madge's parents. But he did have an address and telephone for a Hiram Gaspar. She had just got off the phone with him and had to use some strong arm tactics just to get him to agree to see her.

That was to be expected, but he was more cooperative than she had expected.

"I just got off the phone with him, Alfred, and he'll see us this afternoon at eleven thirty. Not only am I still full from breakfast, but I imagine that Mr. Gaspar might host us for elevenses."

She smiled at him and Alfred nodded.

"Was he cooperative?"

"More than I had hoped he would be. I had to encourage him to see us by suggesting that it was us or Scotland Yard. When I explained that Madge had been receiving some strange letters, he softened and wanted to assure me that he had nothing to do with it. I told him that I'd be most assured if he invited us over to explain in person. He obliged."

Alfred smiled and took a hold of the teapot.

"Tea, my Lady?"

Frances nodded.

"Yes, please. You know, Alfred, I do get ever so tired of this business, sometimes."

Frances looked out at her garden. The grass was green and the rose bushes and other flowers were dotted with color. It was beautiful and picturesque, almost as if one of the masters had painted it. Frances sighed.

"I think that perhaps we should take Lord Declan's advice and move you up to Ambleside after we've finished with this case. I think you could use a break."

Frances nodded and reached for her cup of tea. She squeezed the lemon into it and brought the cup to her lips. It was too hot, but the floral scent of the tea with the lemon juice in it smelled relaxing. She put her teacup back down.

"I think you're right. All this business of violence, threats and war has taken its toll."

"And the war has dragged on, my Lady. Much longer than I had anticipated. And I fear we're in for a few more years. But at least we haven't had any bombs for some time now."

"Touch wood," said Frances, reaching for the umbrella's pole and knocking it.

"Have you thought of retiring my Lady?"

Frances looked over at him. She had been with him longer than Eric. He had been Eric's butler when she married him and Alfred felt more like an older brother to her than a butler. She admired his calming and quiet presence. He could have been so much more, but alas, he was not born to money and as such, in the Britain of the early 1900s, his options were more limited.

And yet he didn't seem resigned to his fate. He was more accepting of it and found a joy and contentment in his station that she admired.

"I don't know if I could ever retire, Alfred. What on earth would I do with myself? Declan takes care of the business. I fear I'd wither and die."

Alfred smiled and his eyes creased and twinkled with kindness.

"There is a lot to do at Ambleside, my Lady. You would have lots of people who would seek your company and wisdom."

"Yes, I know. And I don't mean to complain. I do find this sleuthing rewarding, especially when justice is served. I just tire of the murder and violence on occasion."

"Don't we all. Yet there has been none of that yet on this particular case, and perhaps it will remain so."

"I do hope so," said Frances, "though I fear that time is not on our side."

"I have a feeling that our next meeting with Mr. Gaspar might crack open this case just enough to shed some light into it. I wouldn't be surprised if this secret that Mr. Gaspar has involves Michael as well as Ms. Hollingsberry."

"I wouldn't be surprised. But, as interesting as that might be, it might not put us on the path of these letters, and learning who wrote them."

"Or, it might."

Alfred took his teacup and saucer in both hands and sipped from it. Frances did the same. Just a small sip as it was still quite hot.

"What we need to uncover is the meaning behind the verse that is in every letter that Madge has received so far. The sins of the father."

"Perhaps it has something to do with Michael's father."

"How so?"

"Well, Madge is the mother of Michael and perhaps she put him up for adoption and the father is upset at that. If we start backwards at Michael's birth which was in 1893 and move forward to today, I'd guess Madge's age at late sixties. Perhaps a little younger as she doesn't quite look as good as she might. And if that's the case then she was likely born in the mid seventies. That would make her quite a young woman when Michael was born."

"Very true. And that would be understandable. But why wait so long to seek revenge for something that happened such a long time ago?"

"You've often said my Lady, that there is often little reason or rhyme to the wicked ways of men, and I'd hasten to add, women too. Sometimes ill-will like that festers and grows until it's a boil that must be lanced and some know only one way to excise that sort of festering hatred. Perhaps now is the time."

Frances nodded.

"You have a good point."

"If we find out who the father of Michael is, I'd be almost certain that he'd be our man writing the letters."

"And yet, I can't shake the idea that the boarders, one or several of them, are involved somehow with this terrible situation."

"Perhaps, though I can't see how they would be. I understand that they're unpleasant, except perhaps for Penelope, and yes, all of them don't like Ms. Hollingsberry. But there's an easy solution to that. Leave. That's all they have to do."

"You make it sound so easy," said Frances, smiling at him.

"Well, that would be the easy option for any of them."

"But matters of emotion and of the heart do not often follow the most logical course. Hatred and vengeance are like a madness, they cause people to act out of character, do things they wouldn't dream of under normal circumstances."

"True. We'll get there, I'm sure. By hook or by crook," said Alfred, smiling, and trying to make Frances feel better about the whole affair. For indeed, she was right, this was a sticky mess and they seemed no closer to getting at the truth of it. As much as Alfred liked his theory, it was just that, a theory built on wobbly legs. Time would tell if he was getting any better at detective work like Lady Marmalade suggested he was.

They drank their cups of tea in silence for several minutes. The warm spring sun was nuzzling up Lady Marmalade's calves in a pleasant and comforting manner. She looked up at the sky. It was a baby blue dotted with cotton ball clouds. A perfect day and she smiled at it. And she thought back to The Blitz of September 1940 when the sky was blackened with the mosquito looking Luftwaffe that buzzed and whined above as they dropped their bombs carelessly and recklessly on the good citizens of London below.

Frances had escaped to Ambleside at that time, with Alfred and Ginny. They had left no one behind to watch Marmalade Park, and yet it had stood, resolutely British, proud and unflinching and it had survived by some miracle. As London had survived, as the citizens dug deep and carried on with their daily lives as best they could.

Coming back intermittently until The Blitz ended in May of last year, Lady Marmalade always felt a twinge of guilt for those who had to remain behind. The unlucky ones who had no place in the country to escape to. And yet Ambleside had opened its arms wide to those who needed a place to stay. All rooms were full, and it was a large estate. One of the largest in the country. But it couldn't take in everyone, and that was where the twinge of sadness stained the corners of Lady Marmalade's life during The Blitz.

That seemed like such a long time ago now. So many nights without Germans tormenting them from above that London night life had started up again, tentatively, like a drunk who had stumbled and fallen. Frances smiled at the beautiful sky.

"Twenty three nights," she said.

"I beg your pardon my Lady," said Alfred.

"Twenty three nights we've had no German bombs. Isn't that right, Alfred?"

Frances still looked up at the sky, watching the clouds change into abstract shapes. She thought she saw a dove, but when she looked back, it was gone.

"Yes, my Lady. Twenty three nights, indeed. I believe the Germans are tiring of our British fortitude and determination."

Frances looked over at Alfred.

"I believe you're right. Let's hope for another night free of violence," she said.

"Yes, indeed. That would go down easy."

Frances looked around her garden at the small patch of greenery and color. A few trees huddled against each other in comfort and the hedge was large and thick. She heard the chirping birds in the trees. The sweetest song she had heard in a long time. Sweeter right now, than even Josephine Baker's soulful voice.

Frances wanted to capture this moment and stretch it into eternity. But that was not to be. Madge needed her help and she needed to see Hiram Gaspar who might have the answer to many of her questions.

Thirteen

Hiram Gaspar lived in Kings Cross in a green-brown, bricked townhome that had newly whitewashed trim around the main door and windows that faced onto the street. The door to his home was a bright green and the number on it was thirty-three. These were skinny homes but comfortably sized for a small family.

Alfred parked the Rolls Royce on the side of the street in front of Hiram's home. This brought a few nosy neighbors out to take a look at who might be visiting their neighborhood in such a car. Kings Cross had tasted some of the German blasts. At the end of the street, rubble was still piled up on one side, having not yet been cleared away. It appeared, from where Frances and Alfred stood, that at least two homes had been hit, one of them practically ruined.

As Frances and Alfred walked up the steps to Hiram's front door, she smiled at one of the nosy neighbors. A large woman in hair rollers and a night dress under a night gown. Her arms were folded against her ample bosom and a cigarette stood as erect as a Palace guard in between her fingers. Her face was an unpleasant pinched scowl and she offered no smile in return.

Alfred used the doorknocker to announce their presence. It had just gone past eleven thirty. Through the frosted glass windows on the door, Alfred noticed a figure coming towards them.

The door opened and a large man, tall and thick, stood in front of them. He was the Hiram that Matilda had mentioned. With gray hair and thick bushy eyebrows. His face was meaty but not fat and his mouth was permanently turned down. His eyes were brown and bags of gray smeared ash hung from the lower lids.

"Good day. Lady Marmalade, I presume?" he said.

Frances smiled and held out her hand to him. Hiram hesitated for a moment before accepting it and giving it a quick courteous shake before letting it go, as if she had just offered him a used hanky.

Alfred offered Hiram his hand and Hiram accepted it just like he had Lady Marmalade's. His hand was warm and soft. It felt to Alfred as if he had just shook hands with a patty of warmed minced meat.

"I am Hiram Gaspar, as you might imagine. Come in."

Hiram turned around and walked down the hallway and took the first right into the living room. He left the closing of the door to Alfred, who closed it after him. Frances and Alfred followed Hiram into the sparse living room.

Hiram stood by an armchair and gestured to a worn couch for the two of them to sit on. The living room had a bookshelf across from the couch and in front of the couch was a short table with a few magazines on it. The bookshelf was jam packed full of books. Paperbacks mostly, with some hardcovers mixed in.

The armchair was at the far end of the living room, and behind it, farther into the house, was the dining room which joined the kitchen.

"I'll get tea ready," said Hiram, not waiting for a reply as he disappeared into the dining room and then the kitchen.

The armchair faced out onto the street and through the blinds you could see Lady Marmalade's Rolls Royce. The street itself was quiet and Frances could see no neighbors across from Hiram's home.

Next to the armchair was a round wooden table that held an ashtray and packet of cigarettes and an American lighter, the sort that Frances had seen GIs use. That was the smell that Lady Marmalade had first noticed. The almost oppressive stale tobacco smoke. Frances got up and opened the front window a couple of inches to let in fresh air. The effect was almost immediate. Alfred smiled at her and nodded in agreement.

The carpet was a dark chocolate brown, tightly woven and worn in places. Frances also noticed that it was bunched up in a little ripple where the dining room and living room met. A Persian rug, also having seen better days, was tossed on the opposite side of the table from where Lady Marmalade sat. The one corner had been kicked up and showed its underbelly.

Frances heard the kettle whistle in the kitchen and the closing of cupboards and the clanging of cutlery and china. Frances and Alfred waited in silence for a few minutes more until Hiram came back into the living room carrying the tray for tea. He placed it on the table in front of Lady Marmalade. On it were teacups for three. They were mismatched, each teacup different to the other and all three saucers different still.

The teapot was plain white as was the milk jug and sugar bowl. The sugar was granulated and a large plate that came from yet another collection held several biscuits. Chocolate, ginger nut and Marie.

"I'm afraid that's all I had," said Hiram sitting heavily into the armchair. "We should let it steep for a few minutes."

"This looks lovely," said Lady Marmalade, smiling and trying to lift the dour mood that drenched the very fabrics in the room.

As Frances looked at Hiram, he did indeed remind her of an undertaker. She hadn't yet seen him smile as Matilda had recalled him smiling to her, but he did have the heavy glum mood of an undertaker.

"Thank you for seeing us," said Frances. "I don't think I've had a chance to introduce my butler, Alfred Donahue."

"I know who he is. You mentioned he'd be coming with you this morning."

Hiram's tone was flat and his voice cracked through years of tobacco smoke. He picked at imaginary lint on his right pant leg, not looking at Frances as he spoke.

"Nevertheless, it was good of you to see us."

"I didn't have a choice."

This time he looked up at her and held her gaze.

"Then you made the better choice of the two available to you."

He didn't say anything, but he held her gaze. He was hard to read. His whole manner was flat. Like a man used up and left empty of any emotion. A shell of a living being marching towards the end of his life because there was no alternative.

"I suppose I shan't beat around the bush," said Frances.

"That would be best," said Hiram.

"I've been asked by Ms. Margaret Hollingsberry to investigate some frightful letters that she has been receiving over the past six months. Threatening letters, that seem to have started coincidentally after your last visit to her home."

"Coincidentally," he said.

"You do remember visiting with her, don't you?"

"I do. But I think our tea is ready."

Hiram got up, pushing on his knees with his hands. You could almost hear his old bones creak. Frances put him at anywhere from late sixties to early seventies. He went around to the opposite side of the table from where Frances and Alfred sat. He kneeled down on one knee and poured the tea into the three cups, leaving room for cream and sugar.

Alfred needed neither and took his cup, as well as a ginger nut from the plate of biscuits, dunked it into his tea and bit the soggy end off. Frances added cream and sugar as there were no lemons. Though she felt like cream and sugar on this occasion in any event. Hiram was a big man and his use of cream and sugar matched his stature.

He pushed down on the knee he wasn't kneeling on and stood up with much effort. Frances saw him wince and he walked stiffly over to his armchair where he sat back down. He cradled the saucer and tea cup in his big right hand and put a tower of six cookies on the table to his left.

He had taken three of each and they were arranged in alternative order. Ginger nut first then Marie to perhaps cleanse the palette and then a chocolate and repeat. Hiram took a ginger nut and dunked it in his tea and put the whole biscuit in his mouth.

Lady Marmalade took a Marie biscuit and dunked the tip of it into her tea and nibbled at the wet end. She looked at Hiram.

"When did you visit Ms. Hollingsberry?"

"End of last year," said Hiram, looking at the table with his dwindling tower of biscuits. He took the Marie and drowned it in his tea and put the whole soggy thing in his mouth. A small bit fell off and splashed into this tea like a high diver. Hiram hardly noticed, or he pretended not to.

"One of her boarders said that you spoke to her. Do your remember that?"

Hiram took his tea cup in his left hand and had his first sip. He put it back down in its saucer and then looked at Frances.

"I do."

"Do you remember what you said to her?"

Frances was finding his lack of engaging conversation starting to become frustrating.

"I don't."

"If this is not a good time to talk to you, perhaps I should come back with the police. Hopefully you'll be more responsive then."

Frances got up and Alfred joined her. She had hardly started on her tea and she still held most of her Marie biscuit in her left hand. She was hoping he'd fall for her bluff. She didn't really want to leave but she was getting exasperated.

"Sit down," said Hiram looking at her. "I don't remember the conversation because it was hardly important."

Frances sat back down and looked sternly at him. If he was younger than she it might have helped. But, being her senior, it didn't bother him in the least bit.

"You told her, and this is from her recollection, that bad things were going to happen in Ms. Hollingsberry's house."

"And have they?"

"Yes, I believe they have."

"Then perhaps I'll put a wager on next week's horse race."

"Or perhaps I'd put a wager that you had something to do with this bad business that is affecting Ms. Hollingsberry."

Hiram looked down at his tea, decided he wanted a sip and so he did so.

"I didn't have anything to do with any letters."

"Would you be prepared to give me a handwriting sample then."

"All right."

There was a newspaper folded onto the side of the table by the wireless, and a pen lay on top of it. Hiram took his tea cup and saucer and put it behind his biscuits. He put the folded newspaper on his lap and looked at Frances.

"What would you like me to write?"

"The quick brown fox jumps over the lazy dog."

Frances watched him write the sentence while his lips moved ever so slightly. Hiram handed the newspaper to Alfred who immediately handed it to Frances and they both looked at the handwriting.

Hiram's handwriting was neat but small with flowing loops. It was difficult to read, but not impossible. Very dissimilar to the handwriting on the letter which next to Hiram's looked incredibly elegant.

"No match," said Frances to Alfred.

"No match, my Lady," he agreed.

Frances looked up at Hiram.

"What exactly did you mean then, by trouble coming to the home."

Hiram had placed his tea cup back in his lap and had taken the chocolate biscuit for a drowning in his tea. He plopped the whole thing in his mouth like he had before, tilting his head back and dropping it like a fish into his open mouth.

"I didn't really mean much by it. That boarder you speak of looked like a young sweet thing and I'd just had a difficult conversation with Margaret. I hadn't seen her in years and she was just as ill tempered as I remembered. I thought the young woman should know. Bad things seem to happen to Margaret. That I know for a fact, most of which she brings upon herself. So you might say I was just extrapolating."

Frances took a sip of tea and dunked another small corner of her biscuit into it and nibbled at the dunked end. Alfred reached for another ginger nut and dunked half of it in and ate that part.

"From what I've heard, you went to Madge looking for money."

"Money that was rightfully mine."

"Or rightfully hers. From what I understand, this money was her grandmother's."

"Our grandmother's. I was Lilly's grandson as much as Margaret was her granddaughter."

"Yes, but from what I understand, Lilly Gaspar gave away her small fortune to Madge. She was entitled to do with it as she pleased."

"So you say, and I don't disagree in principle. However, Lilly was spiteful. I was punished for the sins of my father."

Frances looked over at Alfred and he raised an eyebrow at her.

"You find something I said interesting?" asked Hiram.

Frances looked at him carefully for a moment.

"You almost quoted the Bible verse that has been found in all of the letters Madge has received."

"Interesting."

Hiram went back to dunking his second and last ginger nut into his tea cup.

"Interesting? It practically proves your guilt."

Hiram shrugged slightly and finished chewing his biscuit.

"Hardly. If I was guilty of anything the police would be here and not you."

"The police might yet be here, Mr. Gaspar!" said Frances sternly.

"I don't see how the coincidence of that quotation that I just used, which also happens to be in the letters, is any indication of my guilt. It is a common enough saying. I'm sure most people are familiar with it."

"I'm sure they are, but that you used it is suspicious. Especially in light of the fact that your visit to Madge coincides with the beginning of these letters."

"Listen, Lady Marmalade. I just gave you a sample of my handwriting, which I didn't have to do. I did it as good faith to show that I have nothing to hide."

"Handwriting can be changed."

"Yes, it can, but you've come here for my help, and I'd like to help, but you're not making it easy. I am not guilty of any of these things you seem to suggest."

Frances thought that by this time he should have been getting exasperated if not hot under the collar, because she knew she was. But Hiram was still as flat as a Shrove Tuesday pancake.

"Okay, let's try and get back to a more conversational place then, shall we?"

Hiram nodded before taking the last sip of his tea. He tilted the cup almost upside down, not minding the last soggy bits of biscuit crumbs that were in his tea cup. He got up with effort and went over to the teapot and picked it up. He offered to refill Lady Marmalade's tea cup and Alfred's before his own, which they both accepted. He refilled it, topped it with cream and sugar and sat back down.

"Why did you want the money, which Madge had received, from your grandmother?"

"Because I believed that it was owed to me. Or at the very least, the surviving grandchildren, of whom I was one of two, should have received it in equal amounts."

"That I understand Hiram, but why did you need it. Why was it so important that you had to go over and visit Madge and get into an argument about it? And why wait so long?"

"I have got myself into a little bit of trouble over the years, I'm afraid."

"What sort of trouble?"

"Nothing much, but it all adds up. I'm not good with money and I spend it quite liberally, on women, drink and assorted expensive odds and sods. I've also been known to get carried away on horse races."

"I see," said Frances.

"Do you?" asked Hiram rhetorically, his tone empty of animosity. "I saw you drive up in your Rolls Royce. This is not the most prestigious suburb in London and it is hard to fall from higher ground."

Hiram took his penultimate biscuit and dunked it into his second cup of tea. Frances took a moment to dunk another corner of her Marie biscuit and Alfred finished his second ginger nut.

"Tell me about it," said Frances.

"There's not much to tell," said Hiram through a mouth of soggy biscuit.

"But I think there is. I think it is important to tell."

Hiram looked at Frances for a moment in silence, and decided there was no shame in the telling. The shame of his situation had happened decades ago. It had been brushed under the rug for so long, it felt almost comfortable. Anyway, it wasn't really his shame, it was his father's and his family's. He was just an innocent bystander.

"I came from money at one point. My grandparents, the ones we're talking about had done well in business. Lilly and Charles Gaspar. I suppose you know that already. If you've visited Margaret then you've visited my grandparent's home, because she got everything and that house was theirs. The last vestige of real money they ever had."

Frances took a sip of tea and Alfred did the same.

"Around the beginning of this century my grandfather made some atrocious business decisions and terrible stock purchase to try and recoup the losses. But that's not really relevant, because I was long cut out from the will by then."

"Has this got anything to do with the secrets that you threatened Madge about?"

Hiram looked at Frances steadily.

"You've done your homework."

Frances nodded and took another sip of tea.

"That Gaspar house that Margaret lives in doesn't have enough cupboards to contain all the skeletons in our history. The Gaspars are riddled with secrets, though some are worse than others."

"I'd like to hear about those."

"Yes, everybody loves the juicy bits, the gossip, when it doesn't involve them."

Frances still could not detect any acrid tone.

"That's not my interest in them, Hiram, I am interested in understanding these letters and the threats they promise."

"It happened in the early 1890s. It was 1893, if I remember correctly, when my father was struck from my grandmother's will. And that was when my grandparents still had lots of wealth. We're talking several hundred thousand pounds at that time."

"That is a small fortune," said Lady Marmalade.

Hiram looked at her and wiped his left hand across the length of his left pant let, smoothing it out.

"Perhaps for you, but for most, it was a very large fortune."

Frances nodded, that's not what she meant, even though it was not large by her standard, she still recognized it to be a king's ransom to most.

"I was devastated. I had been living on credit as if my grandmother was going to bequeath me a portion of it. My mother left my father at that time and moved back to the country to be with her parents. I was their only child."

"How old were at that time?"

"I was twenty three."

"My father lost all will to live and turned to drink. He wasn't an evil man, though I suppose he lost control of the monster within. He died three years later after drinking all night and falling into a river, where he drowned."

"I'm sorry to hear that," said Frances.

Hiram looked at her and nodded.

"It was a long time ago. Anyway, what my father hadn't managed to squander, and I being the sole surviving heir, I managed to sell his business and I've been living on the meager investments ever since. To the tune of about two hundred pounds a month."

Frances nodded and dunked the last bit of her biscuit into the tea and ate it. Two hundred pounds a month was not a lot by any means, however, she was well aware that many people worked hard labor six days a week each month for not that much.

"I take it your parents had divorced by then?"

"Yes, and it was an easy divorce for my father. My mother didn't ask for anything. Though I sent her a hundred or so pounds each month until she died in the Spanish Flu."

"That was kind of you."

"It was the least I could do, the pain that my father put us through and leaving us all but destitute. So to answer your original question, I went to Margaret on that occasion to ask for money as I had done twice before, thinking that she might have softened over the years. She hadn't, and I suppose in a way I don't blame her. Though why she carries on as if it's my fault I still have no idea. I guess children really do pay for the sins of their fathers."

Hiram grabbed his last chocolate biscuit and dunked it into his tea before putting the entire thing in his mouth. He looked out the far living room window at something out there. Frances followed his gaze but couldn't see what had captured his attention. Perhaps he was looking back into the past.

"May I ask you about the secret or secrets, Hiram?" asked Frances sipping the last of her tea and putting the tea cup and saucer back onto the table in front of her.

Hiram looked over, momentarily confused. He had been dwelling on the past. It wasn't a good place to dwell, but then again, neither was the present for him.

"I beg your pardon?"

"The secret or secrets, can I hear about them?"

"Ah, yes, the damn skeletons."

Hiram looked back out the living room window as if he was expecting them to walk up through the gate to his property at any moment.

"I suppose you'll likely find out somehow. Might as well be from me. I could beat about the bush and try to be delicate about it, but there is just no way to be delicate about some things. And this is one of them."

He looked at Lady Marmalade to gauge her reaction.

"I have been privy to the depths of depravity, sadly, Hiram. Perhaps the direct approach is best."

"Very well." Hiram paused for a moment and cleared his throat. It was still difficult all these years later to give voice to the atrocity. Hiram looked out the window again, avoiding eye contact with Frances. "My father raped Margaret."

The words came out easily, not as harsh or as sharp as the shattered glass he expected them to feel like. They tumbled out of his mouth and rolled slowly and softly across the floor like damp clouds before disappearing. He had expected them to clang bout like raucous children running around clanging bells. But none of that happened. The room went quiet after he had uttered that vileness and the world seemed to stop. Nobody spoke for what seemed like ages. He looked at Frances. She looked at him and gave the softest, slightest sympathetic smile.

"That's a terrible burden to carry around."

Hiram nodded.

"And there was nothing I could do about it. Lilly and Charles decided to sweep it under the rug. The police weren't called and everyone was told very severely that police intervention would not be tolerated. We moved to Manchester for a bit, before my mother left him at around the same time I did."

Hiram paused now, remembering his broken father when his mother left him. She left a grown man sobbing and begging on his knees as she walked out the door. She couldn't blame him, his father had lost control of his monster. Once it was out of the cage, you couldn't put it back in.

Nevertheless, it devastated his father and left him a broken man. Hiram couldn't stand the sight of him either and he left months later. He hated him for the rape, but he hated him more for his lost inheritance.

Over the years he had come to be appalled at his own lack of perspective. The inheritance was the least of it. It was the rape that was the twisted evil seed that had grown the root of misfortune for everyone tainted by it. His father had been truly and gravely remorseful, perhaps if he had been helped, things would have turned out differently. But Hiram hadn't thought of it then, and now in years gone by, he didn't know if such evil could be forgiven and a man who committed such atrocity be helped.

"Can I assume then that Madge became pregnant and gave birth to a boy named Michael?"

Hiram nodded and looked at her briefly then he placed his attention out through the living room window where it felt more comfortable.

"She had the worst of it. Obviously, but that was just the beginning. Her father blamed her and her wicked ways. What sort of wicked ways I don't know, she never seemed improper to me. Nevertheless, she was beaten mercilessly during her pregnancy and for the year following, until her parents were murdered."

"How do you know this?"

"We were close once. That was one of the reasons why I thought she might give me some of the money."

"But she never gave you anything?"

Hiram shook his head wearily as if to do so was trying to rock a boulder from side to side.

"No, I suppose being the son of her rapist, I guess she just couldn't get over that."

"That explains a lot about her temperament," said Frances.

Hiram nodded.

"It does. I don't blame her, really. And if you check with Matilda about the argument we had late last year during my last visit, I'm sure she'll attest to the fact that it was really Margaret who was upset and not I."

Frances nodded. She wouldn't be surprised by that. Hiram looked back at her.

"And that is why I wouldn't wish to add to Margaret's grief by sending her vengeful letters. I believe she's had more than her share of pain."

"If I can make an observation," said Frances looking intently at Hiram. Hiram nodded at her. "You don't seem like the happiest man I've met, and I don't mean that disrespectfully."

"I'm not," he said, trying on a smile and finding it awkward so he took it off. "My life took a turn for the worse in many ways after what my father did. It's a heavy burden to carry around as a young man, knowing that your father is a rapist, and perhaps even the more for him not having been punished for it."

"I've asked my friend, Inspector Pearce, to look into it, but you might know the answer, so I'll ask you too. Were Madge's parent's murderers ever found and brought to justice."

Hiram looked at her and rubbed his hand along his pant leg again.

"She was and whether justice was served is not up to me to judge."

Frances looked at him and waited. Hiram tipped the last of his tea into his mouth and placed the tea cup and saucer on the table next to him. He picked up his packet of cigarettes and his American lighter.

"Do you mind?" he said showing Frances the packet of cigarettes.

Lady Marmalade did mind, but she couldn't disallow a sad man any small comfort in his own home so she shook her head. Hiram turned the packet upside down and knocked one out. He put it to his mouth and lit it. He closed his eyes and inhaled, and for the first time since Frances had sat down on that couch in Hiram's home, she thought she saw a mirage of bliss if not joy color his face for just a moment.

Hiram exhaled the smoke out through his nostrils and rested his right hand, which held the cigarette, on the armrest. He opened his eyes and looked at Lady Marmalade.

"Margaret killed her parents. She subdued them with chloroform one at a time and then drowned them each separately in the bathtub."

"How do you know this?"

"She told me."

"And what happened?"

"She told the police too. She was tried and convicted, but she had the scars as witness to the abuse by her father, and her mother knew about and did nothing. She was found not criminally responsible and sent to a hospital where she was kept in a ward for the mentally deranged until she was twenty one."

"What was this hospital?"

"St. Bartholomew's."

Frances looked at Alfred and he nodded at her. Hiram looked at both of them and sucked on his cigarette.

"Is there something important about that?" asked Hiram.

"It's just that Madge's will has one beneficiary and that is Barts."

Hiram nodded, blowing smoke out his nose.

"That's not surprising. Her baby Michael was born there and cared for there until he was adopted."

"Do you remember his birth date?"

"He was born on the eleventh of the eleventh. The 11th of November as I recall. A memorable day and a heartbreaking day for Margaret."

Alfred looked at Frances and raised his eyebrows. She nodded.

"Why was it heartbreaking for her?"

"She had become attached to him during the pregnancy I suppose, and she wanted to keep him, but that wasn't to be. The last she saw of him, if I recall, was on Christmas day of 1893. What did you find so interesting about his birth date?"

"Not because it's Remembrance Day, that's quite coincidental. But because you've just told us who the letter writer is."

"How did I manage that?"

"All of the letters written so far, except for the first one, were delivered on the eleventh of the month. I don't think that's coincidental."

Hiram blew smoke out of his mouth in one long stream and watched it dissipate.

"I suppose it isn't coincidental, is it?"

Frances didn't say anything.

"No, I don't think it is. Has anyone seen or heard from Michael since?"

"Not that I know. I think he was sent to an orphanage. That's the last I knew of what happened to him. Margaret lost touch of his whereabouts then, too."

Hiram rubbed his leg again. Frances wondered if perhaps it hurt. Maybe he suffered from arthritis or some other such ailment. Hiram watched himself rub his leg.

"I think there's more tea in the pot if you want to help yourselves," he said.

"That's quite all right, I've had my fill, thank you."

Frances paused for a moment and gathered her thoughts.

"So, you think the reason that Lilly, your grandmother, left everything to Madge was out of a sense of guilt and remorse for what her son had done to her granddaughter."

Hiram smoked his cigarette and the smoke exited his nose and curled round his neck like a noose. Hiram closed his eyes for a moment before he spoke.

"I think that's part of the reason, certainly."

"What else, then?"

"Well, would you want to leave anything to a rapist or a rapist's son. I think there was no other choice. So, yes, she felt guilt and shame, but she didn't have anyone else to share the meager amounts with. I certainly understand why she wouldn't have left my father any, and we, I guess I, got painted with the same brush. In any event, even if things had turned out well, I wouldn't have seen the same amount as Margaret. Lilly had always preferred my aunt to my father and even before the rape she had preferred her granddaughter to her grandson. Maybe she just felt she had more in common with women than men."

There was no animosity in Hiram's voice. Hadn't been since Frances had first started talking to him. Now she could feel the dignified resignation, practiced after years and years of dashed dreams.

"How does it feel to know you'll never have any access to the money?"

"At this stage of my life, Frances, I feel indifferent. I could have used it, that's for sure. But I tried three times over the past decade. On this last occasion I even stooped so low as to consider it undignified, but even then, Margaret was resolute."

"How so? What about it was undignified?"

"Several things, I suppose. The first suggesting that I would spill the beans about her rape. That's low, but then I told her about my cancer. I have leukemia you see, and my legs ache from it. Still, she was unmoved."

"I'm sorry to hear that."

"Yes, well, I don't think I'll see the year out, so really, money at this point is not going to make much of a difference to me."

"I suppose not. How old was Madge when she was raped by your father?"

"Can't recall for certain, but she was likely sixteen or seventeen. Thereabouts."

Hiram smoked on his cigarette some more, tapped the ash out onto the ashtray and closed his eyes and rubbed his leg. Knowing now that he had cancer, Frances could see the ever so slight shadow of pain that drifted across his face.

"Michael would be in his late forties by now, I suppose. Almost fifty. You said he was born in 1893?"

Hiram nodded.

"November of 1893, so this year he'll be turning forty nine."

Hiram looked at Frances before taking the last puff of his cigarette and putting it out in the ashtray.

"You really think that Michael is writing these letters?"

"I do."

"But what if he's not even in London anymore. Anything could have happened to him over the past forty nine years."

"That's quite true, though the letters are postmarked in London so whoever is sending them is sending them here from within London."

"That doesn't mean he's the one doing it. He could be working with a friend."

"True, but I suspect not. The letter suggested something bad will happen to Madge tomorrow. If he really was out of town, then I don't suspect that the letters would contain the same threats that they do."

"Do you have anyone you suspect then?"

"No, though now that I know who it is, it should be quite easy to find out what became of this young boy, Michael. I'm sure that Scotland Yard will be able to help with that."

"It could take a day or more though, knowing how the government works," said Alfred.

"Then we should waste no more time."

Hiram looked at Frances and she stood up.

"It was kind of you to talk with us, Hiram, about this difficult subject matter. And thank you for the tea."

"Not at all," said Hiram standing up with difficulty.

He walked them out and Frances paused at the door as they said goodbye.

"I hope that your health improves," she said.

"It won't, but thank you anyway."

They walked down his steps and to the car where Alfred opened the door for her and closed it behind her. He got in the front seat and started the car up.

"I believe I need to speak with Inspector Pearce and inform him of the urgency of getting the information we need about Michael."

Alfred nodded.

"I agree my Lady. Though I fear that time is running out."

Fourteen

Thursday the 11th of June, was a day that dragged along as Lady Marmalade kept waiting at home hoping for a phone call from Inspector Pearce with news on who Michael was. That phone call had not come and the day was stretching its legs into the afternoon.

Frances had called upon Ms. Hollingsberry's home and had reached Lula. In the morning post, there had not been any letter of the kind that they had been expecting. Frances had requested that Lula call at the first moment when the letter came in. She was expecting it to arrive by afternoon mail, especially now that it hadn't arrived by morning post.

Frances was in the living room waiting for afternoon tea. The clock had just struck four and Ginny was preparing the tea with scones, clotted cream and jam. Outside the sky was moody and glum. Heavy gray clouds across its dour face.

Ginny came in carrying a silver tray with all the accoutrements for a pleasant but not obscenely large tea. She placed it on the table.

"Thanks, Ginny. Would you call Alfred? Let's all sit down for tea together," said Frances smiling at her housekeeper.

"Yes, my Lady."

Ginny disappeared and returned not long after with Alfred in tow. Lady Marmalade was already putting a dollop of clotted cream and a dollop of jam on each half of her scone. There were six scones on a plate on the tray. Ginny and Alfred sat down and helped themselves to a scone each. They let the tea steep a little more. All three of them preferring a stronger tea.

"You always make such moist, and yet flaky, soft scones, Ginny. They're marvelous."

Frances took a bite of her one half.

"Thank you, my Lady. I think it's all in your grandmother's recipe that I use."

Frances smiled and thought back to her grandmother. Her father's mother with whom she was terribly close as a young girl. What a wonderful woman her nana had been. Alfred took a big bite out of one half of his scone, and nodded at Ginny.

"A very good scone it is," he said.

Ginny was dotting hers with cream and jam.

"Any word yet from the Hollingsberry's?" she asked.

"Not yet, Ginny, I imagine the letter will arrive by afternoon post. Though I'm most concerned not hearing from Inspector Pearce. That worries me."

"Perhaps when it rains, it'll pour," said Alfred.

"Perhaps, though I wouldn't count on it."

"How long did the inspector say it would take to get the information you need?"

"He said it could take a day or two, depending on how well the files have been kept and whether their location has seen any damage from the bombing. It's not so much the police, but the government agency in charge of children's' services, that will likely be the sticking point."

"That doesn't sound very encouraging, does it?" said Ginny.

"No, I'm afraid not. Though, Alfred and I will pop over this afternoon once I hear that the letter has arrived so that we might be able to assess the situation. I'm hopeful that if we at least show some interest that whoever Michael is will be less inclined to act on these threats."

Ginny took a bite of her scone and looked up at Frances.

"I wonder who this Michael fellow could be?"

"That is the last piece of the puzzle," said Alfred.

"Indeed," said Lady Marmalade.

"If I were to guess," said Alfred, "I think it would be someone we haven't met yet. Someone who is keeping his whereabouts unknown."

"But that could make it difficult to harm her if that is really his intent," said Ginny.

"Or he could be working with someone on the inside. I have my suspicions that one of the boarders is involved, somehow," said Frances.

"Who might that be?" asked Ginny.

"That's another small piece of the puzzle. Could be any of them really, it's quite hard to say. Could even be Lula for all we know, despite her best protestations to the contrary."

"Then why wait so long to seek revenge?" asked Alfred taking a sip of his tea.

"Well, Michael is driving the process and I think we'd all agree, or at least you and I would, Alfred, that Lula is quite the wallflower. Quite retiring and mild mannered."

Alfred nodded and put the last bite of his scone in his mouth.

"So, with that in mind, I think the timing just fits in with Michael's schedule more so than Lula's."

"You know," said Alfred, "come to think of it. You might be right thinking that Lula is involved. I remember what she said to me that first night when I walked her home."

Frances nodded.

"Something about war doing peculiar things to people, my Lady, and that they then seek retribution for their misdeeds. Perhaps she was taking about seeking retribution from misdeeds done up on the righteous."

Frances nodded, and put a bite of scone into her mouth. She finished eating before speaking again.

"What about clouding the minds of the unrighteous?"

"Yes, I remember that. It was all quite peculiar. I can't say I really understood what she meant by that."

"Could be that she was suggesting that those who weren't repentant for their misdeeds would be punished. The mind of the unrighteous person is clouded in a fog and they fail to see the misdeeds they've committed," offered Ginny.

Ginny sipped tea and then ate some scone.

"Could be," said Alfred looking at Ginny, "I like how that sounds." Then he looked over at Frances.

"We might be getting somewhere," said Frances. "I do hope so."

"I wonder why Michael, if it is him who is writing the letters, would wait so long before sending them. Why now, I wonder?" asked Ginny.

"I imagine it's because this is just his first opportunity. I don't think he had a chance to do so before. It's likely, I imagine, that he just found out about Madge within the past year or so."

Ginny nodded and finished the one half of her scone. Alfred had finished his first and took a second from the plate on the tray and dolloped cream and jam on both sides.

"This whole thing seems quite awful. I can't understand why anyone would do something so horrid," said Ginny.

"It is upsetting. It's not enough that we have a war to contend with. People still have to hold grudges and remain vengeful," said Frances.

"I'm thinking, my Lady, about this whole affair. I wonder why he'd have such a grudge against his mother? It hardly seems reasonable," said Alfred.

"The mind can get twisted over the smallest insult Alfred, you know that. But perhaps there is more to it than at first becomes apparent. Maybe he doesn't know that his mother was raped by his great uncle. Perhaps he's begrudged her all these decades for giving him up to an orphanage. We know how miserable some children's lives in some orphanages can be. There could be a myriad of things that he hates, if that's not too strong of a word, about his life because his mother gave him up."

Alfred nodded and drank the rest of his tea and put a big bite of his second scone in his mouth.

"One never knows the blows that life deals to others, unless we're very intimate with them. Even then, who can understand the inner torment that some fragile minds are put through."

"I know. My brother, for example, though he appears to be doing well by all accounts, has suffered decades of terrible depression. On more than one occasion did we fear losing him to his demons."

"What do you mean?" asked Ginny. "Might he had to have been put into an institution?"

Alfred shook his head.

"No, not like that. We feared he might be do himself in."

Ginny reached across the table and patted Alfred's forearm.

"That's terrible," she said. "I'm so sorry."

"Thank you. He's better now, with age, the depression seems to have mellowed."

"I'm glad to hear that Reginald, isn't it?" asked Frances and Alfred nodded, "is doing so much better. He always struck me as a sensitive and sweet man."

"Yes, he's always been sensitive to unkind words and not just those aimed at him, either."

"And that's the thing," said Frances. "Sticks and stones may very well break bones, but words can leave festering wounds that we never see, and this is most dangerous. A mentally wounded man, or woman for that matter, is capable of great fury. It's those wounds we can't see that can often cause long term effects."

Alfred nodded and finished the first half of his second scone.

"I've seen that first hand with my brother."

"So you're thinking that even if this Michael doesn't know that his mother was raped, that his own wounds at the perceived injury of being orphaned might have been festering all these years?" asked Ginny.

Frances nodded.

"That's a good way to put it. But perhaps not just the insult of being abandoned or orphaned. I think there is more to Michael's story than just his abandonment. I think he probably has suffered at the hands of unkind foster parents and/or he's a sensitive boy by nature. I just hope we can prevent him from carrying out any threat he feels he needs to."

"We'll hear from Lula soon and we'll head on over and make sure that nobody is allowed into the house for the rest of the evening," said Alfred. "That should help, shouldn't it?"

"That's what I was planning to do."

Frances finished her tea as the telephone began to ring.

"I'll get that, my Lady," said Ginny.

Frances nodded.

Ginny went out into the main hallway where there was a telephone in a small alcove with table and chair. After she had answered it and spoken to the caller she laid the receiver on the desk and came back into the living room, grinning.

"It's Lula for you, my Lady, she says the letter has arrived."

"Thank you, Ginny."

Frances got up and walked out into the hallway and picked up the receiver.

"Hello."

"Lady Marmalade?"

"Yes."

"It's Lula Beckenswidth, I came by on Sunday evening..." said the soft voice.

"Yes, dear, I know who you are, we spoke this morning, I was expecting your phone call."

"Sorry, yes, I'm just a little nervous. You see the sixth letter has arrived and grandmother is frightfully upset by it and really wants to see you."

"Good, I was planning on coming over as soon as I heard. Alfred and I will be there within a half hour."

"Thank you Lady Marmalade."

Frances hung up the phone and thought how queer it was of Lula to remind her of who she was. But Lula was an odd duck generally. Frances walked back into the living room. Alfred was just finishing his last half of his second scone. He looked up at Lady Marmalade.

"Are we off, my Lady?"

"When you're finished," said Frances.

Alfred stood up, reached down for his teacup, and took the last mouthful. He smiled at Frances.

"All ready to go," he said.

They walked to the front door and Alfred put on his jacket and Frances put on a cardigan. It was cool outside with the heavy brooding clouds even though it was June. They left Marmalade Park with Ginny closing the door behind them.

It was about a quarter to four in the afternoon when Alfred and Lady Marmalade stood at the front door of the Hollingsberry residence, waiting for Jeremiah to answer. He did so in his usual buoyant manner.

"How nice to see you again," he said as he opened the door and bowed deeply at him. Alfred couldn't help but smile.

"Good to see you again, too, Jeremiah," said Alfred.

"I wish it was under better circumstances," said Frances. "Where is Ms. Hollingsberry?"

"She's upstairs, my Lady," said Jeremiah as he stood upright again.

Down the hall Lula came to greet them, walking briskly with her eyes cast down. Behind her, at the entrance to the living room, stood Colin with a childish grin on his face.

"She's in a terrible state," said Lula.

"I can imagine," said Frances. "Will you take me up to see her?"

Lula nodded, her eyes looking around furtively. She turned around and walked down the hallway towards the stairs. Lady Marmalade and Alfred followed her. As they started up the stairs, Colin shouted after them.

"Let the games begin, eh?"

Frances ignored him and followed Lula up the stairs and then down the main hallway past Matilda's room. Matilda's door was open and Matilda was lying down on her bed reading "One, Two, Buckle my Shoe". She didn't look up as Lula, Alfred and Frances passed by. Lula stopped at the end of the hallway and knocked on Madge's closed bedroom door.

"Come in," came a wheezing voice from the inside of the room.

Lula opened the door and entered with Frances behind her and Alfred following her. Madge was propped up in her bed on a few pillows. She looked worse than when Lady Marmalade had seen her last, if that was at all possible.

"Leave us," she wheezed at Lula, waving her off with her hand holding a white tissue, which reminded Frances of a small white dove trying to escape. Lula left and closed the door behind her. Alfred went up to Madge's dressing table and brought back the small cushioned seat for Lady Marmalade to sit on.

"Thank you, Alfred," she said, sitting on the chair and moving it up close to Madge's bed.

There was a bedside table that was clotted with an almost full ashtray, an empty cigarette holder, a packet of cigarettes, lighter, a lamp, a wireless that was not turned on, a glass of water and a carafe of water that was all but empty and also two small vials filled with pills.

Madge tried to reach for something on the side table. She was too fat and her arm couldn't twist that much to get to it easily.

"Let me get it for you, ma'am," said Alfred.

"Thank you, my cigarettes and cigarette holder and lighter."

Alfred got those items for her and he and Frances watched in silence as Madge put a Benson & Hedges into the cigarette holder and lit it with trembling fingers. Frances couldn't be sure she was trembling because she was scared or because she was sicker than she seemed.

On her comforter, above her stomach was what looked like the letter in question. It was a single page as the others had been and it was face down. Madge exhaled and looked at Frances looking at the letter. Madge picked it up and shook it.

"The impertinence," she said, though her voice held very little authority and confidence. She wheezed and took another pull on her cigarette. Lady Marmalade couldn't help but wonder why a woman in her condition would smoke. But then she realized there was no underestimating the power of addictions. Madge handed the letter off to Frances. Frances reached for it and took it.

Alfred stood by her left shoulder and leaned in respectfully to read the letter. It said:

Punish the children for the sins of the father to the third and fourth generation of those who hate me.

You have not repented. The time is nigh. You will die.

Six dash six.

The handwriting was the same as it was in the others, though perhaps even a little more careful and well written.

"May I take a look at the envelope?" asked Frances.

The envelope had been hidden under the letter on top of Madge. Madge picked it up and handed it to Frances. Frances looked at it, as did Alfred, bowing behind her shoulder. There was nothing new about the envelope. It was the same as the other three that Frances had seen. And the postmark was the same as all the others. It had been mailed from central London.

That didn't help. Practically anyone within the UK could get to central London and certainly anyone within the city could mail a letter from that location. It was not particularly helpful; though for Frances it suggested that the letter writer was based in London.

"This must be quite upsetting to you," said Frances.

Madge nodded her head vigorously and then broke into a coughing fit which lasted almost a full minute. Alfred reached for the glass of water on her side table and held it ready to give to her when she calmed down. She took it from him and nodded. A nod that suggested thanks without her having to actually say it.

She handed it back to Alfred and he took it carefully as though it might now be contagious and put it back down on her side table.

"I am very upset, Frances," said Madge taking a puff on her cigarette. "I mean, really, who would want to do this to me? I've never hurt anyone."

Frances didn't say anything for a moment. She looked at Madge questionly for a long time.

"I was hoping that it wouldn't come, you know, secretly?"

Frances nodded.

"Listen, Madge, you need to be very transparent and honest with me. I know about your parents."

"What do you know about them?" Madge asked, trying to look genuinely curious.

"Alfred and I saw Hiram yesterday and he told us how you drowned your own parents."

"Absurd. Why would I do such a beastly thing like that?"

Madge looked away and smoked on her cigarette, she was embarrassed to look at Frances.

"Because your father beat you for getting pregnant."

Frances didn't really want to add to her grief and her current troubles, but if she was going to help Madge, then Madge needed to be open and forthright with her. There was no shame in what had happened to her, but they needed to build trust if Frances could help her as she wanted to. Madge still didn't look at Lady Marmalade and she didn't say anything either.

"There's no shame in what happened to you, Madge," said Frances, softly and compassionately.

Madge looked at Lady Marmalade then, but didn't say anything. She took a nervous puff on her cigarette.

"How can I help you, if we can't talk openly and honestly with one another?" asked Frances. "This is very serious, now that you've received what is most likely the final letter. You need to be frank with me so I can determine the best approach. Please, Madge, tell me what happened?"

Madge took another nervous puff on her cigarette, her hand still trembling.

"My uncle raped me," she said. "What is there to talk about?"

"I need to understand what happened afterwards. I believe that these letters have been written by your son, Michael."

Madge looked at her sideways and frowned. She puffed again on her cigarette, a clump of ash falling onto her pajama top which she carelessly brushed off.

"That's impossible," she said.

"How so?"

"Because I haven't heard or seen him in over forty five years, that's why."

Madge was getting upset. It showed plainly on her face, the facade of decades melting like ice on a hot tin roof.

"When was the last time you heard or saw him?"

"Christmas day, 1893."

Madge blinked her eyes a few time. They were misting up and she couldn't see properly.

"Nothing since then?"

"No. I sent him a birthday card on his first three birthdays and Christmas cards too in '94, '95 and '96."

"Why did you stop?"

"His second and third birthday card were sent back as were the last two Christmas cards. I lost touch and nobody would tell me where he had gone."

Madge blinked her eyes again and tears rolled down her cheeks. Embarrassed, she looked away from Frances and Alfred and towards the window. She pulled out the tissue that had been stuck up her pajama sleeve and dabbed at her eyes.

"Do you know what happened to him after you left him at the hospital?"

Madge shook her head before turning around to look at Frances.

"Barts was really good to me, and him, for the short time they had him. He was sent to an orphanage in the summer of '94. After that, I don't know."

"I understand you wanted to keep him. Is that right?"

Lady Marmalade's voice was soft and warm like honey, soothing on the ears and on the flagging spirit. Madge nodded again and her lower lip trembled. She dabbed at her eyes.

"But they wouldn't let me."

Madge looked away, biting her lip and dabbing her eyes. Even now, more than forty five years later it was plain that the pain still burned hot and stinging in Madge's heart.

"Who wouldn't let you?"

"My father and mother. And I had no place to go. If I wanted to stay with them I had to give the boy up. I was sixteen when he raped me."

She said the last sentence barely above a whisper.

"And my father thought it was my fault. He was an evil man. And my mother, she wouldn't do anything. Weak woman, just turned deaf ears to my cries."

Madge was still looking out the window. She dabbed her eyes and puffed on a cigarette from a shaking hand.

"I'm terribly sorry for what happened to you Madge. I really am."

Madge turned back to look at Frances.

"Why would he write me such evil letters? I never harmed him. I never had a choice. I tried to do right by him. I really did."

And you could hear it in her plaintive voice, that Margaret Hollingsberry really had tried to do the best she could as a young, helpless woman in difficult circumstances.

"I know," said Frances, "but I think that perhaps Michael doesn't feel that way."

Madge blew smoke in a long trail up towards the ceiling. The heat in the room was oppressive. It was a good thing that Jeremiah had taken Alfred's jacket and Frances' cardigan.

"I need to speak with him," said Madge. "Help him understand that I had no choice."

She looked at Frances through pleading eyes. And eyes that showed perhaps the smallest glimmer of hope that she could meet her son again.

"I don't think that's a good idea," said Frances.

"But why not?"

"Well, firstly, we don't know who he is now, or where he is. Secondly, I think you need the police to find him first, and only then, after we know who Michael has become might it be possible for you to speak with him about this. But not before. This is for your own safety, Madge."

Madge looked away and took the last puff of her cigarette and then squashed it out in the ashtray which was now certainly full.

"You are sure you don't know where he is?"

Frances looked at Madge. She wanted to know if Madge was hiding anything from her. Madge looked up from squashing the cigarette.

"No, I don't know where he is."

"Good, because this is really important. Now is not the time to think you can rationalize with Michael. He's been hell bent on revenge for whatever slight he feels and if you reach out to him, you'll just make it easier for him to hurt you."

Madge nodded slowly, as if the dawning realization of what Frances was suggesting was only now making sense.

"Why would my own child do this to me?"

She wasn't really asking it of anyone.

"I believe that Michael is, or was, a sensitive boy, and perhaps the orphanage or foster parents were difficult on him. That's the only way I can explain it. You have to try and come to it from his point of view, Madge. Abandoned by his mother, and he likely has no idea why. It is the reason that you gave him up that offers you solace, but sadly, Michael doesn't know that reason. All he knows is being abandoned by his mother and left to strangers. Perhaps even unkind strangers."

Madge nodded, her breath was shallow and quick. You could hear her wheezing if you listened carefully.

"Such misfortune. Haven't I suffered enough that even now my son wants to harm me."

"Those are questions that can't be answered. I feel for you, Madge, I really do. Only God knows why you've had to travel the thorny path he set for you. But what we need to do is clear the obstacles set before us so that you can travel on without harm for as long as you've been given. That's my focus."

"What do you want me to do?" asked Madge.

"Are you expecting any visitors today?"

"No, I hardly ever get visitors," she said, with a voice and sad and hollow as an empty church.

"I don't want you receive any today, and not tomorrow, either, so long as I haven't heard back from Inspector Pearce I'd prefer you don't entertain anyone."

Madge nodded and looked at Frances through glassy eyes.

"When is your doctor due for his next visit?"

"Tomorrow," said Madge.

Frances nodded.

"Obviously, I don't want you to put your health at risk, so Dr. Dankworth is certainly permitted to visit, but no one else. Please."

Madge nodded.

"Jeremiah!" she screeched, and until that moment, Lady Marmalade had forgotten the shrill screeching that Madge was capable of. Frances winced and shut her eyes, she felt for a moment that her ears might bleed.

"Jeremiah!" she screeched again, this time with greater effort and volume.

Frances put up her hand and opened her eyes.

"Perhaps you'll let Alfred go and fetch him."

"That would be nice," said Madge.

Frances nodded and Alfred went to leave, smiling in gratitude that he wouldn't have to listen to the banshee's wail any longer. As he opened the door, he saw Jeremiah walking down the hall at a good clip towards him. He held the door open for the man and then closed it after.

Jeremiah held in his hand a clean handkerchief that he used to mop the sheen from his glowing, wet face.

"Yes, madam, how may I help you?"

Jeremiah stood, slightly hunched over, his silly smile still plastered on his face, as fake as the apples in a still life painting.

"I want you to listen very carefully to what Lady Marmalade has to say, and do exactly as she says."

"Yes, madam."

Jeremiah turned his attention towards Lady Marmalade. Frances turned her chair ninety degrees and then sat so that she was facing him.

"As you know, Ms. Hollingsberry has been receiving some very threatening letters, that concern me deeply."

"Yes, my Lady."

"Today she received what I believe will be the last one. As such, we must take careful measures to ensure that nothing happens to Ms. Hollingsberry until I've had a chance to speak with Inspector Pearce of Scotland Yard to determine who the culprit might be."

"Yes, my Lady."

The corners of Jeremiah's cheeks were straining to suspend the anchors of his smile. It started to droop.

"I understand that Dr. Dankworth is coming round to pay Ms. Hollingsberry a visit tomorrow."

Frances looked at him.

"That is correct, my Lady."

"Are you expecting anyone else to visit either this evening or tomorrow?"

"No, my Lady, no one other than the postman and the milkman."

"Very well, so the gardener, Silas is not coming round tomorrow?"

"No, my Lady, he is due next week."

"All right then, receive the milk and the mail but don't let either of them into the home. As for the milk, make sure someone tries it before Ms. Hollingsberry has any."

"Of course."

"One last thing. Can you gather the boarders and Lula downstairs, I want to give them clear instructions, too. Alfred and I will be down in a few moments."

"Yes, my Lady. Will that be all?"

Frances nodded and Jeremiah bowed before leaving, closing the door behind him. Frances turned her chair back and looked at Madge.

"Please, don't overrule this decision. I know it might seem inconvenient, but it'll just be for the day. I have every faith that I'll hear from Inspector Pearce tomorrow at the latest."

"If you think it is best, I'll do what you suggest."

"Barring any unforeseen events, I'll be round again late morning, or sooner if I've heard from Inspector Pearce."

Madge nodded and held out her hand. Frances took it in hers and patted it with her one hand as she held it in the other.

"Thank you, so much. I'm sure this has been quite an inconvenience for you."

"Not at all. Try and go about your usual routine this evening and I'll be round tomorrow."

Madge nodded. Frances stood up and turned to leave.

"If you need anything or you think that things are somehow changing, please have Lula call me."

"I will."

"Of course, if things are quite serious, you should call the police first."

Madge nodded and Frances and Alfred left her room with Alfred closing the door behind them. Frances saw Matilda's legs dash into her room. She walked up to the doorway and looked inside. Matilda had just got herself back onto the bed and was pretending to read, but it was easy to see it for the charade that it was.

"Did you get what you needed?" asked Lady Marmalade.

"I beg your pardon?" said Matilda trying to look upset at the intrusion.

"Listening in on my conversation with Madge. Did you get all you needed from it?"

"That's absurd," said Matilda, looking away and back at her book. "I've been reading ever since you came up."

"Really?"

"Yes, really."

"And do you always read upside down? Because you weren't when we first came up."

Matilda looked at her book and it was upside down as Lady Marmalade had indicated.

"Bugger," she said. "Look, I just want to know what's going on. That's all. I know she received the letter today."

"Didn't Jeremiah tell you that I wanted to see you all downstairs?"

"Well, yes, he did, and I was getting there."

"Then get on with it and I'll let all of you know what's going on."

Frances and Alfred stepped aside as Matilda exited the room, tossing her Agatha Christie novel on the bed as she left. They watched her disappear around the corner at the end of the hall, heading downstairs. Alfred turned to look at Frances.

"Dare I say, that the prickly, abrasive Ms. Hollingsberry we first met was nowhere to be found this evening. She was almost pleasant."

Frances smiled at Alfred and nodded her head.

"Quite. Staring death in the face will often have a humbling effect on most, if not all."

They walked down the hall, headed towards the living room, where Lady Marmalade wanted to make a few things very clear to the boarders, especially to one Mr. Colin Abbermann.

Fifteen

Everyone was downstairs waiting for Alfred and Frances when they turned into the living room from the hallway. Colin and Penelope sat on one couch and Matilda and Lula sat on the other. Jeremiah was standing off to the side of the couch where Colin and Penelope sat and Mollie was standing next to him. Colin and Penelope sat parallel to the entrance to the living room and they were the first two that Frances made eye to eye contact with.

Frances took an armchair that was facing Colin and Alfred took the other armchair next to her that was facing Penelope. Frances took a moment to look around the room, her eyes taking a moment to catch everyone's gaze in turn.

"As you probably all know," said Frances, "Ms. Hollingsberry received another of those threatening letters in today's afternoon post."

Frances looked around to gauge the faces of everyone gathered.

"I believe that this will be the last of the letters and so I have instructed Jeremiah not to allow any visitors to the house tonight or tomorrow. Not until I've had a chance to speak with Scotland Yard and make a determination as to who this culprit is who has the gall to write these letters. These letters concern me a very great deal. Are any of you expecting guests tonight or tomorrow?"

Frances looked around the room. Matilda nodded her head and the others all shook theirs.

"You'll have to make other arrangements, then," said Frances.

"But I can't, it's very important that I receive the delivery."

"A delivery of what?"

"I'm expecting a new a dressing table for my room, and I must have it tomorrow."

"That's allowed. I don't want any of your friends coming in. I want no one here other than who might have to be here on official business, in and out. Do I make myself clear."

There were murmurs of agreement.

"What makes you think that you'll be able to determine who the person is who wrote these letters?" asked Colin. "What if he masked his true hand when writing them?"

"I believe that we'll be able to determine that with the police graphologist. In any case, we already know who it is. We just have to find out their true identity."

"You do?" asked Colin a little shocked and surprised.

"Yes, we do. It's someone whose name was Michael as a boy. As Lula informed us when we visited, thank you Lula."

Lula smiled coyly and flitted a glance at Frances.

"Michael was Madge's son who had to be given up for adoption."

"Why?" asked Penelope with genuine curiosity.

"That's not for me to say, but I believe that Michael holds a grudge against his mother, a grudge based on falsehoods, it would seem, but a grudge nonetheless."

"That's awful," said Penelope, "that a son would want to harm his mother."

"Yes, it is. But we're not going to let that happen. If you'll all keep vigilant about not letting anyone into the home for this evening and tomorrow, I'm sure we'll get to the bottom of this without any harm coming to anyone."

"I thought the only harm was pointed at Madge," said Colin.

Frances looked at him.

"Yes, that's true, however, I believe that one of you is involved in this scheme somehow, and as such I ask each and everyone of you to keep a close eye on all the others. Let the police know immediately if there is anything that concerns you."

"Why would any of us be involved?" asked Colin, "that sounds like rubbish to me. I mean what do we have to gain from it?"

"That's a very good question, indeed. And what you might have to gain from it might be something as little as the enjoyment of seeing Madge squirm. She is not the easiest woman to be around, I understand that, but the chance to return her unkindness with this sort of vengeance is likely to be something that one of you would find too good to pass up."

Colin didn't say anything but took to chewing his fingernails. Matilda blew air across her face, making the hair over her forehead dance.

"Well, it is quite the inconvenience," she said, "just to entertain a batty old woman who, I might add, probably sent these letters to herself."

"I take these letters seriously, and I'd sooner have the four of you inconvenienced than Ms. Hollingsberry hurt, or worse. It is a small price to pay, and if as you say, she wrote these letters herself, then I will personally see to it that she gets her just deserts. I'd bet my reputation that she didn't write these letters, someone else did."

"Forgive me for saying so, Lady Marmalade, but your reputation doesn't mean anything to me," said Colin.

"It doesn't have to. It is enough that I have been asked by the owner of this home to intervene on her behalf. If you don't like it, you are free to leave until this incident is over, and in fact I'd encourage you to do the same."

Frances looked at Colin for a while. He held her stare until he went back to chewing his nails. In the corner of her eye, Lady Marmalade saw Mollie put up her hand. She looked over to her and smiled.

"Yes, Mollie."

"I have a roast in the oven, my Lady, if I may go and check on it."

"Please do, Mollie, I have finished what I needed to say."

Mollie looked at Frances much like a small child, smiling happily if stupidly, as she left.

"Does anyone have any questions?"

Nobody said anything for a while. Frances looked at Lula.

"I'll ask you to take especially good care of your grandmother tonight and tomorrow, if you don't mind Lula."

Lula looked up at Frances, smiled, and nodded her head vigorously. Frances stood up and Alfred stood up with her.

"I will be back tomorrow morning, just as soon as I've had a chance to visit with Scotland Yard. Please, be extremely vigilant tonight."

She looked at them all for a moment and as she turned to leave, she heard the clock strike six.

Sixteen

It was eight in the evening when the noise began again. There had been twenty three nights without any bombs dropping from German planes. There had been more nights without the moaning sirens than with. That was a small mercy. But tonight wasn't one of them.

Frances and Alfred and Ginny made their way down to the basement bomb shelter. They took their time and brought snacks with them. They were all enjoying a little glass of port and Ginny had cut up some cheeses and crackers on a board that she was carrying down with her. Each holding steadily onto their glass of port. Alfred strangling the bottle of port in his free hand.

They took their seats in the shelter, Frances sitting on the couch and Ginny on an armchair. Alfred sat back down on the other armchair next to Ginny after turning on the wireless. The two of them sat across from Lady Marmalade with a sturdy wooden table between them.

Ginny had put the wooden board on the table. It contained small wedges of Gorgonzola, Roquefort and Stilton. Alfred put the bottle of port down next to it.

"So glad you saved the port," said Frances smiling.

We have confirmation that a Luftwaffe squadron has been sighted coming across the Channel. Please, calmly but quickly, make your way to the nearest shelter to seek safety. We will keep you informed as details emerge...

"Oh, bugger," said Frances, listening to the announcer on the wireless. "I was hoping we might keep our record going."

"I have a good feeling that we might yet. Don't discount our flyboys too quickly my Lady," said Alfred.

"I do hope you're right, though everything comes to an end eventually. Even these delicious cheeses," said Frances cutting off a small slice of Stilton, her favorite with port, and popping it into her mouth.

"I hope you're right, too," said Ginny bending over the table and cutting a good chunk of Gorgonzola which she put on a cracker and ate half of.

"I think tonight will be my witness," said Alfred smiling. "Though I'll not put a wager on it, as I've been wrong before. Twenty three nights without bombs is a good run. It means we're winning."

"We are indeed. Of that I have no doubt," said Frances. "But you know, you become accustomed to the bombings and the sirens, so much so, that I wonder what life will be like when all this nonsense is finished with."

Frances sat back into her couch and sipped on her port.

"I think it'll be quiet, my Lady," said Alfred smiling.

Frances and Ginny had a good laugh.

"It certainly will be," said Ginny. "Perhaps, too quiet."

"Oh, I don't know, I'm looking forward to some peace and quiet again. These sirens are so bloody loud, one can hardly hear oneself think," said Frances.

"They are indeed, especially topside my Lady. But you have to admit that they're barely an announce here in the basement."

Frances nodded and turned to the wireless.

...squadron is five minutes from London. Everyone should be safely in their shelters by now...

"Hmm," said Alfred. "It appears that they're getting closer. I wonder if this might be a real one this time."

Frances took another sliver of Stilton and placed it on a cracker and bit half of it off.

"It would seem so," said Ginny, looking just a bit nervous.

"No need to be nervous, my dear," said Frances, looking at Ginny. "You know this shelter has withstood The Blitz and all that the Germans have been able to throw at her."

Frances sat calmly. Things of this nature didn't normally ruffle her feathers. She had an almost fatalistic approach to life. When it was her time, it would be her time, but she didn't worry about it. Not that she took undue risks. Indeed, a good part of what reassured her was the engineering and cost that Eric had spared no expense with when he had ordered this shelter built. She was sure it would survive a direct hit. Because he had assured her that it would.

"You're right, of course my Lady, but I just get a little nervous each time the bombs start to rain. And Marmalade Park has not yet taken a direct hit."

"That is true my dear, but I have every confidence that my late husband was right when he assured me that it would survive a direct hit. I am certain if that happens, we'll barely feel it. Though I have a strong feeling that if this does turn out to be a real raid, that Marmalade Park will be spared once again, as she has this war, so far."

Ginny smiled, comforted by Lady Marmalade's confidence.

"I think we could all use a little more fortification for our spirits. Don't you agree?"

Alfred and Ginny nodded.

"Would you do the honors please, Alfred."

"With pleasure, my Lady," he said.

Alfred took the bottle of port and freshened everyone's glasses, starting with Lady Marmalade and ending with himself. He looked down at the board of cheese. Even from where he was seated he could smell them. They smelled like the wet socks of a

World War one soldier who's spent too much time in the wet trenches of Polygon Wood.

Alfred leaned over and took a bit of the soft, crumbly, blue veined Roquefort and put it on a cracker. He put the whole thing in his mouth. He had a love-hate relationship with strong cheese. He loved the taste, the creamy, buttery first impression followed by the salty, tangy afterglow. But the smell, well, the smell kept him away from cheese more often than he would like.

...confirmed bombings started in South London. Brace yourselves ladies and gentleman...

"And so it begins," said Frances. She grabbed hold of the armrest on her side of the couch and waited. "It shouldn't be long before we get a sense of where they're coming in from."

Alfred put his port in his left hand and with his right he held Ginny's left hand softly in his. He smiled at her. She smiled back, a brave smile that felt weak and trembled. She closed her eyes.

You couldn't hear the bombs this deep underground, their whining and whizzing was drowned out by the sirens, and the sirens sounded soft like a mosquito buzzing in close for a morsel. The first bomb took less than a minute before they felt it. Like a soft shake of the earth, as if a giant had fallen down outside and was struggling to get up.

"That seemed closer than I would have liked," said Frances, taking a sip of port and clutching the armchair with her left hand.

Several more bombs landed and the vibration and thuds could be felt through the walls and through their feet on the floors. After several seconds, the bombs moved on farther north, not finding the mayhem they had hoped for at Marmalade Park. After just several minutes, everything had gone quiet and all that could be heard was the whining sirens, still blaring.

...stay where you are, safe in your shelters. We will let you know when it is safe to leave and head topside...

"Well, that wasn't too bad was it, Ginny?" said Frances.

"No, not at all," she said, as she released her hand from Alfred's comforting grip and wiped the back of it across her forehead. She smiled nervously.

"Just like I told you, Marmalade Park has been spared once again, by St. Marmalade."

"Is that even a real saint?" asked Ginny.

"Good heavens, no, that's Eric, up there looking out for us."

And they laughed, using up the nervous tension that the bombing raid had built up within them. And then they sat silently for a while, thinking of those long lost to them and those who had been lost during this terrible war.

Frances could see Eric now, right here in this shelter with her. His arm around her waist as he grinned at her.

"We'll be safe as houses in here, my love, if we choose to stay. Though I think Avalon at Ambleside should be our safe haven if the Germans get nasty,"

Frances smiled at him and kissed him on the cheek. He had always taken such good care of her. He had never had the chance to see how well this shelter had withstood the previous years of bombing. It would have made him proud, she was sure of that.

"My Lady?" said Alfred.

She came out of her reverie and looked over at Alfred and smiled at him.

"I'm sorry, Alfred, did you say something?"

"I was just asking if you were all right?"

"Yes, thank you, I was just thinking of Eric," she said.

Alfred nodded solemnly.

"I miss him, too, my Lady. He was a great man."

Ginny took another slice of cheese, this time she tried the Stilton with its green pockmarked face. She put it on a cracker and put it in her mouth. After she had finished chewing it she took a drink of port. Her glass had a third left and she was feeling the warmth from it in her belly.

The recent bombs were now just a faint memory. Nothing shook through the walls and nothing could be felt through the floors, and yet the sirens still whined on in their sorrowful tone.

It was another fifteen minutes, sitting deep within the bowels of the cold earth before the wireless announcers had confirmed it was safe. As usual they instructed everyone to keep away from any bombs and to call the local police or military to deal with any that might be undetonated or not.

Frances, Alfred, and Ginny got up, each clutching their now empty port glasses. The port bottle was still almost half full, it would survive another day. Ginny picked up the wooden board which still held most of the three cheeses and several crackers with the fallen crumbs of their recently devoured comrades.

They walked up the stairs and entered Marmalade Park. Alfred and Ginny walked to the living room to lay everything down. Frances wanted to call Lula and see how Ms. Hollingsberry was doing through the raid. It would be a terrible calamity to lose her to the Germans when Lady Marmalade was trying her best to keep her safe from Michael. Frances picked up the telephone but the line was dead. She tried the operator but got no response.

Frances walked into the living room and sat down on the couch.

"It appears that the telephone system has been hit by the bombings," she said.

"That's unfortunate," said Alfred.

"Yes, it is, I was hoping to get hold of Lula to see how the raid was for them," said Frances.

"If you'd like, I can take a quick walk over and see how things are," said Alfred.

"That's all right, thank you Alfred. I'm sure they're fine, and if anything is wrong I'm sure we'll get word. No point in fretting about what might be when we have no reason to be worried."

"Very true, I'm sure they've been mostly untouched by the bombs as we were. Not that I can say for certain, but it didn't seem like we felt many bombs landing that were coming from their direction."

Alfred was trying to ease any residual fears that Lady Marmalade had. In truth he couldn't be certain at all. How could he be? When the bombs landed around them and he felt them through the trembling walls and floor of the bomb shelter he couldn't be certain they were landing just above them in the garden or down the street a block away.

Lady Marmalade decided to take another slice of Stilton and put it on a cracker, which she nibbled at. When she was finished she picked up the paper and started reading about international affairs.

Much of the news was filled with the battles raging between the countries involved in this Second World War. The Battle of Midway which had just recently been won was still being discussed as a great victory, while the attack on Sydney Harbor by Japanese midget submarines was being criticized heavily.

Lady Marmalade read with interest, not because she was enamored with the war but because she liked to keep abreast of international affairs. And it seemed to her that the allies were winning. Though it was still early in the war and God knew how much longer the chaos would continue. But the recent and welcomed entrance into the war by the Americans in December of '41 had given Lady Marmalade great hope that victory would come to the allies sooner than later.

Ginny sat next to Lady Marmalade on the couch and picked up the sections of the paper as Lady Marmalade put them down after she had finished with them. Alfred begrudgingly took another piece of Roquefort as his nose and mouth fought with one another, his mouth finally winning.

The smell was nausea inducing but the taste was something just short of heavenly. He closed his eyes and savored the moment. Frances put down the rest of the paper and looked at her watch. It would be nine p.m. very soon, and the port was starting to make her sleepy. She doubted that there would be a second raid tonight and her thoughts turned towards bedtime.

Ginny was mesmerized about an article in the lifestyle section about Cash and Cary. She couldn't, as did most women of the time, quite understand what Cary Grant found in Barbara Hutton. Ginny didn't think it would work, though she was certain she could make Cary Grant the happiest man alive.

"I think I'll retire for the night," said Frances, standing up.

Alfred and Ginny stood with her.

"Would you like some warm cocoa?" asked Alfred.

Frances shook her head.

"I think I've had quite enough for the evening. The port was just what I needed."

The grandfather clock chimed in with nine bells. They all stood quietly until it had finished.

"Very well, my Lady. I wish you a goodnight and we'll see if we can't bring Ms. Hollingsberry some justice tomorrow," said Alfred.

"Agreed," said Frances.

"Goodnight, my Lady," said Ginny.

"Goodnight."

Frances started to walk out of the living room when they all heard a loud and determined knocking on the front door.

"I wonder who on earth could be calling upon us at this ungodly hour so soon after an air raid," said Frances.

"Not sure, my Lady. I'll go and have a look. Perhaps one of the neighbors needs help with something. Let me deal with it."

"Thank you, Alfred."

Frances followed Alfred out of the living room and down the hall where she started up the stairs as he went on to answer the door.

Seventeen

Alfred opened the door and a frantic Lula Beckenswidth greeted him. She looked a mess. Her eyes had been tearing and she was clenching and unclenching her hands and shaking them in front of her as if they were on fire.

"Come in, Lula, come in," said Alfred. "What is it?"

Lula came in and tried to start speaking but she was babbling incoherently.

"It's, it's terrible... bad things... I don't know what to do."

Frances had heard her as she had started up the stairs and she came back down quickly. She walked up to her and put her hand around her shoulder.

"Take a deep breath, my dear, and tell me what happened."

Frances guided her to a chaise lounge that was up against the wall in the hallway just past the entranceway and she sat down next to the visibly upset Lula.

"It's Granny," she said, "she's dead."

Frances looked at her and her face frowned. This was not the news she was hoping to hear.

"What? Did you say that Madge is dead?" asked Frances, not quite believing her ears, at first.

Lula nodded.

"Yes. I went to get her when the sirens started, to take her into the shelter, but she was already dead. I had to leave her there."

Lula started crying and Frances put her arm around her and hugged her in closer to herself.

"Could you get some tissues please, Alfred?" she asked.

Alfred nodded and walked briskly down the hall to the bathroom to collect some tissues for Lula.

"There, there, dear, let it out and then tell me exactly what happened."

Alfred came back just as quickly as he had left and handed the tissues to Lula who took them eagerly. She wiped her eyes and blew her nose and then looked up shyly at Frances.

"I had poured Madge her bath like I usually do and had added her bath oils as always and then I'd helped her into the bath where I left her."

"What time was this my dear?"

"It was shortly after seven."

Frances nodded.

"She usually likes to take a long bath every other day, so I thought nothing of it until the sirens went off at around eight p.m. I went up to help her get dressed and to bring her down into the shelter. I thought she would likely be out of the bath already so I went to her room but she wasn't there. I went back to the bathroom and knocked on the door. I got no answer so I walked in and found her..."

Lula sobbed again and Frances rubbed her back. She dabbed her eyes with the tissues.

"Madge had her last bath on Tuesday then?"

Lula nodded, then stopped and shook her head.

"No, she was supposed to but she took her last bath on Monday evening instead."

"I see, so the door was closed but it wasn't locked?" asked Frances.

Lula nodded.

"She's not allowed to lock the door in case something happens, she's old you know, and not in the best of health."

Frances looked up at Alfred.

"Alfred, please take off to the nearest police station as fast as you can and see if they can't get hold of Inspector Pearce and ask him to join us at Ms. Hollingsberry's as quickly as he can."

"Right away, my Lady."

Alfred left the house, closing the door behind him, and headed off to the local police station which, thankfully, was only several blocks away. He started off at a light jog.

"Tell me what you saw when you got into the bathroom," said Frances.

"I saw Granny in the bathtub, her face was under the water. I ran up to her and pulled her head up out of the water as best I could but she was already dead. I could tell. Her face was blue and she wouldn't respond to my yelling."

"And then what happened."

"I yelled for Jeremiah and he came running up the stairs, followed by Colin. Colin took charge and checked for her breathing. He told me she was dead, that there was nothing we could do. That we had to leave and save ourselves and take cover in the shelter. Then afterwards we could call the police and get it sorted out. I didn't want to leave her there like that. I really didn't..."

Lula took to crying again and Frances comforted her and waited until she composed herself again.

"But you did leave didn't you?"

"I had no choice," Lula said looking at Lady Marmalade with pleading puppy dog eyes. "Colin dragged me out and we all went downstairs into the shelter and waited until it was all over. Then as soon as they gave the all clear I ran here as fast as I could."

"What about the others? Did anyone go for the police?"

Lula shook her head as she balled up the tissues in her small fists.

"No, Penelope was going to go but Colin told her not to. He said that you'd be calling the police in any event as soon as you heard."

"Hmm," said Frances.

Lula looked up at her confused and frightened.

"Should I have called on the police first?" she asked.

"No, my dear, it's all right, you did the right thing. Alfred's gone for the police so the best we can do now is to head back to Madge's home so I can start taking a look around and investigate what happened to her."

"But can't you see, my Lady, Madge drowned. Nobody killed her."

"So, nobody came round this evening who shouldn't have been there, just like I asked?"

Lula nodded.

"It was just the four of us and Jeremiah and Mollie."

"Did anyone else go upstairs to check on Madge from when you drew her bath until you went to get her when the sirens went off?"

"Not any of the boarders," Lula said, nervously. "We were all downstairs in the living room. Colin was sketching Penelope. Matilda was reading a magazine and I was knitting."

"What about Jeremiah or Mollie?"

"I can't say about them, they weren't with us. You don't think one of them would have drowned her?"

"It can't be ruled out my dear. Come, I think we should make our way back to your grandmother's home to keep an eye on things and wait until the police arrive."

Frances stood up and helped Lula. Lula dabbed at her eyes. Frances reached into the side table that was by the front entrance and took the keys to the Aston Martin and they exited

Marmalade Park and went into the garage. Frances opened the garage door, drove the Aston Martin out and closed it again behind her. She did the same with the gate to Marmalade Park and then drove the two of them, at great speed, to Ms. Hollingsberry's home.

"Take me right to Madge, please Lula," said Frances as she got out of the car and followed Lula up the stairs to the house.

Lula walked in and Frances closed the door behind them. They went straight upstairs and headed down the hallway towards Madge's room. Just before they got there, on the right hand side, opposite Matilda's bedroom, was the bathroom.

The bathroom door was slightly ajar. Lula pointed to it feebly, "She's in there."

Lula was afraid to go in, so Lady Marmalade opened the door and walked in. The bathroom was large and in the middle at the back was the claw footed bathtub. It was filled to within just a few inches of the rim, right up to the overflow drain. Madge was half floating half sinking in the bathtub, her face barely under the surface.

Frances walked up to her and looked her up and down. She didn't look as if she had struggled with anyone. There were no signs of injury, and just as Lula had said, it looked as if she had simply drowned. Yet there was an ever so slight sweet smell in the air that hinted of sugared almonds but with a fake chemical hint to it. Lady Marmalade knew exactly what that was.

She looked around and saw the toilet with the seat down and the sink with cabinets underneath and cabinets above. Close to the bathtub, up against the wall by the head of the bathtub was a towel rack with a pair of white towels on it. The floor was tiled in small black and white squares.

Madge's dressing gown lay crumpled by the side of the bathtub and there appeared to be no water that had splashed out of the bathtub and onto the floor. Frances turned around and saw Lula standing by the doorway.

"Where are these bath oils that you poured in for Madge?" she asked.

Lula pointed at the cabinet beneath the bathroom sink. Frances opened it up and took a look inside. There was a large glass bottle that held about two cups and it had a floral paper sticker on it that advertised it as the worlds best lavender bath oils. Frances picked it up.

"Is this it?"

Lula nodded.

"She likes me to use about half of it for each bath. She thinks it helps her skin."

"Then there was only half left this evening?"

The bottle was empty except for a small amount that had settled on the bottom of the bottle. Lula nodded again.

"Though it was strange. It didn't seem to smell as strong as it had on Monday evening when I used it as a fresh bottle. I mean, it didn't smell as strongly of lavender as I remember, it had a slightly different, sweeter almost nuttier smell, but I didn't really pay attention to it."

Frances nodded. She held the bottle away from her and gingerly unscrewed the lid. She brought it back and quickly drew it across and under her nose. She inhaled just the smallest amount and it smelled exactly as she had expected.

"Your grandmother was murdered, Lula, I'm afraid to say. I've seen all I need to in here. I suggest we head downstairs and wait for Inspector Pearce with the others."

"But how? Nobody was in here, at least I don't believe there was. I can't say for sure about Jeremiah and Mollie but surely they wouldn't have drowned her. I put her into the bathtub myself and left and closed the door after myself. She must have slipped or something and drowned. Her health is not the best."

Lula was looking down and shaking her head, trying to understand how her grandmother could have been murdered when there was nobody up here to do it. Frances walked out of the bathroom and Lula followed her into the hallway. Frances closed the door behind them.

"Tell me Lula, did you feel a little different after helping your grandmother into the bathtub? A little queasy or dizzy?"

"Yes, I did actually. But Madge is heavy. I often get lightheaded when helping her into the bathtub and then standing up again."

Frances started walking down the hallway towards the stairs with Lula by her side.

"I don't understand," said Lula. "How could she have been murdered?"

"I'll tell you all when we get downstairs," said Frances.

And they walked in silence down the stairs, down the hallway and back into the living room which felt to Lady Marmalade as being almost as familiar as her own living room.

When they got there, everyone was gathered around. Colin had a tumbler of whiskey in his hand and Penelope and Matilda were drinking what looked like port. They were clearly all quite distraught. Jeremiah stood solemnly to one side and Mollie stood by him, not quite sure what to do with herself. For the first time since Frances had met them, their faces were not crinkled into idiotic smiles, and rightly so.

Colin was standing behind the couch where Penelope and Matilda sat together. He had his free hand on Penelope's shoulder. Lula took the couch next to Matilda and Penelope. Frances sat down in the armchair she had sat in the last time she was here. She looked at them all somberly and rested her eyes on Colin.

"Why did you instruct Penelope not to call for the police?"

"Oh, come on," he said, looking upset already. "Lula had gone to fetch you and I knew you'd be taking care of it. Besides, you're much closer to us than the police are for heaven's sake. And she's been dead for some time, already. Surely an extra half hour isn't that important."

"No, it's not, but don't you think you should have come, a big strapping fellow like yourself rather than sending a young woman out in the middle of the night? Do you have no shame?"

Colin sent her a stern look and swallowed some whiskey.

"Look, we're all quite unnerved by this whole thing. It's the first time any of us have ever seen a dead body. I wasn't thinking clearly. Lula took off like a shot at the first opportunity. I barely had the chance to ask her where she was going."

Frances looked at Lula and she nodded in agreement with what Colin had said.

"Very well. Did any of you disturb anything upstairs in the bathroom when you went in?"

She was looking at Colin mostly. He shook his head.

"I went in after Jeremiah and saw Lula trying to hold Madge's head up above the water. She was crying and hysterical. I checked Madge's breathing and I knew she was dead. I told Lula we had to leave, that we needed to get into the shelter. I had to pull her away. I didn't touch anything while I was in there."

"And you, Jeremiah?"

Frances turned to look at the butler. He shook his head soberly.

"No, my Lady. I got into the bathroom before Mr. Abbermann, but he took charge right away. I stood to the side and watched. I didn't touch anything and I agree with everything that Mr. Abbermann said."

"And you Lula, did you touch anything while you were in there?"

She shook her head slowly and sadly, her head bowed down her eyes flitting from Frances to her own fists that were balled up in her lap.

"I just tried to help my grandmother, that's all. I wasn't even aware of anything else."

"Has anyone else entered the bathroom since Colin, Jeremiah and Lula left?"

Frances looked carefully at Matilda and Penelope.

"Good grief, no, there is just no way that I want to see a dead body. It sends shivers up my spine just thinking about it," said Matilda.

"I agree with Matilda," said Penelope, "I find the whole thing quite grizzly."

Colin squeezed her shoulder in support. Frances looked over at Jeremiah and Mollie standing off to one side.

"The two of you were not with the others during Madge's bath time, can you tell me where, exactly, you were between seven and when the sirens went off?" asked Frances.

"I had finished up dinner for the boarders, my Lady," said Mollie, the smile still vacant from her face, "and I had tidied up the dirty dishes. Me and Jerry were having our dinner during that time."

"For the whole hour?"

"No, my Lady, but after we had eaten, Jerry went and offered after dinner drinks and desserts to the boarders, then he came back and stayed with me in the kitchen and kept me company while I cleaned up."

"So, at no time during that period did you go upstairs?"

"I didn't go upstairs, my Lady. I haven't been upstairs since before dinner when I informed Ms. Hollingsberry that dinner was ready."

"And what time was that?"

"About six p.m."

Mollie looked like she was in trouble, but she wasn't, at least not at the moment.

"Can you corroborate that, Jeremiah?"

"Yes, my Lady, just as Mollie said. We had our supper and then I came out and offered port and brandy to the boarders and some Black Forest cake that Mollie had baked this afternoon. Then I went back and kept her company while she washed up. Just after the sirens started I heard Ms. Beckenswidth yelling from upstairs so I went to help and that's when Colin came in right after me."

Frances looked over at the boarders.

"Can any of you confirm that Jeremiah was out here serving cake and drinks as he says?"

Matilda and Penelope nodded, so did Lula.

"Yes, he was, just like he says. The cake was delicious and so was the brandy," said Colin trying for a bit of levity.

"Why all these questions, I thought that Lula said Madge had accidentally drowned?" asked Matilda.

"Yes, it is very apparent that Madge has drowned, but she did not drown accidentally. Just as I had feared, and even with my best intentions of protecting her, Michael has managed to murder his mother."

"Good heavens," said Penelope. "You can't be serious. How? Nobody's been in the house all night just as you had asked."

"Michael, it seems, knew Madge's schedule quite intimately and he used that to his advantage and used Lula, unknowingly, to be the instrument of his evil plan."

"What do you mean?" asked Lula.

"Michael, whoever he is, must have known that Madge baths every other day or so and that she likes to use ample bath oils with her bath. I believe that he poured most of the bath oils down the sink and replaced it with chloroform. Just leaving enough of the bath oils to mask the aroma."

Lula looked up at Lady Marmalade and blinked her eyes, it looked like she might burst into tears again at any moment.

"So you're saying that I killed her?"

"No, my dear, I'm saying that you poured the bath oils into her bath which had already been replaced with chloroform to knock her out and then cause her to drown."

Lula started to tear up and cry.

"No, no, no... I should have known... I killed Granny," she said.

Jeremiah left the living room and returned carrying a box of tissues which he handed to Lula.

"What an evil and cunning monster," said Matilda. "I thought that it was all just a bit of a joke that Madge was playing on all of us."

Frances shook her head slowly.

"I'm afraid not my dear, this has been, sadly, all too real."

"Then who is this Michael?" asked Penelope.

"I have an idea, but I'm waiting to get confirmation from Inspector Pearce. There is no need to rush now if justice is to be served. We want to be thorough and certain."

"But the letters, what about those letters?" asked Matilda. "They don't look like they're written by a man, that's partly why I thought Madge might have been responsible. Surely they've been written by a woman."

"I agree that they certainly don't look like they've been written by a man, and I do believe that they weren't written by Michael."

"Then who?"

"Time and Inspector Pearce's graphologist will answer that question, though I suspect that the culprit is one of you three."

"Preposterous, you have to be joking," said Colin, gesticulating angrily.

Frances looked at him and then at Matilda until her eyes finally rested on Penelope. Penelope looked at Frances with her eyes wide and raised her eyebrows. She folded her arms under her bosom and looked down at the table.

"You have to be joking. I didn't do it," she said.

"We will see," said Frances, looking over at each of them in turn. "I do believe whoever did do it, that they didn't believe it would end as badly as this. I believe that whoever of you wrote the letters thought it was quite good fun to cause Madge some discomfort as she has caused each and everyone of you in your own way."

"Bloody right," said Colin, "I can't say she didn't deserve to be a little agitated. But none of us would have plotted to kill her, for god's sake."

"That I do believe. Whoever is the letter writer was used as a pawn just as Lula was in fulfilling Michael's sinister plan."

"Look," said Matilda, "we're all out of a home now. Madge made it abundantly clear that if she should die, we'd all be kicked out of here. As much as we might have disliked her, none of us wanted her dead, if only for that reason."

"I understand that," said Frances.

"I mean, it's very difficult right now to find a rooming house," said Matilda.

"Isn't that the truth," added Colin, "I'm going to have to live in my studio until I can find a place, if I don't get caught."

"I think I should be all right," said Penelope, "Mr. and Mrs. Bollingshook have wanted a live in nanny for some time. Matilda said she'd put in a good word with them as she's leaving to head back up to Liverpool to move in with her mum and dad until Max gets back from the war. So I'm sure they'll take me on as a fulltime nanny."

"Is that so?" asked Frances looking at Matilda.

"Yes, I'm fed up with this war. My mum says that Liverpool doesn't have it half as bad as London, and Penelope has been looking for different work for some time."

"Then why did you make such a scene about how hard it is to find a rooming house?" asked Frances.

Matilda looked away and huffed.

"Because you're insinuating that one of us wrote those letters and it wasn't me, I wanted you to realize that."

Frances didn't say anything.

"You shouldn't have said that," said Colin to Penelope.

"What," she said.

"Say that you have a place to move to, it makes you look all the more guilty."

"About what?"

"Well, it makes it look like you had reason to write those letters, because Madge's death and getting kicked out of here doesn't affect you much at all now."

"Really?" asked Penelope, looking at Frances. "What about Lula, Madge practically beats the stuffing out of her and she'll get to stay here, so why am I the guilty one?"

"One of you is guilty," said Frances, "and I haven't made up my mind as to who that is yet, we'll let the evidence decide."

Penelope shook her head.

"Unbelievable, Matilda's not going to be inconvenienced by this much at all, and she's made her plans well in advance. I just learned about the full time nanny position."

Penelope's crossed her arms even more firmly and looked away at the far wall which was jammed with statues and paintings. Colin squeezed her shoulder.

"I'm sure you didn't do it... Did you?"

Penelope didn't answer him.

"I'm just teasing you."

"This is not the time for your stupid jokes," said Matilda, looking at him sternly.

He didn't respond. He put his tumbler to his lips and drained the brandy. He looked longingly at the bar, but didn't head over to it right away. Penelope picked up her port from the table and took the last sip.

"I've sent Alfred to call for the police. They should be here any minute and we'll be getting to the bottom of this shortly."

As if on cue, there was a knock at the front door. Jeremiah looked at Lady Marmalade.

"Will you allow me to answer, my Lady?"

"Of course."

Eighteen

Inspector Pearce entered the living room twirling his very well manicured moustache. He was followed by two constables. They looked like twins, if not in looks then in stature. Large, burly men whom you might expect to be lumberjacks rather than Bobbies. They were clean shaven and wore their Custodian helmets smartly on their heads. They each walked off to a side of the room and stood 'at ease' with their legs apart and their hands behind their backs.

Last in was Alfred, who didn't look particularly flustered. The Hollingsberry's grandfather clock chimed once for half past nine. Nobody stood up to greet the inspector. In fact, the temperature of the room got decidedly chilly.

"Evening. I am Inspector Pearce of Scotland Yard," he said looking around the room and making eye contact with everyone. "If you'll all please wait here, I'll have Lady Marmalade show me to the bathroom."

He looked over at Frances and smiled at her, offering his hand, which she took and shook as she got up.

"Nice to see you again, though we ought to stop meeting under these circumstances."

He gave her a sly grin and she smiled back.

"It's always a pleasure to see you, Devlin. Please follow me, the bathroom is upstairs."

Inspector Pearce followed Frances out the living room and as he did so he nodded at his constables. They were not to let anyone out of the room. They made their way up the landing and down the hall, taking the last right before Madge's room into the bathroom. Frances entered first and stood quietly in the middle of the bathroom as Pearce came up beside her and stood next to her. He looked around.

"No signs of violence," he said.

"No, not at all, Devlin," she answered.

Inspector Pearce looked over at Frances and smiled at her. She looked up at him.

"Are you going to make this harder for me or will you just tell me what happened. I know you've already been in here."

Frances smiled.

"You know me too well," she said. "I'll tell you what I think happened and then you can make your own judgment."

"I haven't known you to get it wrong yet."

"Well, don't jinx me, there is a first time for everything."

Frances turned around and pointed at the door.

"Lula draws Madge's bath every other day or so. Last time she had her bath was on the evening of the 8th of June, a Monday. This evening she drew her grandmother's bath just as she usually does and she adds half a bottle of bath oils."

"That's rich."

"Yes, I agree, but apparently Madge believes that's what she needs to keep her skin smooth and supple. In any event, Lula draws the bath and then helps Madge into it. She leaves and closes the door behind her. From what I've been able to ascertain, nobody else came up here until the sirens started. Then Lula came up to find her grandmother to help her downstairs into the shelter."

Pearce nodded as he looked around the bathroom, noticing the crumpled dressing gown on the floor by the bathtub.

"And she came in here and found her drowned, just like she is now?"

"Yes," said Frances, "though she first checked her grandmother's room, but not finding her there she came back to the bathroom and knocked before entering. She came in and tried to revive her grandmother."

"How so?"

"She tried as best as she could to yank her out of the water as much as she could. But she's a small fragile thing, Lula. I would surmise that Madge was already long dead by this point. Lula yelled for help and both the butler Jeremiah and Colin came upstairs and into the bathroom. Colin took charge, checked for her breathing and determined that Madge was dead. He told me that he had to practically drag Lula down into the shelter."

"I see, so the woman has been stewing in this bath since around eight?"

"No, quite a bit before then. She took her bath at shortly after seven Lula said."

"Right, sorry. I meant she had been left in here since Lula found her when the sirens went off."

Frances nodded.

"It looks to me like a simple drowning. Perhaps she knocked her head or had a mild heart attack and drowned."

"That's what Lula thought at first too. It does look clean and convenient doesn't it. And if we hadn't received those letters from Madge I might agree. But we have, and on a side note I have the sixth letter that Madge received this afternoon to give you."

"Did it suggest something like this?"

"Not directly, but it certainly made it clear that something awful would happen to her. I have it in my handbag downstairs, I'll give it to you when we get down. It said, 'you have not repented. The time is nigh. You will die.'"

"I see," said Pearce, nodding his head. "She certainly wasn't drowned forcibly, otherwise you'd expect a lot of water all over the floor."

"Exactly. This might have been the perfect murder if it weren't for all these letters. She's an older woman, not in the best of health, it could easily have been ruled a natural death."

"Except that the murderer wanted vengeance and part of that was causing her fear before hand."

"Right."

"And you think that this murderer is Michael?"

Frances nodded.

"Any word about that yet?"

"I'm afraid not, but they've promised me they'll have the records delivered first thing in the morning and I'll be meeting with my graphologist first thing in the morning too."

"Good."

"All right, then. So Madge was drowned, I think it's fair to say that was the cause of death. But if this was murder, how was she drowned so easily?"

"The key is that bottle of bath oils I mentioned."

Frances walked up to the cabinet under the sink and opened it up. She pulled out the bottle of bath oils and gave it to Pearce. He looked at it and then looked at her.

"My wife likes the same bath oils. This is hardly intriguing."

"Take the cap off and have the slightest whiff, and I mean the slightest, Devlin."

Pearce looked at her and unscrewed the cap off the bottle and took a faint whiff of the aroma from the contents. He quickly held it away from his nose and screwed the cap back on.

"You trying to put me under?" he asked.

Frances smiled.

"Chloroform with just the barest hint of lavender."

Frances nodded.

"Exactly. I asked Lula if she felt a bit light headed after she had helped her grandmother into the bath and she admitted to feeling that way, but she said she often feels a bit woozy after helping her grandmother into her bath as she's a big woman. But as you smelled it, there is very little of the lavender left in it. I think at least half of this bottle was pure chloroform."

"You could knock out an elephant with that much," said Pearce.

"I imagine so. I think our murderer didn't want to take any chances."

"Do you have any idea who you think it might be?"

"Michael, of course," said Lady Marmalade grinning.

"Yes, but who is Michael?"

"I'm teasing with you, Devlin," said Frances. "But to answer your question, yes I do believe I have an idea about who Michael might be."

"And are you going to share that with me?"

"Not yet, I'd rather get confirmation from you when you have it."

"Very well," said Pearce who had taken to twirling his moustache again. "What about the letter writer?"

"You know, that is something that I'm not sure about. Looking at those samples that I gave you, I thought that Matilda's matched the closest, but I just don't know why she would do that. And then I noticed Colin's signature on his painting in the living room. The A and Bs of his last name are loopy and round like some parts of the handwriting in the letters, but his sample was not like that at all."

"Could be he masked his own handwriting."

"Or, he created a stylized hand for the letters. He is after all an artist."

"But why do it?"

"Oh, I don't know, Devlin, I think any of the three boarders downstairs might have done it just for a silly joke, not realizing the severity of the outcome. None of them really like her and I can understand why. It might have been something as simple as spite."

"Let's see what the graphologist has to say. But one question I do have, is what makes you think it is someone in the home who wrote these letters?"

"That's elementary, my dear Pearce," said Lady Marmalade, smiling at him, "or perhaps it isn't. The way I look at it is this: Michael somehow is aware of Madge's day-to-day routines, otherwise how would he know when to switch out the bath oils or have someone switch them out for him? As such, I think he'd want to use someone from the inside to write the letters so that everything is more easily contained. The outcome is more assured and he can keep an eye on everything from a distance. Additionally, he likely knows how difficult a woman this Madge is, and so those living under her roof are more likely to hold ill will towards her than some stranger who might be more easily put off from writing the letters by the content of them."

Pearce nodded and continued to look around the bathroom. He walked over to the cabinets and had a look inside, not finding anything very interesting. No drugs of any sort except for a small bottle of aspirin. He walked back over to where Frances stood.

"Anything else that I should be aware of while we're here. The coroner should be here any minute."

Frances looked around.

"No, just that bottle of bath oils. I think the rest is reasonably undisturbed. I don't believe our murderer has been in here for some time."

Pearce nodded and they walked out of the bathroom just as the coroner and his two men came up the stairs carrying a stretcher.

"Inspector, Lady Marmalade," said the coroner as they passed by each other.

"Good evening, Dr. Graveson," said Devlin.

"Good evening, doctor," said Frances.

Frances and Devlin walked back down the stairs and made their way to the living room. Inspector Pearce came up to the group who were seated around the living room and started taking down their names. Frances went up to him and touched him on the elbow. He looked at her. She handed Pearce the sixth letter. He'd be needing it now for the homicide file.

"Sorry to interrupt, Devlin, but I'll be heading off. It's been a long night. Will you call me first thing tomorrow morning when your information comes in?"

"I most certainly will. Good night, Frances."

"Good night, Devlin."

Alfred got up and walked with Frances to the front door. Frances looked into the closet and took out her cardigan and Alfred got his jacket. Frances looked into her purse and took out the keys to the Aston Martin and handed them to Alfred.

"Would you mind driving, Alfred? It's been such a tiring night."

"Of course, my Lady."

They let themselves out and Alfred held the passenger car door open for Frances and closed it after her. He got into the driver's seat, started up the car and drove off towards Marmalade Park.

"Quite the evening, what with the bombings and the murder," said Alfred.

"Oh, Alfred, you have no idea. Poor Ms. Hollingsberry, I fear that I failed her."

"You did your best, my Lady. I don't think anyone else could have done any better. We took all the precautions that we could have."

"Thank you for saying so, Alfred. At least perhaps, in a small way, I can comfort myself with the fact that Madge died somewhat peacefully."

"How was she murdered?" asked Alfred.

"It appears that her bath oils, of which she is known to use in copious amounts, were diluted heavily with chloroform. So, when Lula drew her bath and added the bath oils, she was in essence creating a bath filled with chloroform. I'm sure that it was within only a few minutes being in that tub that she succumbed to the chloroform and slipped under the water and drowned."

"Still, terrible to be murdered," said Alfred. "But as you say, it was likely painless. We'll get to the bottom of this. We'll make sure that Michael is brought to justice."

"Yes, we will," said Frances. "I believe that tomorrow will be the end of it. I think we'll find our letter writer and the person known once as Michael."

Alfred mumbled his agreement, keeping his eyes firmly on the road ahead of him. Thankfully, there was very little extra rubble from the evening's bombing raid that had affected the road back to Marmalade Park, and the two of them spent the rest of the journey in silence.

Nineteen

Friday morning was sunny and warm. Frances had taken her breakfast outside overlooking her small garden in Marmalade Park. The grass was green and the flowers colorful. It was quiet and peaceful and she sat with Ginny and Alfred. Birds flew overhead and some perched in a few of the trees in the garden, singing their hearts out. Sitting in the back garden of Marmalade Park, it was hard to appreciate that they were at war, that they had been at war for almost three years now.

Lady Marmalade's garden was a small oasis from the rubble that could be found not far outside of her home and dotted all over London. Ginny had served up breakfast, just a light repast. Lady Marmalade was cracking at the shell of a hardboiled egg and on a side plate she had a slice of toast with butter melting on its warm face.

Frances took the egg out of its holder and peeled the shell of it and placed it back in the egg holder. She dusted Humpty's bald white pate with salt and took the first scoop. Her eggs were never runny, she couldn't stomach them that way. They had to be cooked through. Ginny had learned this the very first day she had come to work for the Marmalades. It was how she preferred her own eggs.

Alfred on the other hand preferred his eggs runny. He had two of them in front of him. Only the top halves of their shells missing. He had taken off the first quarter of the egg and had cut his toast into strips. He was dipping the strips into the runny yolks and eating them with relish.

Lady Marmalade reached for the teapot and topped up her tea. She was having it black with just a small squeeze of lemon. Inside the house the phone started to ring.

"I see the telephones have been fixed," said Alfred, getting out of his chair.

"Yes, that was very fast of them," said Frances.

Alfred went into the house as Ginny and Frances kept eating. By the time Alfred had come back outside, Frances had finished her egg and was about to start on her toast. It had just gone past nine o'clock.

"It's Inspector Pearce for you, my Lady."

"Thank you, Alfred," said Frances, as she got up and went inside. Alfred sat back down only once Frances had disappeared.

Frances walked through the living room and up the hallway until she reached the phone.

"Devlin," she said into the receiver.

"Frances, I have wonderful news for you. We've determined who both the letter writer is and who Michael is. You won't believe it."

"Thank you, Devlin, it's so important that justice be served."

"Oh, yes, it will. I'm heading up the Ms. Hollingsberry's residence to arrest Colin Abbermann."

"Oh, I see."

"Would you like to meet me there?"

"Certainly, when will you be getting there?"

"I think my lads and I will arrive by ten."

"Good, I'll see you at ten then."

The said their goodbyes and hung up. Lady Marmalade walked back outside. Alfred stood up and sat down when Frances did.

"Good news, my Lady?" asked Alfred.

"Yes, indeed. Inspector Pearce tells me that he knows who Michael is and who the letter writer is."

"That is good news," said Ginny.

"We'll be heading up to Ms. Hollingsberry's residence after breakfast. No rush though, Inspector Pearce doesn't expect he'll get there much before ten."

"Did he tell you who they were?" asked Alfred.

"Not exactly," said Frances, "though he did say he was going to the Hollingsberry residence to arrest Colin Abbermann."

Alfred dipped the last bit of toast into this second egg and ate it before speaking.

"The letter writer, I'm assuming; he's not old enough to be Michael."

"That's just what I thought. What I want to know is why he did it."

"Me, too," said Ginny.

"Perhaps, like you said last night, just out of spite. Maybe for someone like that it's that simple and that easy. I never did care very much for him. Quite a brash, abrasive and combative young man."

"I agree," said Frances. "Though I wonder if there aren't other reasons for having done it. I guess we'll see."

Alfred nodded and took to eating the last of his egg and sipping his tea in between mouthfuls. They sat in silence for the rest of the meal and then sat out in the garden for a while just enjoying the weather.

"Isn't it strange how the day is so sunny this morning as if it knew that the blinding light of justice would make good on its promise."

"I quite like the metaphor," said Alfred.

"Well, Alfred, what do you think? Should we be off?"

"I think so my Lady. I wouldn't want to be late to the party. I'd pay good money to see that young man's face when he gets arrested."

Alfred and Frances got up and left the table after saying their farewells to Ginny. Ginny went to tidying up and cleaning the breakfast dishes once they had gone.

It was such a lovely day that Alfred and Frances decided to walk. Alfred was dressed in a light gray jacket and matching slacks with a gray bowler's hat upon his head and he carried a walking stick. Not because he limped, but because he liked it. Frances wore a pale blue summer dress that flowed below her knees and a matching pair of flat blue shoes. Upon her head was a pale blue scarf. The dress had sleeves that fell to her elbows and she had a white handbag that she carried in the crook of her left arm.

It didn't take them much longer than fifteen minutes to walk to Ms. Hollingsberry's home. It was beginning to feel like a home away from home in some ways. They walked through Hyde Park where children with their mothers were playing. Some boys were hiding behind some rubble and others were lying in the craters where bombs had exploded. They were playing war games as only young boys can.

Frances smiled at everyone as she went by and her sunny disposition was greeted with the same. When they got to the Hollingsberry home, Jeremiah answered the door. He was pleasant but not as obsequiously sweet as he had been on the many occasions before. It was a welcome change.

"Where is everyone, Jeremiah?" asked Frances.

"They should be gathering in the living room for tea. We'll be serving it at ten this morning, if you'd care to join us."

"No, thank you Jeremiah. And you might want to suggest to Mollie that she not serve the tea before eleven. Inspector Pearce will be by any moment now."

"Yes, my Lady."

Alfred and Frances walked down the hall and into the living room. Colin was sketching, again. He was looking at Penelope now and then who was the subject of his sketch. She was sitting on the couch across from him. She looked up when Frances walked in.

"Oy," he said, "keep your face steady."

Lula was on a chaise lounge on the far side of the room, behind Penelope and she was reading a magazine. Matilda was standing behind the couch that Colin was on and admiring his sketch. She looked up at Frances when she came in.

"Good morning," she said, matter of factly without much warmth or emotion of any kind.

"Good morning," said Frances.

Colin looked up at her and Alfred.

"Good God, haven't you had enough of this place, already? Shouldn't you be out there finding the murderer?"

"We are, we're just waiting for Inspector Pearce to come by."

"And why does he need to come here?" asked Colin.

"I'm sure he'll tell everyone why he's here."

And with that there was a knock at the door which Jeremiah went and answered. Down the hall you could hear Inspector Pearce's authoritative voice. Moments later Pearce walked into the living room, dressed in a light brown suit and tie. He was followed by the same two constables from last night.

"You beat me to it," he said, smiling at Frances.

"I wouldn't have missed it for the world," she said.

Pearce went up and shook Alfred's hand warmly.

"Thanks for getting us last night," he said.

Alfred nodded and smiled at him. Pearce broke from Alfred's grip and looked around the room.

"You are all probably wondering why I'm here again, this morning."

"Bloody right," said Colin, "I wish you people would leave us alone."

"We will, soon enough. We're here in fact, to arrest you, Mr. Colin Abbermann for conspiring to murder Ms. Margaret Hollingsberry."

Pearce looked at Colin sternly, his left eyebrow raised and his moustache immaculately groomed. Colin looked up at him and stood up.

"Now, look here," he said trying to sound as indignant as possible. "I didn't conspire to murder anyone. I had nothing to do with Madge's murder."

"Perhaps not directly, but we have studied those letters that Ms. Hollingsberry received and our graphologist at Scotland Yard has determined that you wrote them. Do you deny that?" asked Pearce

Colin put his sketchbook down and his pencils on top of them. He took to chewing his nails for a moment, the pastels which had colored his fingers now dotting his mouth like a bruise.

"Well, yes... I mean no, I didn't write those letters."

Colin was staring down at Inspector Pearce's shoes. He had gone back to chewing his fingernails.

"Colin, you didn't?" said Penelope standing up with her mouth wide open and her eyes in shock.

Colin started looking around the room.

"I'm afraid you're going to have to come with us, Mr. Abbermann and you can discuss your innocence down at the station."

Pearce looked around at his constables and nodded at them. Colin looked up and, for the first time since Lady Marmalade had known him, she saw fear in his eyes. He looked around nervously, then leaned down and picked up his sketchbook. He flung it at Inspector Pearce where it hit him, sketch side down, on his jacket before falling to the floor. It left pastel dust on his clean suit jacket which he dusted off with his hand.

Colin ran for the doors in the living room that opened up to the garden. Frances wasn't sure what he was thinking. The garden was small and rimmed with high hedges that she couldn't possibly see him getting over. But out he went with the two constables hot on his heels.

He ran to a bird bath that sat in one corner of the garden and tried to dodge the constables as he tried to buy some time looking for an exit. There wasn't one. There was no gate along the side of the house to exit and enter the yard. Frances looked at Alfred and he was smiling, watching the theatrics. Colin had a very determined look on his face.

Inspector Pearce had his arms folded in front of him and he had a sly smile too.

"What is he thinking? He's only making it harder on himself," said Pearce.

"Don't hurt him Inspector, please don't hurt him," said Penelope. "He's not that wicked."

"He'll be all right, don't you worry, they'll get him in a moment."

And outside, Colin made one last attempt to escape by climbing up an apple tree. He didn't make it far before the one constable was grabbing him by the cuff of his pants as Colin tried to shake him off. The other constable came up and grabbed Colin by the jacket and between the two of them they pulled him down.

It was a hard landing for poor old Colin. He landed flat on his stomach and Frances saw the air get knocked out of him. He was easy to control at that point and the two constables picked him up and walked him back into the house as he limped between them. He had some grass and twigs in his hair.

"Now, why would an innocent man run from the police?" asked Pearce.

Colin looked up at him shamefacedly and tried his best grin.

"Look I did it, I'll admit it. But I was never conspiring to murder her. It was all supposed to be a bit of a lark. She was an awful woman, she was. You have no idea. I thought it would be fun to ruffle her feathers a bit, that's all."

"Who told you to write these letters?" asked Pearce.

"I don't know, honestly, I don't know."

"That's not going to help you, young man."

"Look, it started back in January just after I arrived. I received a letter asking if I could be commissioned for a small job, you see. All I had to do was hand write in any style I liked, six letters. I agreed and then a few days later the second letter arrived with instructions."

"What did it say?" asked Pearce.

"It told me what to write and when to post it so that it would arrive on the tenth. I thought it a bit odd, what the letter wanted me to copy, but ten pounds for such a small job is a lot of money. And heaven's knows I could use the money."

Inspector Pearce looked at Frances and drew his mouth down as if trying to make sense of it all. Frances nodded.

"That's not a small amount of money for writing a letter," she said.

"Exactly. I mean ten pounds for something that barely took me ten minutes. I felt lucky, to be honest. And that letter told me that there'd be five more requests like this and if I carried through with them all there'd be a fifty pound bonus included in the last letter."

"And was there?" asked Pearce.

Colin nodded.

"So you made over a hundred pounds for writing six letters?" asked Pearce.

"A hundred and ten pounds. I thought I was really lucky. I even wrote back asking if there would be more work, but sadly, he said no."

"How do you know the letter writer was a he?" asked Frances.

"I don't, I just assumed so from the writing. It looks masculine. Listen, if I'd known he was really committed to hurting her I wouldn't have done it. Honestly, I wouldn't have. But I won't lie and say that I didn't get a bit of a thrill from upsetting Madge with those letters. She was truly a horrid woman. Wasn't she?"

Colin looked around from Matilda to Penelope. They both turned away from his gaze.

"She was difficult, but you shouldn't have done that, Colin. It's very mean spirited," said Matilda.

Colin hung his head down and shook it slowly.

"They were just bloody letters, that's all. I needed the money. I haven't been selling my paintings much and I needed to pay for next semester."

"I would have lent you the money," said Penelope, "if only you'd asked."

Colin looked up at her and smiled sadly.

"You don't hate me, do you?"

Penelope looked away and then briefly looked back at him.

"No, but I didn't think you were like this, Colin. I really didn't. I don't know if I can forgive you."

"I don't suppose you have any of this correspondence, do you?" asked Pearce.

"As a matter of fact, I do. Not all of it. I burned the first couple of letters like I was asked, but with the tone of what I was writing getting more serious I just had this feeling that I should keep them, just in case."

"That's probably the only wise thing you've done so far," said Pearce.

"Take us to them."

"They're in my room."

Colin, handcuffed, led everyone upstairs to his room. It was on the far end of the hallway, opposite Madge's room and on the right side, as you walked down that part of the hallway, the same side as Matilda's room. The room was small and held a single bed that hadn't been made. There was an easel in the corner with a half finished painting of another nude woman on it. This one was more pleasant to look at, no sign of violence or gore, at least not yet.

Next to the bed on the far side of the door was a bedside table with a lamp, on the bedside table were assorted pastels and pencils. On this side of the bed was a chest of drawers and on the left as you entered the bedroom was a wardrobe. At the foot of the bed was a large trunk.

"Where are they?" asked Pearce.

Colin went and took a seat on his bed and nodded towards the wardrobe.

"In the wardrobe, at the bottom in the left drawer under my vests."

One of the constables went up, knelt down, and pulled opened the drawer. He rifled through Colin's white vests and found a pile of letters. He pulled them out and handed them to Pearce.

"I've found something else too," he said.

"What is it?" asked Pearce.

The constable held in his hands a gold necklace with cross and a pearl necklace. Pearce took those from the constable and held them out in front of him for Colin to look at. Colin shook his head.

"Dammit," he said, "I'd forgotten those were there."

"Would you care to explain why you were stealing from Ms. Hollingsberry, too?" asked Pearce.

Colin looked up and smiled guiltily.

"Like I said, I needed some money. If you'll read the letters, one of the earlier ones, he tells me I should take a couple of pieces of Madge's jewelry. He even tells me which pieces he thinks are valuable and which I could resell for some extra money. Have you seen how many knick knacks and art Madge has around the house? It's stuffed full with valuable artifacts. It's not like she would have missed a few items of jewelry. She could afford to."

Pearce handed the jewelry back to the constable who put it away.

"She did miss it," said Frances, "she told me all about it."

Colin didn't look up at her. He hung his head low.

"I just needed the money. She's got so much of it and she was old anyway, it's not like she spends any of it. I need it to finish college."

"Colin, that doesn't mean you can steal from her just because you felt she had a lot," said Penelope.

"I know. I'm sorry. I made some mistakes and I got carried away. I just thought it was a bit of fun. Just taking the Mickey."

"What about the other items you stole, Colin. Where are they?" asked Frances.

Colin looked up at her.

"I didn't take anything else."

"The hairbrush and the lipstick and the photograph. Where are they?" asked Frances.

"I didn't take any of those things, I only took the two necklaces. I swear it."

Colin was looking at Frances earnestly. She studied him for a moment.

"Perhaps you didn't," she said, and then turning to Inspector Pearce. "Perhaps Michael did."

"Why?" asked Pearce.

"I think Michael can explain. But I believe he took the hairbrush and the lipstick when he was trying to determine ways of poisoning her before he settled on the chloroform. I think he was wondering if he could poison her by putting something on her lipstick or in her hairbrush that could be absorbed by the skin."

"And what about the photograph."

"The photograph that Madge kept was of Celia, the daughter. I think he took that out of spite."

"That sounds about right," said Pearce.

Inspector Pearce opened up the letters and started to look through them. He read the last one.

As promised, you'll find sixty pounds enclosed. Ten pounds for the sixth letter and fifty pounds as the bonus for having done such a grand job, already.

Here's what I want you to write in the sixth letter. Nothing else, just the following: "Punish the children for the sins of the father to the third and fourth generation of those who hate me.

You have not repented. The time is nigh. You will die.

Six dash six."

I hope you've had a chance to make some money on the necklaces I suggested you take. If you haven't, you might think of doing that sooner than later. It's best not to keep anything around that might connect you and I.

Thank you for your help, it's been instrumental in getting me what I wanted, which was to upset Ms. Hollingsberry. You'll not hear from me again.

As always, please burn this letter once you're done with it.

The handwriting was small, neat and compact.

"Interesting," said Pearce to himself.

"Quite," agreed Lady Marmalade.

"Did Michael ever sign any of his letters to you?" she asked Colin.

He looked up at her and shook his head.

"No, that's why I have no idea who this Michael is, other than what you've shared with us. If you say it's Michael then I believe you, but he's never given me any indication, other than in that last letter you just read, why he wanted to have me write these letters."

"I see."

"I even asked him in the beginning why he was doing this, and he basically told me that he wouldn't answer any questions. That it was a private matter and the less I knew, the better."

Pearce opened up the other letters and scanned them with Frances doing the same by his side. It was as Colin had said. None of the letters gave any indication as to who the writer was, nor why they were doing this. The last one was the longest of them all. The others were fairly terse and to the point. Like one of the earlier ones:

Here is ten pounds for the fourth letter. Please write only this: "Punish the children for the sins of the father to the third and fourth generation of those who hate me.

Vengeance is coming wrathfully. Your suffering will soon be over.

Four dash six."

Let me know when you've taken the jewelry I suggested, and please mail the letter for the eleventh of the month.

As always, burn this when you're done with it.

"I've seen this handwriting before," said Frances.

"You have?" asked Pearce, looking up at her.

"I have, do you remember, Alfred?" said Frances looking over at him.

"I do. Would you like me to say?"

Frances nodded her head.

"Very well, this looks remarkably similar to Dr. Dankworth's handwriting. I remember seeing a letter on his secretaries desk as we left which she was in the middle of tying up."

"Exactly," said Frances, smiling at Alfred. "Which means. Well, I shouldn't have to tell you, Devlin. You know exactly what it means."

"I knew exactly what it meant before you said so. But it is always helpful to have additional evidence with a case like this."

"What on earth does it mean?" asked Matilda.

Lady Marmalade looked up at her. She stood on the far side of the bed, behind Colin, she had picked up one of his pencils and was playing with it absentmindedly.

"It means that we know who Michael is. Or it means, I know who Michael is without having to ask Inspector Pearce."

"No, you can't mean to suggest... Can you?"

"For god's sake who is it?" asked Colin. "Who have I been writing these damn letters for?"

"You've been writing them for Dr. Kenyon Dankworth, who is Michael."

"NO!" exclaimed Lula finding her voice all of a sudden. She startled them, they had all but forgotten she was there, having crept into the room behind them and sticking like a potted plant as quietly and unobtrusively in the corner by the door.

"But he's been such a good man. He's taken such good care of grandmother."

Lula wasn't really speaking to anyone in particular, she was rather trying to understand what seemed to her to be madness. Frances turned to her.

"I'm afraid so, and I imagine that Inspector Pearce has the records to show the same. Of course he had to pretend to be kind and compassionate to Madge, he wouldn't have been able to get so close and become so trusted otherwise. Speaking of which, isn't he due here sometime today?"

Frances looked around the room and her eyes settled on Jeremiah who had also come up to see why Colin had written these letters.

"Yes, my Lady, he should be here at any moment," said Jeremiah.

Frances looked at her watch. It wasn't much before eleven.

"I don't see how," said Matilda.

"See what my dear?" asked Frances.

"I don't see how he'd do it. Why go to all the trouble of spending this time with the old woman and getting Colin to write these letters? Why not just give her some poisonous pills and be done with it."

"Because murder is very often not like that, my dear. Murder is often not cold and calculated as you might imagine. Very often it is a passion of the heart. A twisted and sick hatred. Such is the case here, I believe."

From downstairs came a knock at the door.

"Will that be Dr. Dankworth?" asked Pearce.

"I believe so, sir," said Jeremiah.

"Good, go and let him in."

Jeremiah left followed by the others.

"What I don't understand is why he would be coming over when he likely knows that the old woman is dead?" asked Matilda.

"Because he doesn't want to get caught, that's why. He knows he's set up an appointment for today to check in on Madge, and if he doesn't show up it'll only cast greater suspicion on him," said Frances.

They all made their way downstairs and stayed back as Jeremiah opened the door. He greeted Dr. Dankworth and Dankworth stepped into the foyer taking off his hat. He carried in his hand his medical bag. He looked up and saw the constable coming down the stairs guiding Colin by the elbow.

"Perhaps this is not a good time for me," he said, speaking to Jeremiah, though everyone could hear him. "I'll come back later to check on Madge."

"I don't think you should go anywhere, Dr. Dankworth," said Pearce walking up towards him. "We've all been waiting for you."

Dankworth spun around on his heels and darted out of the house as Jeremiah still had the front door open.

"Get him," said Pearce to the constable at his side.

The young man took off like a shot after the doctor.

"Take him to the car and wait for me there," said Pearce, speaking to the constable who had brought Colin downstairs. The constable nodded and took Colin outside to the police car.

"And give McGuffin a hand if he needs it," Pearce shouted after him, then he turned to the rest of the group. "I think we should retire to the living room. I'm sure Dr. Dankworth will be joining us shortly."

They followed him into the living room. Nobody sat down, the tenor of the home was no longer relaxing. In short order McGuffin came back in with Dr. Dankworth at his side. Dankworth did not look happy, and in McGuffin's one hand was Dankworth's hat. McGuffin brought him over to the couch and sat him down firmly and took away his medical bag.

He handed the bag to Pearce who took it and put it down by his feet. Pearce kneeled down and opened up the bag and started rifling through it.

"So, why did you run from us, doctor?" asked Pearce, looking in the bag.

"Obviously, it was because I knew you were busy here; I didn't want to interrupt."

"You know, Mr. Abbermann, your scribe, tried that same stunt earlier and we had to pull him out of a tree in the garden."

Dankworth didn't say anything, he looked nervously at Pearce as Pearce kept digging into his bag.

"Aha, what have we here?" asked Pearce as he pulled out a lady's hair brush and lipstick.

"I don't know how those got in there," said Dankworth not looking at anyone.

"I think you do, Kenyon," said Frances. "I think you were coming to replace them since they were of no use to you anymore."

"What happened to the photograph you stole?" asked Pearce.

"I didn't steal any photograph."

Pearce stood up and looked over at Dankworth. He raised his eyebrow and twirled his moustache until he was satisfied it was just so.

"All right, I'll make it easy for you, Michael Hollingsberry. We know all about your unhappy childhood and how you've always blamed your mother, waiting patiently to exact vengeance. We know you used Colin Abbermann to write your letters for you and we know that you've stolen Ms. Margaret Hollingsberry's lipstick and hair brush. We will also find out in short order that you are missing at least one bottle of chloroform. The bottle used to ensure that Ms. Hollingsberry drowned. The only thing I'd like to know is why?" said Pearce.

"Very well, I don't care. My mother was a vile woman. She gave me up when I was barely a month old. You have no idea how horrible my childhood was, living with that bastard of a clergyman and his wife. The abuse they heaped upon me. It was all that bloody woman's fault. She should rather have smothered me as a baby."

Dankworth spoke with great hatred and vehemence about his past and about his mother. Spittle whitened the corners of his mouth and some of it was ejected occasionally as he spoke, like a fine spray of acid.

"And then she goes on to have a daughter whom she fawns over while I cower from my adopted parents. I took that bloody photograph and burnt it. Nothing gave me more pleasure than that, except for knowing now that she's dead."

"But why, Kenyon, after all this time, couldn't you let it go?" asked Frances.

He looked up at her and there was fire and dark hatred in his eyes. Not at Frances, he barely knew her, but from the smoldering memories and acrid emotions he had stoked over the decades.

"Because she was the reason that my life became a living hell for just about two decades. You have no idea how that festers inside of you, how you can't let it go, because its got you tight in its grip. I had to get my revenge, that serpent wouldn't let me go otherwise."

"And now you'll likely spend the rest of your life in prison, or worse yet, hang from the hangman's noose."

"And I'll tell you something else," spat Dankworth, "it was worth it. I'd do it again in a heartbeat."

Frances shook her head slowly.

"How quick we are to condemn others in whose shoes we have never walked even a single stride," she said.

"What's that supposed to mean?" Dankworth asked her.

"It means, Kenyon, that you have no idea the difficult life your mother lived. She was beaten mercilessly by her father for having been raped by her uncle, through which you were conceived. She never wanted to give you up, she told me that herself. But she was a young woman of sixteen when she was raped and she had nowhere to go and no other recourse than to give you up to the care of Barts who will now receive her whole estate."

Frances watched Dankworth carefully for any sign of remorse, and she thought she saw a shadow of understanding cross behind his eyes. He put his head into his hands and sighed. Pearce nodded at McGuffin who took him by the arm and helped him up and out of the living room. Pearce looked at Frances and nodded at her.

"Justice will be served, Frances, I'll make sure of that."

She looked over at him, smiled sweetly and nodded her head.

"Will it really? Will an eye for an eye put things back together or just make us all blind."

"I'll leave that up to the philosophers, and get back to doing my job, which is to get these criminals off the street."

Pearce turned away then and started to head out of the living room, but he paused for a moment and turned back.

"I'm sorry you weren't able to save her," he said.

"Me, too."

And with that he was gone. Frances turned to Alfred and smiled. It was one of the saddest smiles he had ever seen from her.

"I think we should be going, too."

"Yes, my Lady."

"Perhaps there'll be no more bombs tonight," she said.

"I hope so."

They started out of the living room and towards the front door where they stepped out into bright sunlight, leaving everyone at the Hollingsberry home deep in thought and shock.

"Do you think it makes a difference, Alfred?"

"What, my Lady?"

"Trying to bring justice in some small way?"

"I think it does, my Lady. I think an angel might have just gotten her wings."

Frances smiled and they strode off down the road towards Marmalade Park.

About Jason Blacker

Jason Blacker was born in Cape Town but spent most of his first 18 years in Johannesburg. When not grinding his fingers down to stubs at the keyboard he enjoys drinking tea, calisthenics and running. Currently he lives in Canada.

Under his own name he writes hard boiled as well as cozy mysteries, action adventure, thrillers, literary fiction and anything else that tickles his muse. Jason Blacker also writes poetry and daily haikus at his haiku blog.

You can find his haikus and other poetry at his website **www.haiqueue.com**.

To stay up to date and learn about new releases be sure to visit **www.jasonblacker.com** where you can find more information about his writing and upcoming projects.

If you enjoy space opera in the tradition of Star Trek then take a look at Jason Blacker's pen name "Sylynt Storme". It is under the name Sylynt Storme where you can find both sci-fi and vampire fiction written by Jason Blacker.

"Star Sails" is the space opera series and "The Misgivings of the Vampire Lucius Lafayette" is his vampire series.

www.ingramcontent.com/pod-product-compliance
Lightning Source LLC
Chambersburg PA
CBHW020822260626
47169CB00003B/783

* 9 7 8 1 9 2 7 6 2 3 4 2 8 *